# THE MARKET FOR GLORY

# THE MARKET FOR GLORY

### Fleet Street ownership
### in the twentieth century

## SIMON JENKINS

*faber and faber*

LONDON · BOSTON

First published in 1986 by
Faber and Faber Limited
3 Queen Square London WC1N 3AU

Photoset by Parker Typesetting Service, Leicester
Printed in Great Britain by
Redwood Burn, Trowbridge, Wiltshire

*British Library Cataloguing in Publication Data*

Jenkins, Simon, 1943–
The market for glory: Fleet Street ownership in the 20th century.
1. Newspaper publishing – England – London – History –
20th century
2. Newspapers – Ownership – History
3. Fleet Street (London, England)
I. Title
338.4'707212    PN5124.09

ISBN 0-571-14627-9

# CONTENTS

# PREFACE

This book seeks to explain why certain men have wanted to own newspapers. It was written at a time when the British press seemed to be experiencing a bigger upheaval than any this century: its oligopolies, of both labour and capital, were suddenly at risk. In 1986 the seventeen titles that had constituted Britain's national press for many years were joined by three newcomers, either published or at a sufficiently advanced stage to be recruiting staff. Numerous others were mooted. The book's ambit is solely that of the Fleet Street newspapers. It does not deal with the provincial press or newspapers abroad, products that comprise a different market governed by different motivations. Nor do I discuss, except in passing, the editorial content of newspapers or what is conventionally termed the 'politics of the press'. On these topics, there are already many books, the most prominent of which are listed in the bibliography.

The phrase 'Fleet Street' refers generically to the daily and Sunday newspapers produced in London, some with satellite centres in Manchester and Glasgow. Though the history of the British press stretches back to the Middle Ages, it did not take on the character of a national industry until the end of the last century. Since then, despite the numerical shrinkage of national titles in most Western countries, newspapers in Britain have remained both lively and diverse. The reason is that implied by the title, *The Market for Glory*.

The origins of this book lie in a shorter essay written for Faber and Faber in 1979.* In it, I suggested that the remarkable conservatism of Fleet Street was attributable to the non-pecuniary motives of its owners. At that time, most were fighting a guerrilla war with their unions and most were losing. The structure and behaviour of the industry over the next five years remained remarkably constant. Then, in 1985–6, came Eddy Shah, the move of Rupert Murdoch's papers to Wapping and the prospective launch of new titles. This book examines whether the former thesis is applicable to the new circumstances. Is the search for glory, in its various manifestations, no longer a viable motive for proprietorship? Has Fleet Street been invaded by a more ruthless commercialism?

The book's structure is essentially narrative. The early chapters describe first the Fleet Street of the great proprietors and then that of their sons, struggling against the odds to maintain family empires and the status that went with them. I go on to examine the industrial practices that developed in the shadows of these men, and the way these practices spread throughout the industry. I then discuss the new proprietors, basically nine of them, who arrived in the decade and a half following 1970. Their abortive attempts to reform Fleet Street occupy the second part of the book. The final section looks at the background to the events of 1985–6 and their possible consequences.

Any description of an industry runs the risk of jargon. I have tried to avoid phrases such as the media and up- and down-market except where the meaning is clear and brevity is justified. It is usually convenient to refer to the up-market newspapers as the qualities and the down-market ones as the tabloids. Technical terms, such as direct inputting, are explained where they are unavoidable. There is a short chronology at the beginning of the book and a table of circulation trends in an appendix.

---

*\**Newspapers, the Power and the Money* (Faber and Faber, 1979). This book is now out of print and some of its material forms the basis for the earlier chapters of its successor.

I have not given a detailed reference for every source. The books particularly useful to a study of this aspect of the newspaper industry are listed in the bibliography. I have usually indicated in the text or in a footnote from which of these books any relevant quotation has been drawn. The account of recent events is based on interviews, cuttings and the columns of the *UK Press Gazette*. Much other material is drawn from conversations with proprietors, managers, journalists and printers over my twenty years' connection with the industry. Two of these were spent as editor of the *Evening Standard* in direct contact with one Fleet Street proprietor, Lord Matthews. It was an exhilarating, often bizarre, experience: I have tried to ensure this does not distort the relevant passages.

Many past and present colleagues have offered advice or criticism, including in particular David Gordon, Harold Lind, Brian MacArthur, Dugal Nisbet-Smith, Frank Rogers and Charles Wintour. My father, Daniel Jenkins, read and commented on the typescript. I thank them all.

# CHRONOLOGY OF
# THE NEW PROPRIETORS

1953    Thomson arrives in UK, buys *Scotsman*

1956    Final abolition of newsprint rationing

1957    Pearsons acquire *Financial Times*

1959    Thomson buys *Sunday Times* from Kemsley

1960    *News Chronicle*, *Sunday Graphic* and *Empire
        News* closed

1961    King buys *Daily Herald* from Odhams
        *Sunday Dispatch* closed
        *Sunday Telegraph* launched

1962    Royal Commission on the press

1964    *Daily Herald* closed
        *Sun* launched

1966    Thomson buys *The Times* from Lord Astor

1967    *Reynolds News* closed

1968    King deposed at *Daily Mirror*

1969    Murdoch buys *News of the World* from Carr
        Murdoch buys and relaunches *Sun*

1971    Aitken/Rothermere talks fail
        *Daily Sketch* closed

1975  Royal Commission on the press, interim report

1975–6 *Daily Mirror*, *Financial Times*, *Daily Telegraph*, *Daily Express* launch new technology development plans

1976  Anderson (ARCO) buys *Observer*

1977  Joint management/union programme on new technology, rejected by chapels
Matthews buys Beaverbrook Newspapers from Aitken
Royal Commission final report

1978  Matthews launches *Daily Star*
Murdoch plans Wapping plant, first to be built in Docklands

1978–9 Closure of Times Newspapers

1981  Murdoch buys Times Newspapers from Thomson
Rowland buys *Observer* from Anderson
Matthews starts bingo war

1982  Reuters flotation proposed

1984  Reuters flotation
Maxwell buys Mirror group from Reed International

1985  Stevens takes over Express Newspapers from Matthews
Black buys *Daily Telegraph* from Hartwell
Shah and Murdoch deal with electricians to circumvent chapels

1986  Murdoch moves to Wapping
Shah launches *Today*
Whittam Smith launches *Independent*
Maxwell prepares evening *Daily News*

# INTRODUCTION

In March 1887, a spoiled twenty-three-year-old named William Randolph Hearst asked his father for a present of the ailing San Francisco *Examiner*. His father had at last achieved elevation to the Senate, to which cause the *Examiner* had long been devoted. Old George Hearst was horrified at his son's request. 'It's a sure loser,' he said. 'Instead of holding it for my own son, I've been saving it up to give to an enemy.' His son was outraged at the waste of so potent a vehicle for fame. He would take over the paper, he said, and 'startle, amaze and stupefy the world'. He proceeded to do just that.

After expulsion from Harvard, William Hearst had worked briefly on the New York *World*, then being galvanized by Joseph Pulitzer. Most great proprietors have found success not by innovation but by imitation and Hearst was no exception. He studied Pulitzer's technique and determined that the *Examiner* in the west should become the equal of the *World* in New York. He would outdazzle Pulitzer. Over the next half-century, his newspapers stunned their readers and disgusted the American Establishment by their sensationalism. They made and destroyed public reputations. They exposed corruption in others while being deeply corrupt themselves. They bought politicians and created stars, especially in the developing movie industry. In 1898 they goaded Washington into an unnecessary conflict with

Spain over Cuba for no nobler purpose than to increase circulation over rival newspapers. The incident remains, in W. A. Swanberg's words, 'the acme of ruthless, truthless, newspaper jingoism'. Hearst's papers were emporia in which hyperbole, humbug and hypocrisy were on continuous display. In one of a stream of maxims on his favourite topic he declared, 'The editor of the popular journal does not care for facts . . . he would prefer a novelty that is not a fact, to a fact that is not a novelty.' Papers were run not for profit but for their proprietors' interpretation of the public good: 'Newspapers control the nation because they represent the people,' he declared.

Hearst used newspapers as his father had, to further his own political ambition. He ran successfully for Congress and even put himself forward for the Presidency of the United States. Though cheated of this goal, he came close to securing the 1904 Democratic party nomination, buying and threatening his way to 263 votes before losing to the dull but safe Judge Parker. His papers usually gained in circulation, as well they might in the booming cities of turn-of-the-century America. A few made money, though the *Examiner* lost heavily while Hearst was editing it and his organization came near to bankruptcy between the wars. But as long as the money lasted, the profits mattered little. It was circulation that obsessed Hearst, and the power he believed to flow from it.

Though he yearned to be a leader of men, Hearst shared with many newspapermen a shyness in public which was inverted to become flamboyance in print. He found compensation in the shrillness of his headlines and the purple of his prose. As time wore on and political power eluded him, this shrillness became a parody of journalism. The thrill of newspapers remained with him, but vanity and extravagance corroded his personality and left him friendless and unpopular when he died in 1951. Fiction gave Hearst the pedestal his life denied him: his reputation became inseparable from that of Citizen Kane of Orson Welles's film of that name – for which a furious Hearst branded Welles a Bolshevik. Kane was the press baron of stereotype: rich, arrogant, hungry for power and finally tragic.

Hearst/Kane became a grotesque template for newspaper proprietorship the world over. He represented the principle of a privately owned free press, tested to destruction. Hearst entered supposedly forbidden territory, that of overt mendacity, and did so with a flair that appealed to the public as much as it appalled his critics. The 'big lie' might be a travesty of journalism and a threat to democracy, but once Hearst had opened a door on this temptation, it could never quite be shut. The quickest route to the reader's heart, he suggested, was not through truth but through novelty, however phoney. His means might be those of the showman, but his end was shared with even the most serious of journalists: to capture an audience. Both means and end have beckoned seductively to proprietors ever since.

Newspapers are no ordinary industry. A free and varied press is intrinsic to effective democracy. Government and public rely on it for giving and receiving information – yet it is also a private business that operates, in most democratic countries, independently of government. To survive, the press must either make profits or receive subsidies from public or private sources. Those who control these profits and subsidies thus enjoy a special sovereignty over newspapers, even where they choose to delegate it to trusts or to editors. They have traditionally been known as proprietors, though some may act as proxies for the money or ambitions of others and prefer to be called publishers. Proprietorship became so abused a concept in the 1960s that the Fleet Street Newspaper Proprietors' Association changed its name, Proprietors' becoming Publishers' (NPA). The controllers of newspapers have widely varying degrees of power – as we shall see – but I use the term proprietors throughout, since they all help to determine the character of Fleet Street, whether directly or corporately.

Britain's national newspapers are unlike those of every other Western nation in at least one respect: there are many more of them. At the time of writing (in mid-1986), there are ten on weekdays and nine on Sunday, owned by eight distinct organizations. No world city (except Tokyo) has such varied comment each morning on its politics, economics and culture as does London. Nor, despite the nostalgia of journalists for some golden age (usually coterminous with their arrival in Fleet Street), has there been any marked decline in the appeal of newspapers in the past quarter-century, in the face of competition from television and radio. British quality newspaper circulation over that period has risen both daily and on Sundays (see appendix). Popular circulation has declined by no more than 10 per cent, mostly as a result of the loss of popular Sunday papers in favour of weekly magazines such as *Woman* and *Woman's Own*. The titles themselves have shown an astonishing resilience. The same number of national dailies is sold on the London streets as at the end of the Second World War (two more, if the *Financial Times* and *Manchester Guardian* were not then regarded as nationals). Among dailies, only three have disappeared, but these have been replaced by three new ones.*

The industry was traditionally clustered round Fleet Street, sandwiched between the cities of London and Westminster. Its location was dictated by proximity to Somerset House where, until 1855, papers had to be stamped individually before dispatch. It survived the repeal of the Stamp Acts and even the advent of high-speed presses in the twentieth century. These machines were monsters. Each night their noise would roar out through the narrow lanes off Fleet Street. They would consume huge rolls of newsprint and spit out lorries to race north and west across London to catch the late-night trains. Round them would swarm a host of printers, engineers, messengers, drivers and the flotsam of the nocturnal city. These men (never women) were laws unto themselves and when they were not crowding the machine and publishing rooms of the great titles, they spilled out into canteens, pubs and cafés. Here their ancient freemasonry of 'chapels' met to spin gold out of Fleet Street's hot metal. Printers were the aristocrats of labour, the highest-paid workers in Britain.

*News Chronicle* (1960), *Daily Herald* (1964), *Daily Sketch* (1971); the *Sun* (1964), *Daily Star* (1978), *Today* (1986). *The Independent* is due in late 1986.

Fleet Street has long been treated as the most irrational of businesses. Its dealings are conducted by heroes and villains, saints and sinners. It is peopled by stereotypes: the rich, grasping printer thoughtless of the future of his industry; the pusillanimous manager who talks tough but acts weak; the editor veering between sycophancy towards his proprietor and autocracy towards his staff. But Fleet Street is no less rational than any other British industry, and considerably more so than some. Within its pale, it is highly competitive. It has remained mostly immune to intrusion, whether from asset stripper, trade union official or civil servant. Half a century of industrial change had, until recently, left its industrial traditions and practices intact. Participants in the Fleet Street economy have shown an acute sense of self-interest. They have rarely been fools. They have balanced effort and reward, cost and price, in a generally stable equilibrium.

Crucial to this equilibrium is that most proprietors have been happy, indeed eager, to derive non-pecuniary returns from owning newspapers. Such returns are seldom admitted and often denied. They vary widely: fame, honour, access to power, or just being part of the excitement of newspaper production. Proprietors and their families can usually pass on the cost – often tens of millions of pounds – to their shareholders. For a quarter-century until the mid-1980s, most newspaper companies would have been better off investing in government stock. The romanticism, or foolhardiness, of their owners cost them dear. Some proprietors, it is true, were scrupulous. When the first Lord Thomson acquired *The Times* he transferred it to his family account so the expense would not fall on his shareholders. Mr Robert Anderson, who bought the *Observer* in 1976, saw it as an act of corporate philanthropy wholly unconnected with business. On the other hand, the trustees (and staff) of the *Guardian* gloried in its losses – which had to be met from provincial newspaper profits – as if thus elevated to a loftier plane than their rivals. Yet the fact that these varied returns are unquantifiable does not strip them of economic significance. Fleet Street has its price, and it has been paid gladly by some of Britain's (and the world's) most astute businessmen. This book seeks to explain why.

The concept of non-pecuniary return has not been confined to the owners of newspapers. Their workers have come to share it too. Under the comprehensive agreements negotiated in the 1960s, printers found themselves paid so much for so little work and taxed at such high marginal rates that they opted instead for leisure. Working weeks came down from six to five to four, even to three days. Many used the spare time to make profit in the black economy. This was not, as commentators would claim during every dispute, 'industrial lunacy'. It was a simple reflection of their market position. Printers have mostly been careful manipulators of this market. Their chapel negotiating units, often as small as a dozen members, are dedicated to maximizing group earnings. They may exasperate management and be the bane of national union officials. They may suffer the abuse of their colleagues and the odium of journalists. They may miscalculate, as did Rupert Murdoch's printers disastrously in 1985. But until then, the record of the chapels in maintaining the jobs and earnings of their (existing) members was excellent compared with experience in other industries.

Despite its stability, Fleet Street has been considered a problem industry. Since 1945 three Royal Commissions have inquired into it. Mystified consultants have pored over it. Whenever a newspaper changes hands, the industry's entrails are examined for terminal disease, traces of which are invariably found. Public inquiries into British industry usually prefer moral judgements to practical solutions. Who, they ask portentously, is 'most to blame'? Politicians, trade unionists, consultants, leader-writers and Royal Commissions all produce the same answer: 'Blame for the present condition of Fleet Street rests equally with both sides.' This equal spread of blame has supplied the industry with a running excuse for inaction. It has exonerated both parties from responsibility and implied that 'finding a way out' is a task for a loftier and more potent agent than the industry itself. Besides, since the equilibrium was apparently sustainable, why worry?

12

Fleet Street has begun to change, but only after its equilibrium was upset during the dramatic year of 1985–6. The catalyst was partly a change in the legal and commercial context of the period, but more a change in the motivation of certain proprietors. The drastic fall in labour costs, which came with News International's move to its Wapping plant in February 1986, could have arisen only from a determined decision by its proprietor, Rupert Murdoch. It was bound to involve confrontation with the chapels. The expectation, repeated by almost every Fleet Street inquiry, that the unions should play a part in managing industrial change was a misunderstanding of their role and purpose. The 1977 Royal Commission professed itself baffled that chapels should wish to 'cling to their individual authority rather than grasp the opportunities for greater involvement in decision-making at a higher level'. Yet chapels were not meant to be policemen of newspaper costs, any more than their superior unions were in business to keep them in order. They knew well that reform in Fleet Street meant either lower pay or, much the same thing, a reduced opportunity to gain higher pay. The chapel, as we shall see in chapter four, was an instrument crafted to maintain short-term income. Those who supplied the income, the proprietors, would have to initiate change if change there was to be.

The market for labour in Fleet Street has long been a seller's one. Papers might change owners, but they almost never closed – and chapels knew it. In such conditions, industrial reform was not likely to succeed, nor did it. The only sign of life was when an occasional management, such as at Times Newspapers in 1978, threw itself in frustration against the brick wall of chapel power (see page 144). In each case, terrible injuries resulted. Yet by 1985 the industry was growing lax: while its internal equilibrium was steady enough to survive the costly absurdities of the bingo war, its outdated production methods made it vulnerable to new competition. This came initially from an improbable quarter, a solitary proprietor of free newspapers in the north-west of England.

The challenge hit Fleet Street as it was entering a period of unexpected wealth, with the flotation of the Reuters news agency. Existing typesetting and printing methods had to be replaced by new technology and much of this wealth was to be channelled into new buildings in Docklands. Most newspaper groups were resigned to negotiating deals for Docklands which would leave their chapels with the same leverage over costs as before. When the Express Newspapers group began publishing the *Daily Star* in Manchester in 1978 and the *Daily Telegraph* started negotiating a deal for its Isle of Dogs plant in 1985, chapel power was still regarded as incontrovertible. There might be a 'revolution' in computerized technology for Fleet Street, but there was no simultaneous revolution in industrial relations.

The causes of industrial change can be looked at in several ways. Some observers regarded the events of 1985–6 as preordained, the nemesis of decades of proprietorial indolence and chapel greed. This book takes a different view. It is quite possible that the move to Docklands could have been accomplished under labour agreements that would have enshrined chapel power for another generation irrespective of new union laws or new market circumstances. In the case of most titles, this may yet happen. As it was, Eddy Shah came on the scene in 1985 just at the moment when Rupert Murdoch was being taunted by his chapels beyond endurance, and when he was badly in need of improved cash flow. The result was to upset the old equilibrium and open up the industry to new opportunities. I believe there was nothing inevitable about this. The equivalent of chapel power survives in other industries, in engineering, in the railways, in local government. What was crucial was – as it always has been in Fleet Street – a number of decisions made by individual proprietors. British newspapers are produced in the private sector. Those who control the industry's capital are responsible for its condition. It is to their motives that we now turn.

# 1

## THE GREAT PROPRIETORS

Newspapers have seldom been run for the purpose of making men rich. First and foremost, they were a function of public affairs. From their origin in the dissemination of public information to their role in the growth of factions and parties, their story has been intertwined with politics. In the eighteenth century, Whig and Tory politicians bought the loyalty, and presumed influence, of the dozens of daily, evening and weekly papers that flourished on their subsidies. Walpole was accused of spending £50,000 of 'secret service' money on newspaper bribes – and survived the charge. In its early days *The Times* received a Treasury retainer of £300 a year. The first great journalist/proprietor of modern times, William Cobbett, saw his *Political Register* as a vehicle for his radical conservatism. The *Register* and his other publications brought him many a broken head and were the ruin of his family, but they were more influential, he maintained, than all the 'prattling mouths of politicians'.

Even after the abolition of the Stamp Acts and the growth of *The Times* and the *Daily Telegraph* in the second half of the nineteenth century, most papers were still owned, as a subsequent Royal Commission remarked, 'for the prestige and political and social influence their possession conferred'. In 1881 a young fancy-goods salesman turned vegetarian restaurateur named George Newnes started the magazine *Titbits*. It was phenomenally successful. But his pride and joy was the Liberal *Westminster Gazette* on which, in Francis Williams's words, 'he lost between £10,000 and £15,000 a year with an unruffled cheerfulness for sixteen years'. The newspaper as a handmaid to politics has, for most of its history, been the norm not the exception. Liberals and Conservatives subsidized newspapers to remain loyal to their cause throughout the inter-war (1918–1939) period. Labour was the last party formally to sever a direct relationship with a Fleet Street title, when the TUC finally sold its 49 per cent shareholding in the *Daily Herald* in 1964.*

Whether the replacement of party loyalty by proprietorial whim was an advance for democracy is a moot point to which we shall return in the last chapter. What was clear was that newspaper ownership supplied a short cut to political influence. Instead of a slow climb up a party hierarchy, a newspaper offered its proprietor political seniority 'off the peg'. Yet the marriage of such influence to genuine power was seldom happy. As Hearst's experience demonstrated, the potency of a popular newspaper was usually that of the spoiler, the publicist, the satirist; it tended to be destructive rather than constructive. Sustained influence over current affairs depends on loyalty, discretion and a sense of timing; some quality newspapers have achieved this for a short period, usually under great editors rather than great proprietors. The power of a popular paper, however, is almost entirely to cause nuisance. Ownership certainly supplies a ticket to the front stalls of public affairs but seldom to the stage itself. Those who have leapt from one to the other have usually fallen back to their seats, bruised and disillusioned.

In the early nineteenth century in Britain, there was one exception to this rule, the Walter family's publication, *The Times*. This paper dominated mid-Victorian journalism until challenged (and overtaken) by the less staid, then Liberal *Daily Telegraph* in the 1860s. *The Times* had two characteristics which have been in conflict with the stereotype of proprietorship ever since: it was treated by its owner as

*The Communist Party's *Morning Star* does not declare an Audit Bureau circulation and is not normally regarded as a Fleet Street title.

essentially an adjunct to a printing business, and it was available for its staff (or at least its editor) to express in it whatever opinions they judged appropriate. *The Times*, wrote John Walter as early as 1810, would not take any public subsidy, 'because by such admission, the editor was conscious he should have sacrificed the right of condemning any act he esteemed detrimental to the public welfare'. It was a creed only partly diminished by the fact that Walter was both editor and proprietor at the time.

That *The Times* was able to survive as a commercial business owed much to the flair of its two editors from 1816 to 1879, Thomas Barnes and John Delane. But their freedom was an example of what made *The Times* exceptional. The Walter family saw itself as businessmen-printers as much as proprietors. *The Times* was a testbed of new technology: in the eighteenth century it introduced logotype, a system whereby whole words, not just individual letters, could be pre-set for speedy composition. It was the first to use a steam press in 1814. It introduced the Walter rotary press in 1869, involving a series of plated cylinders to print both sides of paper from a continuous reel and then fold them. Each press could produce 12,000 copies an hour against barely 1,000 before then.

The rise of mass literacy at the end of the century brought new newspaper markets and the scope for new printing techniques. The concept of a mass readership had until then been largely confined to the Sunday press; since the 1840s, titles such as *John Bull*, *Lloyd's Weekly*, *Reynolds News* and the *News of the World* had peddled a varying mixture of information, scandal and radical comment to the lower-middle classes. One paper, *Bell's*, had as its explicit subtitle, 'Sporting and Police Gazette and Newspaper of Romance'. Sunday papers in the later nineteenth century outsold dailies four and five times over. *Lloyd's Weekly* broke through the 1 million circulation barrier in 1896.*

The Hoe and Walter rotary presses and, after 1892, the

*On the Victorian Sunday press, Virginia Berridge in George Boyce, see bibliography.

hot-metal Linotype machine made it easier for this weekly market to be exploited on a daily basis. The swift expansion of the railway network made distribution faster and cheaper: it was now feasible to challenge the up-market *Times*, *Daily Telegraph*, *Daily Chronicle* and *Daily News* with more popular fare. First to do so was the expanding London evening press, many of the titles strongly political in motivation. Papers sold for a penny, then a halfpenny. Lurid front pages were borrowed from the Sunday press and from American journalism. The racing tipster and the crime reporter were the heroes of the newsroom. The flat-capped, street-corner newsboy entered London folklore.

The advent of a mass-market national press lay as much in marketing as in journalism or production. Again the roots lay in the weekly press. George Newnes' *Titbits* was launched as a digest of interesting information and was soon selling 700,000 copies a week. Newnes' editors scoured the press for short items to be reprinted in his magazine. His skill lay as much in his sales ingenuity as in the product itself; competitions offered a 'Titbits house' in Dulwich or insurance cover for life as weekly prizes. One campaign was promoted with automatic railway accident cover to any purchaser of the magazine. On some days, the Post Office had to deliver 200 sacks of mail to the *Titbits* office.

Newnes was a true Victorian entrepreneur. For all his enthusiasm as a journalistic popularizer, his ambitions were increasingly political and philanthropic. An ardent Liberal, he served intermittently as an MP from 1885 until the end of his life in 1910. He founded such periodicals as the *Strand Magazine* and *Country Life*. From 1893 he subsidized the *Westminster Gazette*, a paper devoted to the Liberal cause. When Newnes was created a baronet in 1895 (no press lords then), Lord Rosebery cited his work as a 'pioneer of clean, popular literature'.

One early contributor to the columns of *Titbits* was the son of an Irish barrister then living in Hampstead – Alfred Harmsworth. Like Hearst in America, he was to become a source of admiration and revulsion for later generations of proprietors. Harmsworth began his career as a freelance journalist. On a visit to France, he had been impressed by the French *Le Petit Journal*, which was profitably selling 650,000 copies in Paris on a staple of gossip, helpful hints and scandal. On the principle that it is safer to exploit a proven formula than to invent a new one, Harmsworth began a rival to *Titbits*, which he named *Answers*. His competitions were even more outrageous than Newnes': one prize was simply £2 a week for life. Within five years, the circulation of *Answers* had passed a million.

In 1894 Harmsworth paid £23,000 for the *Evening News*, then moribund after years of subsidy from the Conservative party. Whereas Newnes had 'traded up-market' with the *Westminster Gazette* on the basis of his success as a popularizer, Harmsworth took a leaf from Hearst's book, popularizing the *Evening News* and delighting in its soaring circulation. Within a year, he was dabbling in politics, and the Prime Minister, Lord Salisbury, flattered him on the success of his papers. In 1895 Harmsworth accepted nomination as the Unionist parliamentary candidate for Portsmouth, buying a local evening paper in the town and using it for vote-attracting stunts of embarrassing naïvety: in one instance, a local girl draped in a Union Jack was engaged to sing a specially written song in praise of dockyard workers at a local music hall, while a claque called for encores from the rear. The effort was in vain. The Portsmouth electors rejected Harmsworth and produced in him an aversion to democratic politics and to the House of Commons. As his biographers suggest, he came to resent deeply that 'in a democracy, it is the parliamentary man who has the ultimate power'. Harmsworth was left brooding that 'my place is in the House of Lords, where they don't fight elections'.

Harmsworth, with the assistance of his brother Harold, now devoted himself to building up what became for a time Britain's greatest-ever newspaper empire, supplying almost half Fleet Street's total daily sale. A year after his Portsmouth defeat, he launched the *Daily Mail*, priced at a ½d and aimed at the lower-middle-class readers who so avidly bought *Titbits* and *Answers*. The first issue, on 4 May 1896, sold more copies than any daily paper in history (just under 400,000). It made a

*19*

loss on its production costs but was marketed to build circulation and thus advertising revenue. It was the first paper to declare an advertising rate per 1,000 copies sold. It played on the acquisitive aspirations of its readers, especially female ones, and married these aspirations to those of consumer goods advertisers. The paper benefited from the jingoism of the Boer War. It boasted 'all the news in the smallest space' and reduced many editorials to single paragraphs of opinion. Huge amounts were spent on promotion – a special enthusiasm of Harmsworth's was to give rewards for early aviation feats. By using telephones, an edition of the London paper was produced in Manchester. Another edition appeared in Paris. By the close of the century, the *Daily Mail* was selling almost 1 million copies and Harmsworth's personal income from his new Amalgamated Press was put at £150,000 a year.

With money burning holes in their pockets, the Harmsworth brothers bought the *Weekly Dispatch* and turned it into the best selling Sunday paper in Britain. Then, in 1903 they launched the *Daily Mirror*, its title chosen specially to appeal to women. It was written largely by women and the first issue was distributed with a gilt and enamel hand mirror. The paper was a flop. 'Women can't write and don't want to read,' was Alfred Harmsworth's dismissive conclusion. A year later, with losses running at £500 an issue, he sacked most of the women: it was 'like drowning kittens' his manager recalled. The *Daily Mirror* was turned into a picture paper and sales began slowly to improve, but Alfred's heart was never with it and in 1914 he sold it to his brother for £100,000. Harold's more cautious acumen brought it success and Alfred was furious when its circulation eventually overtook that of his beloved *Daily Mail*. Harold later (in 1931) transferred the *Daily Mirror* to an independent company under its own directors. It went on to prosper mightily, until falling under the proprietorial sway of its founder's great-nephew, Cecil Harmsworth King.

By 1905 Alfred Harmsworth was at the height of his entrepreneurial power. He bought the *Observer* and was created Baron Northcliffe by a Conservative cabinet eager for his support – an honour undimmed by his reported comment,

'When I want a peerage, I will buy one like an honest man.'

In 1908 he acquired *The Times*. The paper had been eclipsed by both the *Daily Telegraph* and the *Morning Post* and was selling a paltry 40,000 a day for almost no profit. Its owners, various members of the Walter family, had lost enthusiasm for their inheritance and were ready to sell. Mindful of the sensitivities of the staff and readers to the prospect of joining the 'yellow press', Northcliffe declared his hand only as 'Mr X'. He eventually paid £320,000 for the title, with promises of continued independence for the editorial staff.

Newspaper historians have made much of the parallels between Northcliffe's experience with *The Times* and that of subsequent proprietors of that paper. They are remarkable. Initially Northcliffe concentrated on the production and business departments. As his secretary, Arthur Bates, told *The Times'* historians, Oliver Woods and James Bishop (see bibliography), 'My impression was that he intended ultimately, though not immediately, to have some influence on the news and views of the paper . . . His main aim was to see *The Times* again a great national organ.' Yet he found the staff intractable, calling them 'black friars' after the ancient occupants of Printing House Square. He began to intervene in every decision, enlivening presentation, constantly stressing 'topicality', becoming obsessed with price and circulation. Daily memoranda were sent from wherever in the world his increasingly restless wanderings took him. Steadily he badgered the paper back to security; its sale rose eightfold to 314,000 in 1914. As his biographer, Geoffrey Dawson, noted,* 'The hasty verdict that Northcliffe ruined *The Times* is grotesque. The truth is that at a critical moment, he was wholly responsible for saving it from extinction.'

As Northcliffe fell victim to clinical paranoia, *The Times* entered the darkest period of its history. Annoyed by what he saw as the priggishness of its staff, Northcliffe forced the paper to join the *Daily Mail* in support of his mercurial interventions in First World War policy. Alternately vilified and praised, cabinets scarcely knew how to treat him. He was asked to

*See *Dictionary of National Biography*.

perform a variety of war tasks, including Director of Propaganda and a mission to America. He declined to become air minister, and was consoled with the offer of a viscountcy, which he accepted. After the Armistice, he campaigned virulently for the trial of the Kaiser and finally broke with Lloyd George, whom his propaganda had helped to install in Downing Street.

Northcliffe let it be known that he expected to be a full member of the British delegation to the Versailles Peace Conference. When the appointment failed to materialize, his newspapers showed the Government no mercy and attacked at every turn. In so doing Northcliffe overstepped the mark. In one of the most devastating comments on proprietorial arrogance, Lloyd George told the House of Commons in April 1919:

> When a man is labouring under a deep sense of disappointment, however unjustified and however ridiculous the expectations may have been, he is always apt to think the world is badly run. When a man has deluded himself that he is the only man who can win the war . . . and there is not a whisper, not a sound, it is rather disappointing.

Northcliffe was, said Lloyd George tapping a finger against his temple, suffering from the 'disease of vanity'. He had made too many enemies and been loyal to too few friends to find any defender. The proprietor's bluff had been called.

Northcliffe's last years were as sad as those of Hearst. His delusions of grandeur strayed far beyond the confines of politics. Like Hearst, he had a Napoleon fixation. He delighted in collecting Napoleonic memorabilia, especially portraits suggesting any physical similarity between himself and the emperor. He was childishly pleased to find that one of Napoleon's hats was actually too small for him. By the time of his death, following a world tour in 1922, his paranoia had become acute: he was convinced that a German gang was after him and kept a loaded revolver beneath his pillow. His last instruction to *The Times* was that 'the best man on the night' should be put to writing his obituary.

The Northcliffe empire was swiftly reduced in size on his

death. Harold Harmsworth (created Viscount Rothermere in 1919) had been the businessman of the partnership and much of his energy had gone into restraining his brother's extravagance while steadily going his own way. He lacked journalistic flair and had scant affection for most of the titles which had so enthused his brother. In 1911 Northcliffe had already sold the *Observer* to the American William Waldorf Astor. Astor spent most of his time in Italy and left the paper in the care of its editor, J. L. Garvin, watched over by his politician son, Waldorf Astor. Astor senior was not, however, averse to a Lloyd George viscountcy, granted in 1917, which meant that his son had reluctantly to give up his Parliamentary seat and go to the House of Lords when his father died in 1919. (The seat in Plymouth, passed to his wife, Nancy, who became the first woman to sit in Parliament.)

On Northcliffe's death, a flock of vultures gathered over the corpse of *The Times*, left in his deathbed will to his wife. They included Lloyd George and friends (with Lloyd George as putative editor), Rothermere, and members of the Walter family, who had an option to buy back *The Times* 'at market price' on Northcliffe's death. The family was secretly backed by another of Viscount Astor's sons, John Jacob, who was supported in turn by *The Times*' influential managing director, a Canadian named Campbell Stuart. John Jacob Astor's motive in wanting to acquire *The Times* was to become a familiar one in the subsequent history of Fleet Street: prestige. His American bankers told Stuart that he was 'very anxious to save *The Times* and knew quite well that he could never hope to make a penny out of it'. He eventually had to pay an exorbitant £1,580,000 to top an astonished Rothermere's final bid. It was a sum well in excess of the company's commercial value and could be justified, say Woods and Bishop, 'only by the prestige of *The Times*'. It was the same justification used by Lord Thomson when Astor and his son finally tired of the struggle in 1966. John Jacob, later Lord Astor of Hever, remained proprietor-in-chief throughout those forty years, combining it, for half the period, with being Conservative MP for Dover. Northcliffe had been the last native-born Briton to own Britain's most famous newspaper.

Rothermere did not dwell on his failure for long. He sold the Amalgamated Press magazines to the Berry brothers. He acquired fourteen local newspapers. The Hulton provincial paper group was bought and resold at a profit. In a complex share deal in 1922, he took 49 per cent of Lord Beaverbrook's newspaper interests, selling them back to him in 1933. He survived the crash of 1929 with greater aplomb than most, reputedly making £3 million by manipulating the bear market on Wall Street. In 1931 he hived off the *Daily Mirror* into a trust, telling Beaverbrook that 'for ten or fifteen thousand a year in directorships you can certainly get twenty trusty's [sic] to carry the burdens of newspaper management without forfeiting an overriding influence'. He continued to behave as sole proprietor of the *Daily Mirror*. Even the shy Rothermere, labouring so long in his brother's shadow, could not resist the blandishments of proprietorship. At Northcliffe's prompting, he had already served briefly in Lloyd George's wartime Government: he now assumed his brother's role of mentor and thorough nuisance to the British political Establishment.

Sometimes in league with Beaverbrook, sometimes on his own, Rothermere used his papers to rail against both Labour and Conservative Governments. Always a solitary figure, he developed a particular distaste for the gregarious Stanley Baldwin. In 1930 Rothermere decided to set up a new party, to be called the United Empire party. It was to be composed of what amounted to Rothermere's chosen list of MPs. Beaverbrook was hailed as 'the next Prime Minister' – though Beaverbrook himself denied any intention of wanting the accolade. One parliamentary candidate was told by Rothermere

I cannot make it too abundantly clear that under no circumstances whatsoever will I support Mr Baldwin unless I know exactly what his policy is going to be, unless I have complete guarantees that such policy will be carried out if his party achieves office, and unless I am acquainted with the names of at least eight or ten of his most prominent colleagues in the next ministry.

Once again, a Harmsworth had overstepped the proprietorial mark and invited ridicule. When Baldwin heard of what he termed this 'preposterous and insolent demand', he pointed out that an elected Prime Minister would have to offer the monarch a cabinet that was not his own but Lord Rothermere's. The affair – and the new party – ended with Baldwin's series of furious speeches in 1930 and 1931. He remarked that nothing was 'more curious in modern evolution than the effect of an enormous fortune rapidly made and the control of newspapers of your own . . . It goes to the head like wine.' With the *Daily Mail* and the *Daily Express* and their associated evening papers showing him no sympathy and, as he saw it, damaging the Conservative cause at a time of political turmoil, Baldwin threw down the gauntlet. In March 1931 he said that the Beaverbrook and Rothermere press 'are not newspapers in the ordinary acceptance of the term. They are engines of propaganda for the constantly changing policies, desires, personal wishes, personal likes and dislikes of two men.' He added what has become the most famous aphorism in Fleet Street's history: 'What the proprietorship of these papers is aiming at is power, and power without responsibility: the prerogative of the harlot down the ages.'* It was an opportunistic attack: Baldwin used press lords for his own ends when it suited him and at one point asked Lord Camrose to raise money for a London evening paper to plead his cause.

Rothermere shared with his brother a gaucheness and lack of political touch that embarrassed the comparatively sophisticated Beaverbrook. It removed the sting from his editorial campaigns and rendered him vulnerable to counter-attack. He went on to campaign tediously against government waste, under the *Daily Mirror* slogan of Squandermania. He, like Northcliffe, was a strong advocate of air power, though with little effect on government policy. Following a visit to Hungary, he was offered (by one faction) the crown of that country, thus becoming the only press lord to have had kingship within his grasp. As the 1930s progressed, he strayed into the political wilderness, toying with Mosley and praising Mussolini and Hitler. He died in 1940.

The Harmsworths' rival and occasional ally, Lord Beaver-

*Quotes in the above passages from Koss, see bibliography.

brook was a proprietor of a very different stamp. The historian Francis Williams wrote that 'Northcliffe began as a journalist and finished as a propagandist seduced by his own headlines. Beaverbrook travelled the road the opposite way.' Both men practised a journalism that was a means to the end of self-aggrandizement. Beaverbrook may have been a journalist by instinct, but he never pretended his papers were other than the financial and editorial fuel for his wayward political ambition. As he reminded all who cared to listen – few proprietors have so mesmerized their senior employees – a newspaper must have a sound commercial base. But he would insist his papers prospered only to 'make propaganda'. He loved to hear the howls of Fleet Street progressives whenever he said it.

Max Aitken, as Beaverbrook was then, arrived in Britain from Canada in 1910, a thirty-year-old financier eager for a new life and fascinated by British politics. He had already established a business relationship with the future Prime Minister, Bonar Law, and swiftly obtained a seat as Conservative MP for Ashton-under-Lyne. He assisted his advancement by lending £25,000 to support the ailing *Daily Express* in the Conservative cause. The *Daily Express*, however, needed more than loans to keep it afloat and in 1916 Aitken bought it outright. He used it, as Northcliffe used the *Daily Mail*, to further his (and Bonar Law's) campaign to bring down Asquith and replace him with Lloyd George. In later life, he referred to this campaign as 'the biggest thing I ever did'.

Like Northcliffe, Aitken confidently expected a senior appointment from Lloyd George in return, but, also like Northcliffe, he was merely offered a junior office and, in 1917, a peerage. Aitken refused the office but took the peerage as Lord Beaverbrook. (He accepted a senior post under Churchill in the Second World War.) Instead, he plunged into the labyrinthine intrigues that consumed British politics during and immediately after the First World War and of which he was to be a consummate historian. Yet a proprietor's influence is ultimately a function of that of his friends. As the latter's fortunes waned, so too did Beaverbrook's access to power. He was, of course, no longer an

MP, and after the fall of Lloyd George's Coalition and Bonar Law's death in 1923, he was effectively 'out of office' and left only with the columns of his newspapers in which to express his point of view.

Beaverbrook immediately took steps to ensure that these columns, at least, were safe from the vagaries of fortune. In 1923 he bought and sold the newspaper and magazine empire of Sir Edward Hulton, swapping shares back and forth with Rothermere like gambling chips. From the Hulton deal he took his next catch, the London *Evening Standard*, 'as commission'. In 1931 he constructed the black-glass, art deco building in Fleet Street that became his headquarters. But financial dexterity was not an end in itself. Beaverbrook was adamant that his intentions were merely to provide a secure base for what remained his family of three titles, the *Daily* and *Sunday Express* (the latter was started in 1918) and the *Evening Standard*. Not until 1933 did he finally gain three-quarters voting control of them. With Rothermere sometimes in tandem sometimes in opposition, he settled down once more to his hobby of political manipulation.

Beaverbrook was fortunate (compared with most proprietors) in having such adoring Boswells as A. J. P. Taylor and Michael Foot. Both have portrayed him as an impish genius and a gifted propagandist. Yet his proudest campaign, on behalf of the British Empire, hardly needed his jingoism to maintain public appeal, nor could he do anything to forestall its decline when its day was past. His squabbling with Baldwin seems petulant in retrospect. His alliance with Rothermere against Baldwin in 1930–1 was clumsy and half-hearted. Beaverbrook, unlike Rothermere, loved conventional party politics too much to subvert it wholesale. To him, proprietorship was not so much about propaganda as about making mischief; his malice towards often innocent 'enemies', like his obsessional generosity to friends, displayed an insecurity common among newspaper owners. The *Daily Express* was basically a paper of prejudice, not thought. However, he was certainly a master journalist. He had an instinct for news and a belief in the authority of a good reporter to command the reader's attention. His papers, while he lived, were both popular and prosperous, and he was, perhaps, a nobler British answer to Hearst/Kane than either of the Harmsworth brothers.

Beaverbrook took little pleasure from one of the more bizarre episodes of newspaper history, the circulation battle of the 1930s. The inter-war period was one of swift expansion in newspaper sales. Marketing techniques pioneered by Newnes and Northcliffe spread to other groups. Consumer goods became more widely available to be advertised nationwide. In 1921 there were still forty-one provincial morning papers in Britain; by 1937 thirteen had closed or been merged with others, and a quarter of the London dailies had gone also. In the same period, though, the sales of national morning papers had risen threefold. To gain a bigger share of this market, proprietors (even those supposedly more concerned with political influence) disregarded commercial caution and chased sales in a manner still recalled with awe by Fleet Street veterans.

The instigator of the sales war was yet another proprietor disarmingly eager for public recognition. Julius Elias was the son of a Hammersmith newsagent. He began as an office boy in the printing firm of Odhams, working his way up to become managing director in 1920. Odhams published *John Bull* and the *Sunday People*, whose circulation Elias took from 300,000 to 3 million within three years. Never averse to an old gimmick when it had proved successful, he borrowed Newnes' concept of turning each copy into a free insurance voucher.

In 1929, Odhams took a 51 per cent stake in Labour's *Daily Herald*, the Trades Union Congress (TUC) taking the other 49 per cent. Elias's intention was to turn it from a political propaganda sheet into a popular daily strong enough to challenge the *Daily Mail* and the *Daily Express*, and he became a fanatical warrior in the battle for circulation. The *Daily Herald* was relaunched in 1930 with an editorial appeal broadened from its trade union roots, though still supporting Labour. Elias's staff both admired and satirized his efforts: 'We have no party, creed or bias; we want a peerage for Elias' ran an office song. Free and cut-price offers of bewildering variety – vases, cameras, pens, dictionaries, volumes of Dickens – were carried round the country by an army of canvassers in search of subscriptions. Other proprietors sought to resist the challenge, but eventually the *Daily Express*, *Daily Mail* and *News Chronicle* felt they had to follow suit to retain market share. The nation was awash with clothes and kitchenware, free books and free insurance. The *Daily Herald* achieved its goal of 2 million sales, but Elias found he was spending some £3 million a year keeping them. The losses mounted and he had to take his paper ever more down-market to maintain sales, to the disquiet of its TUC shareholders. Francis Williams recalls a cynic who remarked that the only way to get socialism into the *Daily Herald* was to write it on the back of a bathing beauty. It was an ironic preview of Labour's dismay when the *Daily Herald* eventually became Rupert Murdoch's *Sun*.

Elias's rivals were having to spend similar sums to stay level. Between 1924 and 1935 the number of staff working on national newspapers rose by 72 per cent, of which 40 per cent were canvassers. Beaverbrook was the first to become disillusioned with short-term sales promotion, and sought to bring his fellow proprietors together to call a truce, but when at one point he called off his canvassers, the *Daily Express* lost 250,000 sales in a day – though no one calculated how much money he might have saved at the same time. Beaverbrook began to invest instead in editorial coverage, and was vindicated by the end of the decade as his sales passed the *Daily Herald*'s much-vaunted 2 million. Elias took comfort from his elevation to the peerage as Lord Southwood in 1937, raised to a viscountcy in 1946. He described himself as a 'Tory democrat' but voted with Labour in the House of Lords and even served as a Labour whip.

There was less consolation for the Liberal *News Chronicle*, product of a merger in 1930 between George Cadbury's *Daily News* and the *Daily Chronicle*, owned by the Pearson family's Westminster Press. After a tortured series of negotiations, the Pearsons sold full control to the Cadburys in 1936. The new paper, with a combined sale of 1,400,000, suffered from the same disease as afflicted the *Daily Herald*:

internal and external argument over its political commitment. It had been founded on the basis that 'consistent support should be given to the promotion of unity in the Liberal party', but as the 1930s progressed many of its readers were clearly more interested in the doings of Labour. The result was sniping back and forth between party officials, the Cadbury family and the editorial staff, during which the paper's managers had to maintain a presence in the circulation war with the *Daily Express*, *Daily Herald* and *Daily Mail*. By 1937 they had lost. The *News Chronicle* slid to fourth place, further decline being halted for a decade by wartime newsprint rationing.

Of all the newspaper families founded around the turn of this century, the most unobtrusive also proved one of the most lasting. At an early Harmsworth company general meeting, Alfred Harmsworth was much impressed by questions put to him from the floor by a young Welsh reporter from the Commercial Press Association named William Berry. He asked to see him afterwards and immediately offered him a job. Berry declined. One of three sons of a Merthyr Tydfil estate agent, he had begun his career at fourteen on his local newspaper, leaving to seek his fortune as a journalist in London five years later. The sight of Harmsworth in full flood kindled in him a desire to be his own man. In 1901, at the age of twenty-two, he launched his first publication, *Advertising World*, reputedly writing every word of its first issue. *Boxing* magazine followed eight years later, with William as editor/writer and his brother Gomer as business manager. Other titles were launched and by 1915 the brothers had earned enough to acquire the moribund *Sunday Times*. It was then selling 50,000 a week, a quarter of the sales of its rival the *Observer*. William became its editor-in-chief.

The Berry brothers were a close team with an ascetic lifestyle – they shared a flat near the Strand and had a joint bank account until both were well into their fifties and married. Acquisitions proceeded apace. In 1919, the brothers bought the St Clement's Press, which included the *Financial Times*, from Sir John Ellerman. Five years later came the

Hulton titles, including the Manchester *Daily Dispatch* and the *Daily Sketch*. The Berrys joined with magazine publisher Edward (later Lord) Iliffe to form Allied Newspapers, buying failing provincial titles, merging, closing or galvanizing them where appropriate. In 1926 Berry bought the Amalgamated Press magazine group from the Northcliffe estate, creating one of the largest publishing groups in the country. Nothing in Fleet Street equalled the competitive carnage seen in the provincial press between the wars as the Berrys and Rothermere carved their way through an industry still rooted in its nineteenth-century local ownership. In 1929 the score was 25–14 in the Berrys' favour.

Finally, in 1928 the opportunity came to acquire a prominent daily. The Gladstonian-turned-Unionist *Daily Telegraph*, *The Times*' rival as torch-bearer of independent comment during the Victorian era, was relinquished by the Levy-Lawson family who had owned and run it since 1855. As so often in the history of a newspaper, the founding family had run out of proprietorial steam as one generation succeeded another. The last representative, Viscount Burnham (another Lloyd George peer), departed to join the Indian Statutory Commission. William Berry took over the reins, cut the paper's price from 2d to 1d and doubled its circulation to 200,000, a figure last achieved in the 1870s. The paper's revival was symbolized by its move into a splendid, if pompous, neo-classical palace in Fleet Street. Its great clock, jutting out over the pavement, has warned generations of post-prandial journalists of an imminent deadline and seems to feature in every Fleet Street documentary, most recently as a backdrop to tales of industrial woe.

Within a year of acquiring the *Daily Telegraph*, William Berry was created Lord (later Viscount) Camrose, while Gomer became Viscount Kemsley. (Even their elder brother, Seymour, back in Merthyr, was found a peerage, becoming Lord Buckland.) Camrose eschewed the methods used by Northcliffe after buying *The Times*. He respected the political independence on which Burnham had so prided himself: Burnham, although an MP and then an active peer, had refused ministerial office lest it damage this independence. He also refused to engage in the sales war then consuming the resources of the popular press. Instead, Camrose expanded by acquisition. In 1937 he bought the Conservative *Morning Post* with some 100,000 new readers. That year, Camrose and Kemsley decided to go their separate ways. Kemsley took the provincial papers, the *Daily Sketch* and the *Sunday Times*. Camrose took the *Daily Telegraph*, the magazines and the *Financial Times* (which was sold and merged with the *Financial News* in 1945).

All the Berry papers were strongly Conservative. Though proprietorially independent, there was little sign of the detached editorial judgement of *The Times*, the *Observer* and the *Manchester Guardian*. Both Kemsley and Camrose were proud of the nineteenth-century tradition of proprietor as editor-in-chief and Camrose at the *Daily Telegraph* bequeathed it to his son, the future Lord Hartwell. Of the two brothers, Kemsley was the less balanced personality. He was a keen supporter of the Conservative leadership and, like Rothermere, made crude interventions into political controversy. Visiting Hitler at Bayreuth in July 1939, he was emphatic in discounting Churchill's significance. Chamberlain subsequently reported that 'While giving every credit to Mr Winston Churchill for his ability as a writer and as a speaker, he [Kemsley] reminded Herr Hitler that Mr Churchill had been unfortunate in his campaigns on at least four occasions in the past.' Kemsley later asserted that 'if it had been left to him, he could have managed Hitler and he could have stopped the war,' (quoted by Koss). The arrogance that proprietorship could induce, even in the hard-headed son of a Merthyr alderman, apparently knew no bounds.

Camrose was more circumspect. He was certainly committed to the Conservative cause: during the Second World War Churchill always read the *Daily Telegraph* last, 'knowing that would be all right'. He craved a viscountcy but had to await one from Churchill in 1941 (a contemporary said he really wanted an earldom). Yet he was not a party man. Unlike most of his fellow proprietors, he neither stood for Parliament nor sought political office, though he later agreed to be a wartime adviser to the Ministry of Information. When the Conservative leadership became deeply split in 1939, the Berry titles were divided in their sympathies, with Kemsley's *Sunday Times* remaining loyal to Chamberlain and Camrose's *Daily Telegraph* siding, for a time, with the pro-Churchill faction. (The Astor titles also divided.) Camrose remained an aloof figure but always kept his eye firmly on what he regarded as his first responsibility – his papers. He never diversified or distributed his profits into other activities, as Rothermere was to do. By 1939 he had taken the sales of the *Daily Telegraph* to 750,000 and given it a financial security that survived until 1985. When the crash finally came, his son could say truthfully, 'My family have lived only for their papers.' Camrose died in 1954.

The outbreak of the Second World War brought newsprint rationing and a truce in the battle for circulation. By then, the papers born of the Northcliffe revolution had matured into solid institutions, and during the war their combined sales rose to more than 15 million. The *Daily Express* and the renascent *Daily Mirror* took the lion's share, with the *Daily Telegraph* topping 1 million. After a century in which titles had been bought and sold in the political saloon, the press had now largely freed itself of overt party control. The MP who in 1918 protested, 'Who elects the press? Any rogue with a million of money,' was merely reflecting his own profession's final loss of leverage over Fleet Street. Lord Northcliffe might have cut a ridiculous figure as a pseudo-politician but his commercial innovations led to huge circulations that meant financial independence of cross-subsidy at least for half a century. Unstable though he might have been, Northcliffe was never guilty of being under any politician's thumb for long.

The political potential of this independence was never put to the test. Daily newspapers are about the novel, the revelatory, the mischievous. Politics, especially politics in government, must concern itself with quite different qualities: consistency, confidentiality and collective loyalty. As Delane wrote of the press in 1852, 'We cannot admit that its purpose is to share the labours of statesmanship or that it is bound by the same limitations, the same duties, the same liabilities as that of a Minister of the Crown . . . the Press lives by disclosure.' British political parties were co-operative, democratic organizations that had to be capable of evolving and sustaining policies over time, in and out of office. The newspapers they and their backers sustained up to the Second World War – such as the *Morning Post* or *Daily Herald* – were anaemic products as a result. They were edited with both hands tied and could not compete with publications free of this burden.

When the press lords themselves strayed into politics, they were no more successful than when politicians strayed into journalism. The life force of Lord Rothermere's United Empire party was no more than a series of daily lectures, dumped on the nation's breakfast table and limp by lunchtime. There were times when the Harmsworths and Beaverbrook came near to a common front, during the Asquith/ Lloyd George confrontation and again in 1930. It is possible that the Berrys and the Astors might have formed a potent alliance in the late 1930s. Neither happened. Whenever a conspiracy came near to hatching, proprietorial egotism got the better of it and left proprietors an easy target for ridicule. Most of the first generation of mass-market proprietors were self-made men dazzled by the ease with which they could ascend the social ladder. The blasts of grapeshot that emerged from the Northcliffe and Beaverbrook presses could certainly unnerve a politician, but flattery, cajolery and honours proved reasonably solid defences against it and served to show proprietorial influence for what it was – mostly bluff.

The proprietor eager for political influence had (and still has) to imitate his nineteenth-century forebears, by entering the inner councils of the political Establishment, becoming part of its structure and accepting its disciplines. In doing so, he had to disregard the commercial interest of his paper. With the brief exception of Beaverbrook (and possibly Brendan Bracken at the *Financial News*), no twentieth-century proprietor enjoyed both political confidence and journalistic success. The newspapermen who exerted most influence prior to 1939 were not those who could claim the 'mandatc' of vast circulations. They were not proprietors but editors: H. A. Gwynne of the *Morning Post*, J. L. Garvin of the *Observer* and Geoffrey Dawson of *The Times*. The last named believed in assiduously 'supporting the Government of the day', but he maintained an independent criticism of its policies, developing under Baldwin and Chamberlain an influence considered greater than that of most cabinet ministers. Such editors enjoyed power through their private contacts and the force of argument expressed in their writing. It did not matter that few of the electorate ever read their pages.

The proprietors also had to cope with competition. Their American counterparts were able swiftly to build local quasi-monopolies on the basis of limited urban circulations. As such, they could establish an 'extra-democratic' political status. British press lords had to accept that their readers were spoiled for choice. When Northcliffe trumpeted that 'the whole country will think with us when we say the word', his critics could retort that much of the country preferred to think with the *Daily Express*, the *Morning Post*, the *Daily Telegraph* or the *Daily Sketch*. Many others enjoyed Northcliffe's papers but never read his editorials.

By the outbreak of war in 1939, the concept of the political proprietor had lost both its relevance and its appeal. The recession, the amalgamations of the early 1930s and the resulting circulation war had taken their toll on proprietorial morale. Running newspapers had become a hard and, in some cases, desperate slog. *The Times* and the *Observer*, under the benign control of the Astor family, were in the hands of strong editors. Beaverbrook's friends were out of power, though he returned to active politics under Churchill. Rothermere's influence became more eccentric as war approached, by which time his son Esmond had taken over the direction of the *Daily Mail*. The *News Chronicle* and *Daily Herald* were struggling to establish an identity by shaking off the chains of political partisanship. And how much did a paper's politics really matter? In 1938 the first survey of newspaper opinion from Political and Economic Planning suggested that few readers perceived the political stance of the paper they read. The era of the proprietor-as-politician appeared to be over.

There is no sadder evocation of the passing of this era than A. J. P. Taylor's account of Beaverbrook's declining years. Though the time was the early 1960s, Beaverbrook's outlook remained rooted in the 1920s. He was still concerned that his papers were financially sound, but sound only for his propagandist ends. 'I don't care whether whether you make money,' Taylor has him barking at his manager E. J. Robertson. 'All I want to see, Mr Robertson, is a great newspaper strong in reserves.' Beaverbrook was proud of this strength: £100 invested with him in 1930 was worth £983 in 1960, compared with just £171 with Rothermere's holding company, Associated Newspapers. But his dreams were still of wheeling and dealing among his cronies, campaigning forlornly for the Empire and against the Common Market. Great thoughts would pour forth to his staff: 'Repetition is the principal secret of successful propaganda.' 'Spend less money on foolish propaganda, more money on wise propaganda.' When asked whether he would support Sir Alec Douglas-Home as Prime Minister, he replied, 'If he goes for the Common Market, we go in the other direction!'

Beaverbrook refused, with minor lapses, to diversify or otherwise protect the long-term future of his group, convinced that producing 'good' newspapers alone was sufficient security. 'We are newspapermen,' he said. 'If we divert our activities, we will undoubtedly damage our newspapers.' His printing plant was antiquated. Investment was minimal. Profits were generously distributed and put into family trusts. Managerial initiative was crushed.

Shortly before Beaverbrook's death in 1964, the writer Hugh Massingham interviewed him on his life and work.* The old man's mind, he said, was 'like an echoing gallery through which stump the great figures of half a century –

*Quoted in Taylor, see bibliography.

Churchill and Lloyd George and F. E. Smith and Bonar Law
and Stalin and Arnold Bennett'. Massingham asked Beaverbrook about his most passionate campaign, the Empire Crusade. 'One suddenly becomes aware of the ticking of a clock
in the unexpected silence. And one suddenly realizes that the
old man is weeping. It is what he feels is the real failure of his
life, and there he sits in his stockinged feet, fishing for a
handkerchief.' Eventually Beaverbrook replied, 'I was
unworthy. I thought I could carry on the great policy of Joe
Chamberlain. But I failed.'

It is astonishing that a man who, for fifty years, had run
one of Britain's most successful newspapers, could believe
that he had failed, and for such reason.

# 2

---

# CRUMBLING PALACES

The passing of a proprietor is treated by those working on his newspaper like the death of a constitutional monarch. He may not have been admired – he may even have been hated – but he was the king. He embodied the identity of the paper and had, for the duration of his reign, presided over its survival. However small his influence over its daily life, however prominent the influence of his editors, his going marks the end of an era. A new proprietorship means not just a change of policy, it implies a new order – or possibly none.

The heirs to the pre-Second World War proprietors had a difficult task. Their fathers had been the founders of an industry, big men whose public antics had brought fame, if not distinction, to their respective houses. Beaverbrook and the brothers Harmsworth and Berry had all made their own fortunes. They were first-generation proprietors who left a personal stamp on their titles. They had come to regard proprietorship as a means to social or political status, and had inflicted their ambitions on their sons. Gomer Berry of Merthyr prepared the second Viscount Kemsley for industrial leadership by putting him through Marlborough, Oxford, the Guards, a Conservative constituency and marriage to the daughter of a marquess. Esmond Harmsworth went virtually straight from Eton into Parliament at the age of twenty-one. Young Max Aitken, who wanted only to fly and sail, had to endure five years as MP for Holborn. The first (American) Viscount Astor saw both his sons through Eton and Oxford and both became Conservative MPs. Young Waldorf Astor loved politics and was mortified when forced to resign his seat on succeeding to his father's viscountcy. John Jacob remained an MP until 1945.

Few of the heirs possessed any special journalistic or entrepreneurial talent, of which a newspaper requires at least one to survive. The most their readers could expect was that they would choose capable editors and managers. The commercial competition that returned to Fleet Street in the 1950s and 1960s, unlike that of the 1930s, proved terminal for the losers. The pre-war circulation battle may have depleted the profits or increased the losses of proprietors, but it sold a lot of papers. Total daily circulation rose from 9 million in 1930 to 10½ million at the outbreak of war. The threat of closures receded as imported newsprint was rationed and paper sizes shrank. Publishers reduced the number of pages per edition to maintain sales. Wartime demand was high, even with higher cover prices, and soared in the case of the downmarket *Daily Express* and *Daily Mirror*. Rationing distributed advertising more evenly, thus benefiting the weaker titles. *The Times* registered the biggest profit in its history in 1944. Readers often bought two or three different papers a day, a habit that pushed Fleet Street's total circulation above 15 million by the end of the war.

Newsprint rationing mostly ended in 1949 and papers could once again afford to expand their editorial coverage and advertising. Pagination increased, and the public read more newspaper, if not more newspapers. From consuming 0.5 per cent of household budgets in the 1950s, papers rose to consume 0.8 per cent in the 1970s. It would appear that the 'elementary education' market exploited by Northcliffe was saturated by 1945 at a ratio, very roughly, of one daily paper to every four people. Since then, it has been a matter of competing for what has been a gently declining number of purchasers (from 16 million to 15 million over forty years). The quality titles fared best, roughly doubling sales over this period, benefiting from expanding secondary and higher education and the growth of white collar and professional employment. This growth more than compensated for the threat that obsessed Fleet Street managers in the 1950s: that television, and especially televised advertising, would steadily erode their markets. Television's impact was remarkably small: in the quarter-century since the war, no investigator of Fleet Street has been able to show that either sales or revenues have suffered as a direct result of its growing popularity, possibly the reverse.*

It did, none the less, affect the character of Fleet Street. In particular, it drove the popular press down-market. The two leading dailies in the mid to late 1940s, the *Daily Mirror* and the *Daily Express*, had topped 4 million sales by the end of the 1950s largely through the rivalry of two masterful editors, Guy Bartholomew and Arthur Christiansen. Bartholomew was described by Francis Williams as being 'like a labour boss on the San Francisco waterfront in the tough days'. He had fought his way up from the bottom, 'piling up anger, frustration and a cynical contempt for most of the accepted shibboleths of good taste on the way'. He read little and wrote less. He had a 'passion for crude, practical jokes, a ruthless determination to trample on anyone who got in his way and an occasional odd flash of genial charm'.

Like many journalistic popularizers, Bartholomew was convinced that most people preferred looking at papers to reading them. No *Daily Mirror* story should extend beyond 100 or so words. Producing a mass circulation paper was an exercise in presentation and display. He took the paper from a sale of 720,000 when he became editorial director in 1934 – when it was still saddled with Rothermere's tedious propaganda – to 4,500,000 in 1950. His finest hours came during the war, when he gave the *Daily Mirror* a tone of voice to echo that of the soldier at the front and the civilian at home. The newspaper, still owned by the trust into which Rothermere had deposited it but freed from his influence, contrived to distance itself from Churchill and his leadership without appearing in the least unpatriotic.

*Hirsch and Gordon; Henry; see bibliography.

Bartholomew found what seemed to be a new newspaper market among the working class, as Northcliffe had found one among the lower-middle class. He was not a proprietor and was robustly uninterested in serious politics. In a Mass-Observation report published in 1949, only 3 per cent of *Daily Mirror* readers polled said they read its editorials. Bartholomew's aversion to political coverage infuriated the Labour party, whose more up-market *Daily Herald* was hit by the *Daily Mirror*'s success. To Francis Williams (who worked for the *Daily Herald*), the *Daily Mirror* demanded 'almost a new race of journalists with none of the inhibitions ruling in other newspapers . . . a frenzied gusto in dredging the news for sensational stories of sex and crime, and a complete lack of reticence in dealing with them'. Such editors had been the despair of serious-minded journalists before Bartholomew and have continued to be so since.

Arthur Christiansen was likewise a journalistic technician rather than an architect of political strategy. For the quarter-century after he became editor of the *Daily Express* in 1933, he made it not just the mouthpiece of Beaverbrook's propaganda but a meticulously edited news machine. 'The policies were Lord Beaverbrook's, the presentation mine,' he wrote in his memoirs. Like many editors, he had to be obsequious in the presence of his boss while maintaining a dictatorial relationship with his staff. He managed to achieve the former, like Bartholomew, by a studious unconcern with politics. The latter came from a ruthless sub-editorial pen. His task, he said, was 'to simplify news in such a way that it would be interesting to the Permanent Secretary of the Foreign Office and to the charwoman who brushed his office floor'. Any story had to be told best in the *Daily Express*. Linked with the more traditional fare of gossip and jingoism, this professionalism took the paper far ahead of its rivals. Christiansen made the Express building in Fleet Street vibrate with 'active' journalism, creating news as much as reflecting it. Long after he had gone, the short-lived editors who sat in his chair in the 1970s were always conscious of his shadow.

The *Daily Mirror* was able to protect itself against the appeal of television by supplying a sensational journalism to which television had as yet no answer. Its popular rivals were more vulnerable. The *Daily Express*, *Daily Mail*, *Daily Herald* and the *News Chronicle* relied heavily on placing dramatic news and pictures on the nation's breakfast table each morning. Television could do this the night before. In addition, nationwide circulations were, at first, unable to supply advertisers with the regional variations offered by the new commercial television companies. Nor could they compete with the quality press in the rapid growth of up-market classified advertising, which was unsuitable for television. It was in this middle band of popular journalism that the impact of television on the character of Fleet Street was most apparent. In 1948 it comprised 60 per cent of daily circulation; by 1965 it had fallen to 47 per cent and today (1986), with only the *Daily Mail* (and *Today*) in the field, it is down to 17 per cent.*

Those who had fared less well in the struggles of the 1930s were the first to feel the pressure. The *News Chronicle* was running in fourth place in 1939. The Cadbury family regarded it as held in trust, if rather ambivalently, for the Liberal cause. At the turn of the century, George Cadbury had seen the proprietorship of its forerunner, the *Daily News*, as a crusade: 'I can enter into it with real pleasure and joy as . . . the opportunity for good is vast. The churches have not preached ethical Christianity and we must do it.' He later told his son Edward,

> I want you to know that the money I have invested in these papers would otherwise have gone to charities. I have a profound conviction that money spent on charities is of infinitely less value than money spent in trying to arouse my fellow countrymen to the necessity for measures to ameliorate the condition of the poor.

By the mid-1950s, the *News Chronicle* was in severe commercial difficulties under the direction of Lord Layton and George Cadbury's son, Laurence, who was at the same time running the family chocolate business. Stephen Koss quotes a

*Michael Mander refers to this middle band of the market as Fleet Street's 'Bermuda Triangle', papers with predominantly working-class readership being especially vulnerable. In Harry Henry (ed.), see bibliography.

contemporary as saying that Cadbury 'suffers from weakness and timidity and lack of news instinct, while the aristocratic Lord Layton was captive of his somewhat unworldly political aims'. Cadbury, in an attempt to maintain the family tradition, made a practice of having the *News Chronicle*'s worthy editorials read over to him each night. He would have been better occupied reading its accounts.

By 1960 the *News Chronicle* and its stablemate, the London evening *Star*, had been losing money for four years. Sales were falling by 15 per cent a year. In 1957 savings had been attempted in discussion with the unions, but they were not enough to salvage a hopeless position. Offers had been entertained – and purchasers sought – for both titles. Talks were held with the Beaverbrook Newspapers and Odhams groups. There was mention of a 'daily *Observer*'. The first of what was to be a wholly new genre of Fleet Street proprietors (see chapter six), the Canadian Roy Thomson, was approached. He drew back at the prospect of a redundancy liability of £3 million if he subsequently failed. 'I think I could have saved it,' he said later, 'but I could not afford the gamble.' (He was to prove less fastidious with his gambles at *The Times*.) Eventually, the *News Chronicle* and the *Star* were sold to Associated Newspapers, after Rothermere had ascertained that there was no way of keeping them alive. He was effectively removing competition from his *Daily Mail* and *Evening News* for the price of meeting the *News Chronicle*'s debts.

The sudden closure of the *News Chronicle* shocked Fleet Street. That a Liberal newspaper should have gone to the right-wing Rothermere was more than many a commentator could stomach. That a paper should be sold like any other company seemed outrageous. The *Observer* commented that it had been 'sold with its editor, staff and readers as a nineteenth-century Russian estate was bought and sold with its souls', an analogy the *Observer* forgot when it was itself later put up for sale by the Astors. A Royal Commission was set up to inquire into the future of the press and it investigated the *News Chronicle*'s demise in morbid detail. Each rival proprietor was invited to tell the Commission what he thought had gone wrong. Each castigated the family's direction of the paper, most of them hypocritically avoiding any reference to their own problems. Sir Geoffrey Crowther, a member of the *News Chronicle*'s controlling trust, agreed that 'supreme blame must rest with the management'. He added disconsolately, 'I suspect that had we chosen to go in for pin-up girls, they would not have been good pin-up girls.' Laurence Cadbury gave a suitably proprietorial excuse when he explained that had his son Julian not died in a car crash in 1950, his other son Adrian would have been able to devote himself full time to the newspapers rather than concentrating on the main family business of chocolate. 'We might have raised the money to continue the fight,' he said.

Despite a circulation at its demise of 1,200,000 copies, the *News Chronicle* was the most likely first casualty of the post-war decline in middle-ground newspapers, but it was also clear that the proprietor's true legacy, the will 'to arouse my countrymen' and find the resources to do so, had long since been spent. The first palace had crumbled.

The *News Chronicle*'s chief rival for the progressive middle-of-the-readership market, the *Daily Herald*, momentarily rejoiced at the prospect of a surge in sales from its demise. Yet it too was short of money and losing market share to the *Daily Mirror*. The indulgent hand of Lord Southwood was no longer at the helm. (His death, in 1946, was not without a flourish. His successor, A. C. Duncan, was a keen spiritualist and relied on regular 'consultations' with his deceased boss, a proprietorial immortality not even Northcliffe could equal.) A new editorial agreement between the *Daily Herald*'s majority shareholder, Odhams, and the minority shareholder, the TUC, was signed in 1957, reaffirming the paper's future as 'Labour's daily newspaper'. Yet the days of a 'bought' party press were gone, however badly Labour needed a voice of its own to pit against the Conservative press. Circulation continued to slide: by 1960 the *Daily Herald*'s 1,400,000 was dangerously close to the level at which the *News Chronicle* was about to fail. The TUC was persuaded to relax its claim to uncritical support for Labour in the editorial columns, a stance that was proving lethal to the paper at a time of Conservative ascendancy. But this was of no help. The

*Daily Herald* was in the commercial control of Odhams, and where Odhams went it would have to go too.

In 1959 Odhams had acquired its old rival, the publishers George Newnes, but within two years found itself the subject of predatory interest from the Mirror group. It sought rescue in an attempted amalgamation with Roy Thomson. In 1953 Thomson had gently lifted the *Scotsman* from the hands of the elderly Sir Edmund Findlay, to relieve him of worry over death duties. In 1959 similar anxieties drove the Kemsley family to approach Thomson with the same end in view. Viscount Kemsley (see pages 30–3) was still chairman and editor-in-chief of the *Sunday Times*, the *Sunday Graphic*, the *Empire News* and a collection of provincial titles, eighteen papers in all, with his son Lionel as deputy chairman. The group was run conservatively by members of the family – there were four Berry sons on the board. Their papers supported the Conservative party with uncritical loyalty, though the down-market *Daily Sketch* (later sold to Lord Rothermere) held short of endorsing Churchill in 1945.

Lord Kemsley was now seventy-five (he died in 1968) and after tortuous negotiations an agreement was reached to sell the group for £5 million. The sum was well above its apparent value and indicated a determination on Thomson's part to do more than sit still and watch decline continue. The departure of the Kemsley branch of the Berry family was gloomy. Thomson professed himself shocked by their apparent indifference to the commercial health of their inheritance. The Sheffield paper, which was losing £100,000 a year, was run by a cousin who, Thomson discovered, arrived at the office every morning with two Borzois, his only management experience being as a Guards officer.

Thomson was fascinated by the Berrys' obsession with their cars. Berry directors all had Rolls-Royces or Bentleys with chauffeurs, and usually second cars for their families. Since some of the family remained on the payroll for a time, Thomson ordered that each could have only one car and that all Rolls-Royces must be replaced by Rovers. He recalled in his memoirs, 'This caused more distress among the members of Lord Kemsley's family than anything else we did then or later. They all wrote asking us to give them a little time and they would buy the cars from us.' Thus passed the glorious house of Kemsley.

To Thomson, Odhams offered an opportunity to add a chain of successful magazines to his fast expanding group. To the *Daily Mirror*, on the other hand, Odhams' *Woman* and *Woman's Own*, along with the *Sunday People*, offered a near-monopoly of British weekly magazines. With Bartholomew gone, the leadership of the Mirror group passed to Cecil King, son of Northcliffe's sister. King had gone to work in this backwater of the Harmsworth empire in 1929 and become editorial director of the *Sunday Pictorial* in 1931. Educated at Winchester and Oxford, he was a big man who physically and intellectually towered over those around him in the company. He was unlikely to derive much stimulus from the content of his publications, but was ambitious enough to see in them the vehicle for corporate and political aggrandizement. King was unique among second-generation proprietors in the degree to which he sought to emulate the first generation. His papers were a means to the end of political influence, with high circulation the index of electoral potency. In 1952 the editorial direction of the *Daily Mirror* was taken over by Hugh Cudlipp, a rough-and-tumble journalist with Bartholomew's flair but with an added belief in the paper's role as a voice of working-class opinion. He possessed, in Francis Williams's words, 'the capacity to translate serious political issues into terms that even the politically illiterate can understand'. The skill answered precisely to King's ambition.

Whatever might be the wider implications of the Odhams take-over battle in 1961, the fate of the *Daily Herald* was what attracted most publicity. It was Labour's turn to be as shocked as the Liberals had been over the demise of the *News Chronicle*. The *Daily Herald* was the one paper whose loyalty to the party was beyond question; most Labour leaders regarded the *Daily Mirror* with contempt. They also found it hard to believe that one company would want to keep two competing popular papers in existence. Both Thomson and King understood that they were moving into politically sensitive territory. As their organizations and ambitions expanded, so public and

Government reaction to their actions became more important. Labour in opposition had no power to forestall the *Daily Herald*'s sale, but it had the leverage of a putative future government. Trade union and Labour leaders were courted by both bidders, and it was only when King and Cudlipp capped an improved share offer with an extravagant undertaking to keep publishing the *Daily Herald* for seven years that Thomson withdrew from the field. 'I didn't realize at the time what a blessing it was that I had been kept out of Odhams,' he recalled. 'For there is no doubt had that merger taken place, I would never have got *The Times*.'

The *Daily Mirror* gave a public pledge that John Beavan, the *Daily Herald*'s editor, would continue in office and that 'the *Herald*'s future as a separate entity will be fought for with the utmost energy'. The Government decided not to refer the take-over to the Monopolies Commission – a remarkable decision given the concentration of magazine publishing involved – and the Odhams group duly changed hands. Fierce pressure from the political Establishment had engineered the transfer of a loss-making but politically important product from one benefactor to another. The Labour movement had proved a source of salvation to the *Daily Herald* while the *News Chronicle* a year earlier had fallen victim to the dwindling strength of Liberalism.

The emotion that surrounded the sale of the *Daily Herald* did more than save it. Although in one sense the Labour interest was now wholly at Cecil King's mercy, he too had a restricted range of options. He could take the *Daily Herald* down-market, though that would compete with his profitable *Daily Mirror*. He could leave it to decline, and argue in a year or two that the paper was bankrupt and his pledge could no longer be honoured, though he would be accused of deliberately undermining it. Or he could make the best of a difficult job. He chose the last. Despite growing losses, King and Cudlipp subjected the *Daily Herald* to an expensive facelift and even a change of name. In September 1964 it re-emerged as the *Sun* under the slogan, 'a newspaper born of the age we live in' (not to be confused with the present version of the paper, reborn after the *Sun*'s later sale to

Rupert Murdoch). Its market was intended to be younger, wealthier, more dynamic and more female than that of its previous incarnation. It was self-consciously the paper of the Swinging Sixties.

King's *Sun*, however, was born not of any emerging new spirit but of market research guided by wishful thinking. For all its fine intentions, it turned out to be directed at precisely the declining middle-ground market that the *Daily Herald* and *News Chronicle* had found infertile. Its pages had the patronizing air that journalists find hard to avoid when writing to someone else's brief. It was a case of middle-class writers earnestly searching for a language with which to appeal to working-class readers. King was hoping that either the *Daily Mail* or the *Daily Express* would go under, but it was a faint hope. Within three years, the *Sun* was losing £175,000 a year and its circulation resumed the *Daily Herald*'s downward path. At the expiry of the guarantee period in 1969 (after King's departure), it was put on the market and acquired by another newcomer to Fleet Street, Rupert Murdoch. He did to it what Northcliffe had done to the *Evening News* and Bartholomew to the *Daily Mirror*. He took it ruthlessly down-market, bringing it far more working-class readers than years of TUC and Labour tutelage had done.

Cecil King did not stop at presenting himself as the saviour of Labour's own newspaper. He idolized his uncle, Lord Northcliffe, and regarded himself as inheritor of his public status. When he took over as chairman of the *Daily Mirror* and *Sunday Pictorial* in 1951, he became head of a group already approaching the market strength enjoyed by his two uncles. He reacquired Northcliffe's old Amalgamated Press from the Berrys, with its miscellany of weeklies, periodicals, books and annuals. He added provincial and foreign newspapers, eight book publishers, a record company and holdings in television, paper, entertainment and contract printing. The Mirror group was renamed the International Publishing Corporation (IPC), boasting it was the largest newspaper publishing enterprise in the world. King took to using Northcliffean phraseology, describing his papers as 'my papers' and the *Daily Mirror* readers as 'my people'. As many said, and he doubtless thought, his uncle would have been proud of him.

The *Daily Mirror* had supported Labour, with fluctuating degrees of enthusiasm, throughout the thirteen years of Conservative rule, though it denied the party its specific endorsement at the 1955 election. In addition to saving the *Daily Herald*, King ingratiated himself with most of the party's leaders and regarded himself as power broker in the party's fortunes. 'The *Mirror* might not be able to win you the next election,' Cudlipp had told Richard Crossman, 'but if we turn against you we can certainly lose it for you.' With the return of Labour to power in 1964, King awaited his reward. Yet the new Prime Minister, Harold Wilson, proved a careful student of twentieth-century press history. Taking a leaf from Lloyd George's book, he invited King to the first lunch held after his arrival in Downing Street. He offered him his heartfelt thanks, a peerage and a junior ministerial post at the Board of Trade.

The offer was almost precisely what had been offered to Northcliffe, Rothermere and Beaverbrook. King was deeply offended. Wilson, critically short of governmental talent after so long in opposition, was appointing nonentities from the back benches to Government jobs. He could not even argue that King was an outsider to parliamentary politics – Frank Cousins of the Transport and General Workers' Union (TGWU) was found a seat and given a cabinet post. The message was clear. For the modern Labour party, the trade union movement meant more than the support of the *Daily Mirror* and the *Sun*. King refused both job and peerage and his newspapers soon began to show his resentment.

Cecil King's diary is a remarkable record of the extent to which a newspaper proprietor has access to the corridors of Government yet is powerless to turn that access to account. King was fascinated by his fame. 'My seat in the front row of the political stalls is increasingly interesting,' he wrote. He was contemptuous of fellow second-generation proprietors for not accepting the status to which he felt they were historically entitled. On one political occasion he records Sir Max Aitken (Beaverbrook's son) as talking 'complete nonsense; it is hard to see what can be done with such a man'. He was shocked to hear that Aitken actually believed in the archaic policies for which the *Daily Express* campaigned. He wrote disapprovingly that the second Lord Rothermere 'wants the status and prestige of a major newspaper proprietor but has no ambition to do the job . . . He seems to know very little of what is going on in the world.'

By 1968, admittedly a low point in Wilson's leadership, King had convinced himself that the man who had so slighted him was no longer fit to be running the country. King had become a director of the Bank of England, a perk he had happily accepted from Wilson along with membership of the National Coal Board and National Parks Commission, and from his position at the Bank he claimed to see the British economy crumbling on all sides. He would summon politicians to his luncheon room high in the orange-glass Mirror building at Holborn Circus where he sat in state under a portrait of his uncle. 'Iain Macleod to lunch,' he recorded. 'He wanted to know how I saw things, as I had been right all along! Evidently a crash was coming and equally evidently nothing could be done about Wilson until it came.'

In May 1968 King took the step against which both his Harmsworth uncles might have warned him. An editorial appeared in the *Daily Mirror*, to be quoted in full in 'his' other papers, the *Sun* and the *Glasgow Record*, under the headline 'Enough is Enough'. It was written and signed by King himself and said the country needed a new Prime Minister* and Labour a new leader. Though the article had the agreement of Hugh Cudlipp, his deputy chairman, it was proprietorial overkill, especially from a man who had so identified himself with Labour's return to power. It was not until after it appeared that King asked his editors if they agreed with it: they dutifully said they did.

The article was predictably ineffective. The iron law of such hostile journalism is not to mount so strident an attack that it adduces sympathy for its victim. Wilson's enemies

---

*Lord Mountbatten seems to have been King's favourite choice, see Philip Ziegler, *Mountbatten*, Collins, 1985.

were legion but a hyperbolic attack in the *Daily Mirror* was counter-productive. More serious for King, the article became a weapon in the hands of internal critics. King lacked one lever in the hands of a traditional proprietor: he did not control his own company but was its salaried employee, responsible as chairman to a board and shareholders, none of whom held more than 5 per cent of the stock. However great his admiration for his uncle, he was the victim of Northcliffe's lack of interest in the *Daily Mirror* and the dispersal of its shares by Rothermere in 1931. By 1968 the expansion over which King had presided had begun to falter. The printing division was losing money, mostly through union restrictive practices which King did nothing to curb. The board felt its chairman should be concentrating on business rather than politics. Now he had committed not just a newspaper but a major British corporation – IPC – to a vendetta against the Prime Minister of the day.

If the company's financial position had been more sound, King might have survived. As it was, colleagues who for years had laboured under his lofty shadow summoned up their courage and fired him. King's reaction was suitably majestic. In a rage, he called the news media to Holborn to witness his downfall. To his subsequent satisfaction, television interrupted the afternoon's racing at Epsom to give a somewhat baffled nation news of his demise. Radio, television and the rest of the press were at his disposal and he told himself, 'I shall still be in the public eye for quite a while yet.' He went on to dabble in the favourite pastime of the politically dispossessed: the construction of a 'ministry of all talents' with himself as a prominent member. The official reason for King's dismissal was given as his 'increasing preoccupation with politics'. For a Harmsworth it was a fitting epitaph.

If the deaths of the *News Chronicle* and *Daily Herald* put an end to the concept of a partisan press, the growing insecurity of *The Times* in the 1960s was seen as a national humiliation. While Cecil King was seeking proprietorial renaissance, the Astor family was watching helplessly as the papers it had bought from King's uncle slid towards bankruptcy. The Astors had, with the Berrys, been custodians of

British quality journalism since the 1920s (at least among national proprietors). In 1962 Lord Astor was driven to involuntary tax exile in the South of France as a result of budget changes which could have involved *The Times'* finances in his estate duty. His son Gavin was left to cope with the consequence of his unbusinesslike approach to the paper.

In the early 1960s *The Times* made regular small losses, covered by revenue from investments and subsidiaries (notably the *Times Educational Supplement*). Its journalistic supremacy was being challenged not only by its ancient rival, the *Daily Telegraph*, but by the expanding *Financial Times* and the newly 'national' *Manchester Guardian*. All attempts at managerial or editorial reform were firmly resisted by Lord Astor in messages from his Mediterranean retreat. He continued to regard the paper, as many remarked, like a stately home of which he was honoured custodian and to which no alterations could be made. Lord Astor was proving true to the message conveyed to Northcliffe's trustees in 1922, that he 'knew quite well that he could never hope to make a penny' from the paper.

Change came to *The Times* but, as so often in this story, too little and too late. A report from the accountants, Cooper Brothers, in 1958 advocated a higher circulation, news on the front page, an end to anonymity and a more aggressive editorial and commercial policy. This gave rise to a tortuous internal debate, conducted through letters, memoranda and committees over the next five years. An advertising campaign, 'Top People Take *The Times*', inched the circulation up from 230,000 to 250,000 by the mid-1960s, in part through an expensive student discount scheme. A costly rebuilding of the Walters' old Printing House Square was completed in 1965. A year later came Operation Breakthrough: again a plan to put news (instead of classified advertisements) on the front page, while the inside pages were to be adorned with a political cartoon, a gossip column and a women's page.

The impact was reminiscent of the coming of Northcliffe. In six months the circulation climbed to 300,000. Since the price per copy, 6d, covered only a quarter of the run-on cost and advertising rates could not be increased until the higher sale was sustained and audited, the result of the rise was a devastating increase in costs. Newspapers are a business in which cash flows are so large that the smallest percentage alteration in costs or revenues can undermine stability. In 1966 *The Times* suddenly faced a loss on the year of £300,000. The board estimated that the new plans would eventually require £4 million if they were to succeed. In 1963 Gavin Astor had had to find £250,000 to buy out the last Walter shares (10 per cent) to prevent them falling into the hands of Roy Thomson, already sniffing round Printing House Square. The Astors had no more money. As Woods and Bishop recall, 'The assumption by the staff of *The Times*, the general public and even some members of the board, had long been that, come what might, the Astor millions would always safeguard the paper.' Those millions did not exist. *The Times* was as mortal as any denizen of Fleet Street.

Gavin Astor became exasperated and disillusioned as *The Times*' executives ruminated and stalled over the rescue plans of the early 1960s. He later wrote the staff a sad reflection on the lot of a newspaper owner: 'I have come to realize that to carry the entire financial risk as Proprietor no less than the full legal responsibility as Chairman for the success or failure of the Company, without also carrying executive power, is not a satisfactory situation.' It seemed a far cry from Rothermere's admonition to leave 'twenty trusty's' to do the hard work while the proprietor enjoyed the fun. Yet Astor did nothing to disabuse his staff of the thesis that newspapers were a sacred business unlike any other, and that *The Times* was most sacred of all. *The Times*, he said, 'is a peculiar property in that service to what it believes are the best interests of the nation is placed before the personal and financial gains of its Proprietors'. (Proprietor always deserved a capital P in the Astor hagiography.) The thesis made no allowance for personal and financial losses.

To the chagrin of his staff, in 1966 Gavin Astor sought a purchaser for the paper. Talks were held with the *Manchester Guardian*, then the *Observer* and then the *Financial Times*. None had the resources which might have secured *The Times* intact. The paper's only asset was the building at Printing House Square, yet, as Astor explained, *The Times* was nothing without its building. To have rendered the paper homeless, he believed, would have destroyed it. By thus tying a large annual loss round the neck of his one asset, the building, Astor drastically reduced the value of the company on the open market. Eventually, the board took a deep breath and accepted what it regarded as inevitable, a standing offer of £2 million from the newly ennobled Lord Thomson and alliance to his *Sunday Times*. In September Astor travelled to France to tell his father that the paper he had bought for an exorbitant £1.5 million in 1922 was now sold to a Canadian for (in real terms) a fraction of that sum. He then went to Hove to inform John Walter, now ninety, that his family's last link with the paper had been severed.

The Monopolies Commission inquiry into the sale of *The Times* was similar to the Royal Commission that followed the closure of the *News Chronicle*, an extraordinary parade of Fleet Street self-importance. Thomson owned no national newspaper and the reason for a monopoly reference (under a Labour Government!) was his unconventional background and the special status of *The Times*.* It was an Establishment initiation rite, Thomson remarked with rare acidity, 'to see if I was worthy of their trust'. The Astors, like the Cadburys before them, were regarded as abdicating before their time and from a throne of symbolic significance. Such an event could not pass without investigation and comment.

For once an inquiry into Fleet Street punctured its pomposity. The Commission placed the blame for the condition of *The Times* squarely on the shoulders of the proprietor and management. It expressed surprise that the paper was being sold just at the point when new investment should be about to yield a return. After years of delay, the right strategy had at last been adopted; it needed only a steady nerve and

---

*In 1966 the Mirror group controlled 36.8 per cent of national and provincial daily newspaper circulation; Beaverbrook had 18.1 per cent; Associated Newspapers had 10.9 per cent; Thomson (even with *The Times*) only 6.5 per cent.

access to transitional finance, which on the existing prospectus should not be hard to find. Yet the management had given up. The Commission concluded, 'It is plain that the company no longer had confidence in its own ability to carry on successfully, and this in itself makes change desirable.' The Astors, in other words, had merely lost their nerve.

The Commission also addressed itself to the question of whether *The Times* was, as Gavin Astor had implied, in any way special. It decided it was not: 'Its prestige and the authority with which it speaks should depend entirely on the quality of the newspaper itself.' The Commission accepted, however, that the paper's closure would be a serious matter and that there was a national interest in its surviving as an independent organ. To this extent, it found the Thomson Organisation a satisfactory guarantor. The take-over was approved.

Even in departing, the Astors were able to exact a heavy price from Lord Thomson. A subsidiary board for Times Newspapers was set up separate from the Thomson Organisation, with one-half composed of Astor nominees. To the end, Lord Astor refused any deal which would have allowed Thomson personally on to this board. Astor was the son of a transatlantic *arriviste* and had acquired the paper through the influence of a Canadian manager, yet he could not bring himself to allow another such *arriviste* the full dignity of proprietorship. Thomson also had to promise (or at least felt it tactful to promise) that the paper would be cross-subsidized from the profitable *Sunday Times*. If that proved insufficient, then money would be transferred from family holdings rather than be a charge on shareholders in the Thomson Organisation. The object was 'to continue publishing these papers as quality papers in the national interest. This undertaking will continue for twenty-one years and will be binding on our successors,' said Thomson.

Lord Thomson had described his earlier acquisition of a Scottish commercial television licence as 'a licence to print money'. *The Economist* described his purchase of *The Times* as a licence to lose it. As we shall see in chapter six, he was none the less delighted. Gavin Astor, on the other hand, was

55

exhausted. The old proprietorship, he said in a valedictory message to his staff, was an anachronism. 'The new scheme [for *The Times*] recognizes that the age when proprietors could successfully run their newspapers as a sideline is fading into an age where the survival and prosperity of newspapers depend upon brilliant commercial and professional management.' Thomson would not be 'hampered by the peculiar inhibitions which had grown in the traditions of Printing House Square and which my father wished to see preserved at all costs'. What particularly irked Astor was that Thomson was acquiring *The Times* in part with profits from television: an investment he himself had urged but which had been obstructed both by his father and by *The Times*' managers. Astor knew that things had to change at Printing House Square. Yet another of the ironies which have dogged *The Times*' history this century is that Astor's lament at his father's conservatism was echoed fourteen years later by Lord Thomson's son as he gazed on a similarly depressing scene at the paper in 1979–80.

# 3

## SINS OF THE FATHERS

Within two years of the fall of the house of 'J. J.' Astor in 1966, another ancestral proprietor saw his inheritance slip from his grasp. The Sunday *News of the World* had, for over a century, enjoyed the biggest circulation of any newspaper in Britain, at one point rising to 8 million copies. As we have seen, its mix of fiction, sensationalism and occasional radicalism predated any product of Newnes or Harmsworth. The Carr family had controlled it since 1891, with Sir Emsley Carr as its editor for an extraordinary half-century to 1941. It had become the epitome of down-market journalism, with barely credible 'human-interest' stories combining prurience with titillation. Its disregard of politics – it failed to endorse either party at the 1964 general election – would have been castigated in a 'new' proprietor, yet was viewed as merely eccentric in the Carrs. The paper's management never changed, despite a flash of expansionism when Sir Emsley's son, Sir William, made an abortive bid for Odhams' magazines in 1959. The Carr family treated the paper unashamedly as a milch cow. Profits were devoted to such Carr pastimes as champagne, a company stud farm and private golf courses. By the mid-1960s circulation was falling steadily from its 8 million peak and profits were declining.

As the shares were divided between increasingly dissident relatives, the company was vulnerable to take-over. In 1968 Robert Maxwell, an energetic Czech immigrant, Labour MP

57

and owner of Pergamon Press, made an offer for the paper. Sir William Carr was appalled. His editor and friend Stafford Somerfield wrote an editorial of ill-concealed contempt for Maxwell. The Carrs, he said,

> followed a great family tradition. Would this attitude and policy be continued by a complete stranger, as far as Fleet Street and this newspaper are concerned, a man with no newspaper experience and a Socialist MP? . . . I believe Mr Maxwell is interested in power and money. There is nothing wrong with that but it is not everything . . . This is a British newspaper, run by British people. Let's keep it that way.*

The attack earned Maxwell some sympathy in liberal quarters. Chauvinism was rarely a successful defence against Fleet Street predators and although Carr fought off Maxwell, he did so only by falling foul of another overseas entrepreneur eager to win his proprietorial spurs.

Rupert Murdoch presented himself to the Carrs – advised to do so by his bankers – not as an aggressor but as an ally against Maxwell. Never was wolf so skilfully camouflaged in sheep's clothing. After two months of acrimony, deft footwork by Murdoch and a widespread belief that Take-over Panel rules were being bent to keep out Maxwell, the Murdoch/Carr faction won the day. Murdoch created new shares in the company on the basis of his Australian interests, sufficient to give himself a commanding position. It was ironic that Murdoch's arrival in Fleet Street was purportedly to save an institution that declared itself 'as British as roast beef' and was in defence of an old proprietor against a new one. 'Rupert is a gentleman,' Carr was reported as saying, when a defeated Maxwell warned him Murdoch would have him out 'before your feet touch the ground'.

Maxwell was right. Murdoch had promised Carr he could remain as chairman as well as joint managing director; in addition, Murdoch would not increase his personal shareholding to give him full control of the company. Within six months, he had overridden these and other undertakings given to the

---

*Quoted by Leapman, see bibliography.

Carr family. In June 1969 Murdoch blandly ousted Carr as chairman and took full control of the company. He professed himself as amazed at the Carrs' naïvety as Thomson had been at the Kemsleys'. The soft underbelly of Fleet Street had been probed and found vulnerable. Murdoch later boasted that his acquisition of the *News of the World* was 'the biggest steal since the Great Train Robbery'.

No sooner had the Carrs been vanquished than IPC's hold on the *Sun* began to weaken also. With King gone and Cudlipp's seven-year guarantee to the TUC expired, the *Sun* was down to 850,000 sales. Cudlipp decided either to sell the paper or close it. Once again Maxwell was first into the fray. Aware of the mesmeric hold the *Daily Herald* tradition still had over the *Daily Mirror*'s boardroom, he offered to take the title for nothing, run it on a non-profit basis with reduced staff and commit himself 'unalterably that the newspaper shall give clear and loyal support at all times to the Labour movement'. But the unions would not buy the staff cuts and the journalists were suspicious of Maxwell's integrity. The ball was back in the board's court. Cudlipp now felt he could not, in all (socialist) conscience, refuse another bid should it come forward, even if the survival of the *Sun* might one day threaten the *Daily Mirror*. Fleet Street tradition, with a dose of Labour sentiment, overruled commercial prudence.

Rupert Murdoch now possessed spare capacity at the *News of the World* press in Bouverie Street and a conviction that he could turn the *Sun* into a successful rival to the *Daily Mirror*. To Murdoch, says Michael Leapman, Cudlipp's *Sun* 'was getting above its readers, trying to push them up-market against their will'. Instead, he would give them a true Bartholomew tabloid, 'modelled on the *Mirror* of the 1940s and 1950s, before it had become seized by ideas above its station'. Murdoch bid just £1 million for the *Sun*, bought it, moved it from Covent Garden to Bouverie Street and redesigned it as a racy tabloid, the first edition appearing on the streets on 17 November 1969. After a year in the hands of Murdoch's first editor, Larry Lamb, the circulation had doubled (even before it featured a naked girl on page three). The *Daily Herald* was emphatically dead, though it gave a dying kick when Murdoch decided the *Sun* should still support Labour at the 1970 general election.

The 1960s had by now seen the Cadburys, the Kemsleys, the John Jacob Astors, the Carrs and Cecil King depart the scene. We return later to those who took their places. Three more of the great pre-war houses remained to fall, each after despairing efforts to shore themselves up. The *Observer*, founded in 1791, had been treated by the Waldorf Astors with the same reverence as their cousins had shown *The Times* – though not without some tumultuous rows between Waldorf and J. L. Garvin, its editor from 1908 to 1942. At the end of the war, the Astor family transferred the *Observer*'s ownership to a trust, its profits to be devoted to newspaper charities.

By the early 1970s, the most urgent object for such charity was the paper itself. The *Observer* was being undermined by a new *Sunday Telegraph* and by Thomson's revitalized *Sunday Times*. David Astor, son of the second viscount and Nancy Astor, had been editing and largely running the paper since 1948. His literate, rather genteel, radicalism transformed the *Observer* into a crusading weekly in 1956 through its opposition to the Suez adventure. This cost it many Conservative readers and severely damaged its finances. But a paper's survival seldom depends on commercial viability alone. As the one tenuously left-wing quality Sunday, the post-Suez *Observer* could rely on vocal support among 'opinion-formers' should its future ever be in doubt.

That thesis was soon tested. In the middle of 1975, David Astor announced that the paper was facing a loss on the year of £750,000. It could not afford to continue. Urgent consultations took place with the print unions, resulting in an unprecedented concession of a 25 per cent cut in regular and casual jobs. This was achieved only after much haggling – bitterly contested by the *Observer*'s chapels – backed by a formal promise to the unions from the NPA that the cut would not be treated as a precedent elsewhere. It was an extraordinary promise. Eight rival companies were in effect agreeing to sustain 25 per cent overmanning to keep a ninth in existence. The Fleet Street cartel's love of a quiet life knew no bounds. Astor stepped down as editor, handing over to his deputy, Donald Trelford. Circulation continued to fall (to 670,000 in 1976) to half that of the *Sunday Times* and less even than the *Sunday Telegraph*.

By the following year it was clear that the cuts had been in vain. Purchasers began their now-familiar courtship. Associated Newspapers was considered and rejected. The food manufacturer Sir James Goldsmith declared his hand. City consortia were mooted. As with *The Times*, no one seemed able to offer either sufficient cash or sufficient assurance that the paper's integrity would be maintained. Lord Goodman, *Observer* chairman at the time, opened negotiations with Rupert Murdoch, but the latter left him in no doubt that he would want to alter the paper's leadership. The staff, not surprisingly, were shocked at the prospect of exchanging the great and good Astors for the owner of the *Sun* and the *News of the World*. Yet for once it seemed that a newspaper in need of a proprietor might have to be beggar not chooser.

Not for long. An American writer on the staff of the Colorado Aspen Institute, Douglass Cater, happened to be in London at the time (November 1976). He heard of the *Observer*'s plight and telephoned his benefactor, Robert Anderson of the Atlantic Richfield Oil Corporation (ARCO), and asked him to 'save' it – not from extinction but, by implication, from Murdoch. For Anderson, the money involved seemed small at the time and the cause was noble. Primed by Cater and others to appreciate the *Observer*'s historic status, he announced that the purchase of the paper was an obligation to its 'long and illustrious past'. Taking it for a symbolic £1 note, Anderson said, 'I have spent many years working with institutions engaged in the development and exchange of ideas. It is in the spirit of renewing and building a vital institution for communications that I welcome this opportunity to become a member of the *Observer* partnership.' The staff was relieved and delighted. Murdoch retreated, not for the first or last time humbled in Fleet Street's seller's market. The *Observer*'s losses vanished into the maw of ARCO's $4,000 million assets – for a while.

No sooner had the last Astor money left Fleet Street than

clouds gathered over the most idiosyncratic of proprietor-ships. No departure was to prove more protracted or more painful than that of the Aitkens from the *Daily Express*. Locked in ancestral combat with the Harmsworths, the Beaverbrook empire had come to seem a creature from a lost world. It was moving ever more slowly, bemused by chang-ing surroundings and new rivals. Its traditional domain, the middle-ground broadsheet market, was in swift decline. No new market offered itself. Following Beaverbrook's death in 1964, the group passed to his son Sir Max Aitken. A shy, pleasant man most at ease on the deck of his yacht at Cowes, Aitken even refused to assume his father's title, though he retained his baronetcy. 'There will only be one Lord Beaver-brook,' he said in renouncing the peerage. Yet while he could eschew his father's name he had no alternative style of industrial leadership to adopt. The result was a diluted ver-sion of the old regime. He pursued his father's political campaigns but with little flair and no flexibility. He continued to refuse to diversify. He did not push the paper into new markets. He peopled the organization with men he and his father had known. While the *Sunday Express* made money and the *Evening Standard* (usually) lost it, Aitken struggled to return the circulation of the *Daily Express* to the heights of the 1940s and 1950s.

Cecil King wrote of his similar efforts at the *Daily Herald*: 'There is no more difficult task in journalism than to conduct a newspaper wisely once it is in full decline. There is enor-mous pressure to try formula after formula and to give none of them a long enough test. Each experiment is abandoned as inevitably it fails to win instantaneous success.' Both the *Daily Express* and the *Daily Mail* became case histories of this syndrome under second-generation proprietors. As their chosen market declined, both papers went through editors, image changes and relaunches. They searched for an elixir to recapture past glory, or at least drive the rival to the wall and leave readers to spare for them.

In the second Lord Rothermere's last decade, a new editor was appointed to the *Daily Mail* roughly every two years. The same became true of the *Daily Express*. In 1971 the sixty-one-year-old Aitken and the seventy-two-year-old Rothermere met at the latter's Warwick House in St James's, last of the Green Park mansions still a private residence. Their executives had conducted informal meetings with a view to merging the two groups into a joint publishing company, producing one morning and one London evening paper. All five of their respective daily and evening titles (*Daily Express* and *Evening Standard*, *Daily Mail*, *Daily Sketch* and *Evening News*) were believed to be losing money or at best breaking even at the time. Subsidy was coming, in Associated Newspapers' case, from non-Fleet Street revenues and, for Beaverbrook Newspapers, from the *Sunday Express*. Yet despite the logic of such a deal – joining titles, markets, printing plant and properties to their mutual benefit – it came to nothing. The fathers might have done it, but the sons felt the weight of their inheritance too heavy on their shoulders. They had never been taught how not to fight each other. They pulled apart and made ready for yet more battle.

Rothermere promptly retired and handed over the running of his companies to his son, Vere Harmsworth, who succeeded him as third viscount in 1978. Harmsworth had the appearance of a plump, ineffectual schoolboy. Not a good public performer, he was shy of journalists and had no conversation for the politicians and financiers with whom a proprietor was expected to associate. Yet his humility was his salvation. Diversification had brought to Associated Newspapers a wider pool of management talent, men who regarded the *Daily Mail* as their proprietor's personal foible. Harmsworth, unlike Aitken, was happy to leave it that way. His grandfather's principle of finding others to carry the burden of corporate responsibility was vindicated.

Vere Harmsworth now shelved any thought of a merger with Beaverbrook Newspapers and closed the group's diminutive tabloid, the *Daily Sketch*. This Fleet Street curiosity had been bought from the Kemsleys in 1953 and printed on the *News of the World*'s presses. By 1958 its down-market 'working-class Tory' stance had pushed its sales to a hesitant 1.3 million. It limped on for another decade but was finally doomed with the revival of the *Sun* under Rupert Murdoch. It thus became only the second national daily to close in the past thirty years. In 1971 it was merged into a new, tabloid *Daily Mail*, under the *Daily Sketch*'s former editor, David English. This wrongly led many to assume it was the *Daily Mail* that had been closed – resulting in an outcry against Harmsworth similar to that against Cadbury for closing the *News Chronicle*. At such times, the more 'up-market' a title the greater the outcry.

David English did to the *Daily Mail* what Aitken had been trying and failing to do to the *Daily Express*. He kept its market position steady, appealing to a middle-class, Conservative audience, but concentrating on youth and women. It was a strategy that required time and commitment: the *Daily Mail* continued to lose sales in English's first year. Harmsworth marked the change from his father most emphatically by keeping English at his post for fifteen years (he is still there). It was this need to find and retain the services of able lieutenants that probably did more to save the *Daily Mail* than any other factor, aided by Harmsworth's departure 'off-shore' for tax purposes. The paper did not make money, but it steadily closed the circulation gap with the *Daily Express*, and thus honoured its owner's inheritance from his father, grandfather and great-uncle. It was a Fleet Street triumph.

Meanwhile, Associated Newspapers emerged as a successful conglomerate. Its managing director, Michael Shields, achieved what Beaverbrook had demanded of his managers, 'secure reserves'. The group developed its provincial titles and moved into North Sea oil, property, wood pulp, taxi companies and restaurants. By 1975 non-newspaper interests yielded £2 million on a turnover of £20 million; the newspapers, including the provincials, yielded just £3.8 million on £83 million. The motivation of proprietorship lived on and at a high price, but at least the Harmsworths could afford it. Today, the *Daily Mail* is once again profitable, an impressive testament to the only Fleet Street family to have survived three generations with its empire intact.*

*The Pearson family's involvement in newspapers had been as long but more tangential. Its provincial Westminster Press supported the *Westminster Gazette* (later *Daily News*, later *News Chronicle*) from 1908 to 1938. In 1957 S. Pearson acquired the *Financial Times*.

No such prospect faced Beaverbrook Newspapers in its black-glass building on the other side of Fleet Street. The failure of the 1971 talks with Associated led to the worst sort of corporate panic. A forward planning group had already recommended a £5-million re-equipment of the company's antiquated printing machinery and an amalgamation of the 200-yards-apart *Evening Standard* and *Daily Express* plants. Spending began on this plan but was hampered by lack of capital. Profits in the early 1970s ran at under 4 per cent of turnover, too low to finance the necessary borrowing. Sir Max's response was to seek inspiration in the policies of his father. 'We are in business to sell newspapers,' he would tell his staff time and again. 'We just have to sell more newspapers.' Selling more papers without holding down labour unit costs could be, as we see in chapter five, the road to ruin.

Sir Max now mimicked the second Lord Rothermere: he sent the *Daily Express* scurrying round the middle-ground market in search of new readers wherever they could be found. Derek Marks had been appointed editor in 1966 with a brief to attack the *Daily Telegraph*. In 1970 Ian McColl was brought in and told to revert to the attack on the *Daily Mail*. The executive floor hummed with planning groups and relaunch projects with flashy titles such as *DX 80*. Despite this, the group's bankers demanded action to stem the losses. Sir Max dropped his old sailing partner, John Coote, as managing director and appointed Jocelyn Stevens, fresh from enlivening the *Evening Standard*, in his stead. Stevens's first step was the courageous (and long overdue) closure of Lord Beaverbrook's pride and joy, the *Scottish Daily Express* in Glasgow. Fourteen million pounds was raised, partly in America, to fund the re-equipment programme.

The editorial uncertainty continued. McColl was dismissed in 1974 and replaced by Alastair Burnet, editor of *The Economist*, with a brief to return up-market. He lasted no more than a year before being replaced by Roy Wright. Once again the market profile was 'lowered', yet it was too late for such hesitancy. The oil-price rise of 1974 coincided with a rise in newsprint costs and an industry-wide squeeze on advertising. The paper was to be relaunched, expensively, as a tabloid in 1977 but Lloyds Bank warned that the overdraft would not be renewed beyond April of that year. Objectively, it should have been possible to rescue the company. The re-equipment plan, property development, cost reduction and the as-yet-untested relaunch of the group's main product at least merited a period of grace.

As with *The Times* ten years earlier, the proprietorial will to fight had gone. Sir Max was recovering from a stroke. In his absence, Stevens, together with the joint deputy chairman Peter Hetherington and Sir Max's twenty-five-year-old son Maxwell, went as supplicants to Associated Newspapers and offered to sell them the *Evening Standard* for £10 million. It would be merged with the *Evening News*. It was a fair return for Rothermere's sale of the *Sunday Dispatch* to Beaverbrook Newspapers in 1961, from the closure of which the *Sunday Express* had so profited. The money was to bail out the *Daily Express*, but the negotiating team also put forward a version of the old Warwick House deal, whereby the *Daily Mail* and *Daily Express* would both be printed separately on the *Daily Express*'s new plant.

Already news of the Beaverbrook Newspapers group's troubles and the illness of its proprietor had stimulated increased interest in a possible change of owner. Despite losses on the *Evening Standard* running at over a million pounds a year, the option of a separate future for the evening paper was widely canvassed. As its editor at the time, my engagement diary became a *Who's Who* of actual and potential Fleet Street entrepreneurs: Tiny Rowland of Lonrho, Shell heiress Olga Deterding, Denis Hamilton of *The Times*, Sir James Goldsmith (at the time a 35 per cent shareholder in Beaverbrook Newspapers), Rupert Murdoch, Nigel Broackes of the Trafalgar House property and construction group. All expressed varying degrees of interest; all wisely decided to await the anticipated crisis.

This arrived in the spring of 1977 with Stevens in direct conflict with his board colleagues, Hetherington and Maxwell Aitken. A flamboyant personality, Stevens led by a combination of bullying, back-slapping and frenetic energy. He disliked journalists but had a fascination for the marketing of newspapers and also for the underworld of the production chapels. They soon came to regard 'Joss' as a soft touch. Hetherington and Aitken now tried to sack Stevens, in the traditional Fleet Street fashion when he was on holiday. Stevens returned, fought back and Hetherington left instead. With Sir Max desperately unwell and his son too young to assert authority, the scene was now one of classic corporate degeneration. Three senior executives left, exasperated at Stevens's erratic behaviour. Then in late April, as plans for the merger of the *Evening News* and the *Evening Standard* leaked out, Stevens found himself fighting his closest ally, Charles Wintour, former editor but still chairman of the *Evening Standard*. Behind the paper stood a London public for whom it had become a daily institution. By underestimating the potency of such opinion whenever a title is under threat, both Stevens and Harmsworth made what turned out to be a crucial mistake.

As the talks reached climax,* the acceptability of the merger proposals to Wintour (alone on Beaverbrook Newspapers' board at the time) depended on the extent to which the merged evening paper would be recognizably the *Evening News* or the *Evening Standard*. This in turn resolved itself into the question of who should edit it and from which title should most of the senior staff be chosen. Associated Newspapers could buy the paper, said Wintour, but the *Evening Standard*'s character must live on and its personnel, including myself as editor, were the only guarantee of that. To Stevens, never one for editorial nicetics, this mattered little. To Harmsworth it was as crucial as it was for Wintour. He was eager to publish a paper with the reputation of the *Evening Standard* but he refused absolutely to concede the symbol of defeat, a Beaverbrook editor. He insisted that the editor be Louis Kirby, then editor of the *Evening News*. He courteously offered me the deputy editorship and I refused it.

Each day of stalling proved a day gained. Although by the end of April 1977 it seemed the *Evening Standard* was indeed

---

* A full account appears in Chester and Fenby, see bibliography.

doomed, a last-minute, formal expression of interest by Goldsmith induced Stevens to change horses. He withdrew at the last minute from a final signing ceremony with the Associated Newspapers team, saying that Sir James Goldsmith, already negotiating an alliance with Tiny Rowland, should be allowed six weeks to arrange an alternative which might forestall the closure of the title. The following weeks were bleak for all involved. Sir Max, his son Maxwell and his close adviser Lord Goodman were all averse to Goldsmith. It was clear that simply to sell the *Evening Standard* would not resolve Beaverbrook Newspapers' troubles and the family was determined that it should not pass to a man it did not trust – despite improved offers from 'Cavrho' (Goldsmith's Cavenham in collaboration with Rowland's Lonrho). The company's advisers, Rothschild's, were seeking alternative help, as was a slowly recovering Sir Max himself. Rothschild's approached Nigel Broackes of Trafalgar House, who expressed formal interest. Sir Max saw Rupert Murdoch.

The result of this activity was a firm offer from Murdoch of £10 million in cash, with an insistence, cleared with Sir Max, on a clean sweep of the management. By June the board felt confident enough to refuse the Goldsmith offer. Yet as at the *Observer*, Murdoch had again wrongly assumed a buyer's market. His frankness to Sir Max secured the antagonism of Stevens and his surviving colleagues before battle was even joined. Stevens promptly returned to Associated Newspapers, who improved their old offer and added a promise that the *Evening Standard* would remain in existence. The basis of the deal was a corporate merger, with an amalgamation of printing plant in return for £10 million, roughly matching Murdoch's bid.

A virtually bankrupt newspaper empire thus found itself pondering four separate suitors – Goldsmith, Murdoch, Trafalgar House and Rothermere – all rich in cash and all promising to keep in being its principal liability, its loss-making titles. After further negotiations, Trafalgar House raised its bid to £13.7 million and won the day. Stevens had effectively shut out Murdoch and saved his job. It was a remarkable performance. The Beaverbrook empire passed into the hands of a property developer, Nigel Broackes, and his deputy, Victor Matthews, a building contractor. Sir Max and his family departed immediately. Broackes installed Matthews as chairman of Beaverbrook Newspapers and the group was renamed Express Newspapers. Only the 'Beaver's' impish face, carved by Epstein, was left to gaze down on the art deco hall of his palace, reminding *Daily Express* staff of the feudal hold he once exerted over their labour. His spirit had kept the paper in suspended animation for thirteen years after his death. The spirit of his rival, Northcliffe, might have suffered a tactical defeat, but it still patrolled the ancestral corridors of Carmelite House in the substantial form of Vere Harmsworth. Northcliffe could be awarded the last laugh.

And still the Berrys survived. Fifty yards up Fleet Street in a building as ponderous as Beaverbrook's was jazzy (both now listed as historic), Lord Camrose's son, Michael Berry, sat aloof and splendid as proprietor and editor-in-chief of the *Daily Telegraph*. Shyness was a characteristic shared by most second-generation proprietors, growing up under dominant fathers. Berry was a virtual recluse. Only his marriage to the gregarious Lady Pamela, daughter of Lord Birkenhead, and her constant flow of entertaining kept him in the public eye. He had begun his career as editor of the *Glasgow Sunday Mail* at the age of twenty-three, moving on to the *Financial Times*, then owned by his father. But since the latter's death in 1954, Berry's life was the *Daily Telegraph*. His senior executives were family friends and he was happy to keep them growing old round him. Only two substantive innovations were made under Berry, both cautiously defensive: a *Sunday Telegraph* was begun in 1961 and a weekly colour magazine in 1965. He allowed himself just one eccentricity: in 1968 he accepted a life peerage from the Labour Government to become Lord Hartwell.

The *Daily Telegraph* was a Fleet Street loner. Berry rarely collaborated with his fellow proprietors and preferred to avoid clashes with his print chapels. Though the Sunday paper never made a profit (as a private company the *Daily Telegraph* did not publish detailed accounts), it helped absorb overheads. The daily paper carried the group. It outsold the rest of the quality market put together and could claim the lion's share of classified and display advertising. Yet it had no alternative cash resources on which to draw in time of trouble and was peculiarly vulnerable to strike action. As Hartwell told his staff in the course of one of the paper's rare disputes: 'Alone in Fleet Street we are not part of a great conglomerate. Oil, shipping, paper manufacturing will not come to our aid. We spend all our energy and resources on our newspapers.' In a sigh for the old days he added, 'This used to be taken for a virtue.'

In 1978 the *Daily Telegraph* was hit by a strike arising from a comparability dispute in its telecommunications room. The National Graphical Association (NGA) at the paper – disowned by its national officers – stopped work and the paper was off the streets for two weeks, previously declared by Lord Hartwell to be the maximum his cash resources could stand. He pleaded with the staff that 'bankruptcy will ensue . . . There is nothing to be gained from heroic gestures nor is there money for ransom.' The ennobled son of Viscount Camrose declared that on the *Daily Telegraph*, 'Us and Them are the same people.' The workers involved backed down reluctantly but the paper was plagued with blank spaces for weeks. It limped into 1979 when Hartwell finally put all the titles in the hands of a discretionary trust. It was designed, so he said, to 'ensure the independence of the newspaper until the end of the century'.

The fall came abruptly, precipitated as so often by decisions too drastic for an unreformed management to implement, in this case a move to new printing plants in Manchester and in London's Docklands. Hartwell initiated the move on his own, with only the most rudimentary advice. The re-equipment would cost £105 million, including a generous redundancy scheme for employees estimated at £38 million. The raising of this money in 1985 was a mortifying experience for Hartwell, involving the surrender of 40 per cent of the equity to new shareholders. Cazenove & Co, the City brokers, found great difficulty in placing the stock: new money for Fleet Street normally comes from entrepreneurs interested in control, not from anonymous investors interested only in yield. When 14 per cent of the shares, worth £10 million, were still not taken up, an offer was made in June 1985 through intermediaries to forty-one-year-old Canadian businessman Conrad Black. Hartwell met him in New York and accepted the money. Black demanded and received the right to appoint two directors and the option on any further shares which might become available. Hartwell's family was presented with a *fait accompli*.

For four months, Hartwell staggered on. The costs of the new buildings in London and Manchester were draining him of cash he did not have. By October he was told he needed to raise a further £20 million in working capital immediately to meet current bills. Despair enveloped the corridors of the Telegraph building, where a once-loyal staff passed a motion of 'composite distrust of a management that has brought these great titles to the brink of ruin'. A sensible way of raising money to finance future growth had become a begging for cash to meet day-to-day expenses. Shares in Reuters and a printing ink company were sold. The chapels, as if oblivious to the family's troubles, submitted new demands in the course of the summer for the manning of the Manchester plant. They knew that another source of largesse would soon have to be found. (It has been a standard chapel tactic to squeeze lucrative agreements out of a dying management on which a new and enthusiastic one would be reluctant to renege.) The demands were duly conceded.

The stage army of buyers gathered once more, with exotic additions: the Egyptian Al Fayed brothers (recent purchasers of Harrods), David Stevens of United Newspapers and the Australian Fairfax group. Hartwell's second son, Nicholas Berry, a successful book publisher and heir apparent, was strongly in favour of a Fairfax deal. Yet there was no way round the option clause offered to Black by his father. Despite strenuous efforts by Nicholas Berry to circumvent this clause, by December all other routes seemed closed. Black injected an urgently needed £30 million of cash in return for new shares, which brought him 50.1 per cent of the company. He installed the editor of *The Economist*,

Andrew Knight, as chief executive, who in turn appointed new editors for both the daily and Sunday titles. Hartwell remained titular chairman and editor-in-chief, issuing forlorn edicts from his lonely room at the top of his father's building. With Nicholas Berry out in the cold, his brother, Adrian, continued only as the *Daily Telegraph*'s science correspondent.

By then, the fall of an elderly proprietor could no longer move Fleet Street emotions. There seemed no risk of the *Daily Telegraph* having to close. The institution would survive. The money was waiting in the wings as usual. Hartwell had long acquiesced in some of Fleet Street's worst labour practices. He had refused to modernize either his journalism or his management. His end was one more nemesis of the second generation. Yet he had been a dignified custodian of the *Daily Telegraph*'s long and independent tradition: he never stood for Parliament nor diverted his energies into public or other business life; he courted no reward beyond the satisfaction of proprietorship. Protected for decades by high costs which limited competition, his papers supplied a comfortable residence both for his friends and for the old-fashioned Conservatism they espoused. Only when the roof and walls of that residence needed renewal did the rot become evident. With the first tap of the hammer, the structure sighed and collapsed.

# 4

# THE AUGEAN STABLES

Shortly after his purchase of the *Sunday Times* in 1959, Roy Thomson visited the paper's London offices to meet members of the staff. Among them was a representative from the printing works. 'How do you do,' said Thomson. 'I'm Roy Thomson, the new owner of this paper.' 'You may own it,' replied the man, 'but I run it.' The aura of potency that surrounded the newspaper proprietor did not also surround his relations with his own workforce. Beaverbrook's editors might reverentially transcribe the great man's thoughts on the issue of the day. Northcliffe's staff might quake at his approach. Ministers might pale as their secretaries began, 'Sir, have you read this morning's *Daily* . . .' But once the hallowed words had been typed, subbed and sent 'down the hole' to the composing room, an altogether different power structure took over. Managers on the bridge could turn wheels and pull levers. But the cables linking them to the rudder and the engine room had long rotted away. This relationship between capital and labour in Fleet Street was crucial to the fate of the old proprietors, and to the challenge facing the new ones. More important, it determined the ability of the whole industry to accept innovation and change.

London printing is rooted far deeper than any of the newspapers I have described so far. Its freemasonry long antedates the formation of trade unions. Its associations can trace their history back through early apprenticeship laws and guild regulations to before the Elizabethan Statute of Artificers. In 1587 the Stationers' Company promulgated a limitation on the number of copies that could be printed from each page of composed type before it had to be broken up and reset: 'No formes of letters be kept standing to the prejudice of Workemen at any tyme.' It is the first record of a Fleet Street restrictive practice.

The nomenclature of chapel for a combination of workers in the printing industry is first found in 1688, according to the *Oxford English Dictionary*, though by then chapels were said to have existed 'since time out of mind'. The word almost certainly derived from the early Puritan associations, as did the head of the chapel, known as the father. In 1725 the young Benjamin Franklin, finding work in a printing house in Lincoln's Inn Fields, was shocked at the sight of a rum bottle by every press. He was equally surprised at the demarcations between his fellow workers, and he was enraged to learn that he had to pay no less than 5s to secure entry to a new 'companionship' if he wanted to transfer from one craft to another. These skill companionships – combined into chapels – are the true ancestors of modern trade unions. Some numbered half a dozen members, few more than fifty.

Unskilled print workers did not combine effectively until the late nineteenth century. Though their groups had more the character of trade unions, with national offices, banners and a tradition of political activity, in Fleet Street they adopted the customs and practices of their skilled colleagues. The modern print unions thus remain, as far as national newspapers are concerned, loose confederations. They have little power to help or discipline a Fleet Street member, whose allegiance is strictly to his chapel. A Fleet Street printer is not, first and foremost, a trade unionist. He defines himself and his work by his skill and his chapel, and may well regard the union to which it is allied as an alien, unsympathetic institution.

The story of Fleet Street printing is the story of the growth of chapel power. It was based on a desire to guard entry into what was a skilled and therefore potentially lucrative trade. It was in the printers' interest that apprenticeship be lengthy:

seven years in the Middle Ages, reduced to six only since the last war. This drawn-out process suited both sides. While the employer received continuity of production and a skilled workforce, the employee was protected against cheap labour and sudden dismissal. The skill involved in carving and setting type was considerable, and printing required a sequence of such skills, all markedly different from each other. Each thus developed its own apprenticeship and its own chapel: the composing of pieces of type into a line; setting these lines into a 'forme'; proofing the forme; holding the manuscript page ('copyholder') while the 'reader' checks it; inking the rollers; loading the paper; supervising the printing machine.

Printers are like lawyers, meticulous historians of their labour and articulate defenders of its privileges. While, like lawyers, they will gently deride any restrictive practice out of hours, they fiercely protect it 'on the shop floor', knowing it underpins their earning power. Each stage in the production cycle developed not only its own negotiating structure but its tradition of seniority and earnings differential. And since newspapers required these skills to operate in formal series throughout the production cycle, differentials became enshrined in agreements of great complexity. This chapter is about these agreements. Though many, indeed most, are now in the process of drastic renegotiation as computerized technology finally pushes into Fleet Street, they are inherent to its history and crucial to the strengths and weaknesses of its proprietors.

Newspaper production should by its nature be vulnerable to rapid technological change. In the mid-nineteenth century, the ancient and laborious 'flatbed' method of printing sheets of paper by hand straight off the formes, in use since Gutenberg's invention of 1440, was first improved by the steam press and then supplanted altogether by the rotary press. This machine was evolved from innovations by Walter's chief engineer, Augustus Applegarth, at *The Times* in London and by William Hoe in Philadelphia. It involved a cylindrical cast being made of the forme and attached to a revolving drum. A continuous sheet of paper (known in the trade as newsprint) could be fed through a series of such drums, printed on both sides at once and then folded automatically. The whole unit was called a folder and the principle survives to this day. At the time of Hoe's press, however, the actual type in the formes was still being set by hand, letter by letter or at least word by word.

In 1889 the first Linotype composing machine arrived in Britain from New York, reaching Fleet Street three years later. A typewriter keyboard lifted a brass letter font on to a row in front of the operator, where he could arrange them into a complete line of type. The line was then swung into a miniature foundry attached to the back of the machine and instantly moulded into a 'slug' from a hot-metal pot. This line slid into a tray at the operator's side where he could read it (in reverse) to check that it was correct. The brass casting fonts were returned automatically to their original position for re-use. A paragraph of type could thus be set in a matter of minutes. Only headlines had still to be set by hand. Though obsolete, Linotype machines are still in use in Fleet Street (and in some Third World countries) wherever the 'new technology' has not yet been introduced. When working at full speed they remain marvels of industrial archaeology.

Both mechanical presses and Linotype* machines overturned traditional printing functions, but the chapels survived them both. Each innovation was fought to the point where it could no longer be resisted and was then accommodated on terms dictated by the printers themselves. Some of the fights were bitter. In 1814 John Walter wished to install new German steam presses at Printing House Square. Knowing his printers would object and fearing loss of production, Walter had the new machinery smuggled into a secret room at the rear of the building. While his staff awaited the order to print as usual, he had the entire edition run off without their knowledge to prove he could do without them if need be. Woods and Bishop record him thrusting the new product at his astonished employees, saying 'there would be no redundancies in consequence and that any necessary staff reductions would be effected by normal wastage', but he

---

*Initially a trade name, but used here generically.

would take firm action against any Luddism. (It was no idle threat: four years earlier Walter had had nineteen of his printers sentenced at the Old Bailey for conspiracy.)

With the coming of the Linotype, the tradition of hand-setting individual letters in a line of type – for which the typesetter was paid a piecework rate per letter – was simply transferred to the new mechanical process. The typesetters retrained to work the machines and charged a piecework rate for each slug of type they set. No attempt was made to integrate the old printing shop functions. The headline set-ters ('piece-case workers') remained separate from the type-setters. The 'timehands' putting the slugs into the formes remained distinct from the men who took proofs from them. Another group took the papier mâché 'flongs' from the 'chase', from which the foundrymen cast the plates. All this survived until the arrival of computer technology and 'cold type' in the 1960s, and in some Fleet Street offices survives to this day. The cauldrons of molten metal spitting away in Dickensian composing rooms formed my earliest and most exhilarating impression of Fleet Street.

From the composing room the plates entered the machine room, scene of struggles between machine 'minders' (nowa-days called managers but still colloquially minders) and their 'assistants' at least since the early nineteenth century. Only on the *News of the World* are there no separate minders, for unexplained reasons dating back to its foundation in 1843. Rupert Murdoch tried to extend this useful easement to the *Sun* when he amalgamated the two plants in 1969. He was told this was impossible: the *News of the World* had 'always' been different. The printing room (normally known as the machine room) was, and is, also staffed with brake-hands, oilers and reel-hands, machine engineers and electricians. As the folded newspaper comes off the presses, other demarca-tions take over in the packaging and dispatch departments, known as the publishing room. When new baling and stack-ing machines were introduced in the 1970s, requiring the press of a button to do what two separate chapels had done before, each chapel (though part of the same union) had to have a separate button of its own to start the same machine.

Despite decades of amalgamation, the crafts and tasks retained their individuality in the production cycle. When *The Times'* management embarked on its ambitious but disastrous confrontation in 1978, it discovered sixty-five distinct chapels buried in the substrata of its industrial relations.

The advent of trade unionism and of big national newspapers at the turn of the twentieth century led the chapels to come together to enjoy the protection of union legislation and the benefits of collective wage bargaining. It was not until 1964, however, that an array of skilled craft societies (never 'unions') formed the NGA. In 1966 an amalgamation of the semi-skilled and unskilled societies, the National Society of Operative Printers and Assistants (NATSOPA) and the Union of Printing, Bookbinding and Paperworkers formed the Society of Graphical and Allied Trades (SOGAT), also embracing such exotic relics as the Pattern Card Makers and the Papermould and Dandy Roll Society. The smaller Society of Lithographic Artists, Designers and Engravers (SLADE), was formed to represent the block makers and processors involved in illustrations. It merged with the NGA in 1983.

None of these amalgamations was more than a marriage of convenience for the Fleet Street members. Of the NGA's 132,000 members (in 1985) 95 per cent have nothing to do with Fleet Street. Only one member of its thirty-five-man executive is from the national press and the executive – and the union generally – resents the constant projection into the public eye of its Fleet Street members with their high earnings. The NGA has always been politically moderate. Its headquarters in Bedford concerns itself with pay and conditions in provincial and contract printing and with the genteel politicking that is a feature of union head offices. It earned itself ostracism from the TUC in the early 1970s when it registered under the Heath Government's Industrial Relations Act, in order to protect its considerable assets. It has proved less adept at protecting them from attack under the Thatcher Government.

Within each 'office' the chapel remains supreme. When SOGAT was formed in 1966 it found itself having to divide into Division A and Division B, to respect the differences between, for instance, the machine assistants (NATSOPA) and the publishing room staff. Such were the strains that in 1970 the union split into NATSOPA and SOGAT again, re-amalgamating in 1982 as SOGAT '82. Periodic attempts are made to join chapels within offices, including the setting up of NGA 'imperial composing chapels' to cover the main composing room functions. They have rarely proved effective. As long as the craft companionships remained in being to negotiate pay and task bargaining, the chapel was the centre of industrial power. The 'imperial father' often found himself merely an intermediary between the head printer and the individual fathers-of-chapel (FOCs). The recent and costly practice of 'buying out' old agreements under new technology has eroded some of the worst nonsenses. Many remain.

Key to the chapel system is the control it can exercise over a worker's career and earnings. Managements in the national newspaper industry have no normal rights of hire or fire over printing staff. The pre-entry closed shop was a tradition of the industry before national papers were invented. As Graham Cleverley, a former newspaper manager, puts it: 'The craftsman's self-image is not that of an employee. His view of his relationship with the newspaper management is still that of the independent journeyman hiring out his services (via his union) on equal terms.' The fee he charges is based not on a wage agreement but on a formal scale of piecework and timework prices.

The printer enters the industry as an apprentice under the aegis of the national union somewhere other than in Fleet Street (which has no apprenticeships). Should a vacancy occur, it will theoretically be notified by a chapel, not the employer, to the London branch office of the relevant union. However, the chapel may fill the job itself, either (since the 1960s) by simply sharing the cash negotiated for that shift round existing chapel members, supposedly working harder, or from its own pool of applicants. These will usually be friends or relatives of existing members. Vacancies are sufficiently coveted for them to be a preserve of long-standing printing families. The son of a printer would normally be placed as an apprentice outside Fleet Street. When he is qualified, he is expected to do two years in the 'general print' before enjoying the lucrative pickings of Fleet Street. Finally, he is initiated into the chapel with ritual solemnity. For compositors, there is much daubing with ink, chalk and loud banging of chases. Such initiations are not unique to Fleet Street and are common in the British engineering industry (not to mention the public schools and the armed forces).

The flow of new recruits into Fleet Street has understandably slowed to a trickle. In addition, national unions have tried to stamp out chapel patronage, especially in the casual areas where unemployment tends to be higher. In 1981 the NGA attempted to institute a system whereby every member out of work for whatever reason took his turn on the London branch call book. Yet names tend to melt off the book as printers get new jobs through friends and relations and branch offices are more involved in supplying newspapers with casual staff, particularly at night-time and weekends. Casualization has often been regarded as the curse of Fleet Street, a hangover from the days of high unemployment and cheap unskilled labour. The Saturday night allocation of SOGAT '82 casual shifts is still a depressing affair. Elderly workers sit waiting for a 'call' at branch headquarters, knowing that those with the best contacts will already have found a shift somewhere. It is Fleet Street's version of *On The Waterfront*. Yet for many an old-timer it is better than no work at all. 'Casual casuals' (that is, men without a regular part-time shift to go to) have long been a familiar part of the Fleet Street night-time scene.

Also many ordinary print workers regard a second job, especially at weekends, as a valued supplement to earnings. The 'regular casual' system gives immense patronage to chapel officials involved in Saturday night working for Sunday newspapers. Some of these officials achieve tycoon status, both for their wealth and for the number of jobs under their control. In the late 1970s the head of the *Sunday Times* machine assistants, Reg Brady, doubled as NATSOPA boss at the *Evening Standard* with hundreds of 'shifts' theoretically at his disposal. Part of the *Observer* machine room was under the patronage of chapel officials from the *Daily Mirror*. I recall one such official bemoaning his waning power: he had made his members so rich they could afford to disobey him.

For villainy perhaps nothing has compared to the machine room at the Mirror building in the 1960s, when it became a notorious place of criminal resort, especially on a Saturday night. Blue movies were shown on the company's premises. The Mirror building poker schools had stakes as high as in any West End club, reputedly operated under the wing of the East End's Kray twins. Management at one point protested to the machine chapels for being expected to employ two convicted murderers at one time, one of whom was terrifying the other staff. Employees could order any consumer durable they wanted, to be obtained 'off the back of a lorry' and delivered on a Monday morning. (Even at the *Evening Standard*, a weekly shirt sale was held: an elderly printer would ask deferentially if 'there is anything else sir would like?')

Once inside a Fleet Street companionship, a printer's first loyalty is to his fellow members.* Branch and chapel dues are far higher than national union subscriptions. They cover administration, strike and sickness pay. Chapel committees and their FOCs are elected annually and are responsible to their companionship. The union has no control over them and cannot dismiss them, any more than management can. Agreements signed by national or regional union officials are frequently treated as 'nothing to do with us' by Fleet Street chapels; the job of Fleet Street officer of a print union is a miserable one. During one of the many disputes that plagued the *Observer* in the early 1980s, the NGA's national leadership was so incensed at its machine minders at the *Observer* rejecting a nationally negotiated settlement that it formally withdrew their union cards. This theoretically prevented them from working elsewhere. The chapel thumbed its nose at the union, knowing that it and its friends controlled

---

*Fleet Street printing, like proprietorship and management, is all male. A novel feature of Murdoch's Wapping plant is the presence of women and ethnic minorities in jobs that had previously been confined to white males.

minders' jobs on national newspapers, not the union. After this experience, the NGA had to accept that withholding cards was not a credible discipline in Fleet Street.

A printer has tenure of the job for as long as he wants it and as long as the companionship is ready to keep him. Since his lifestyle may have improved to match his new earnings this can mean well into old age. Only a total incapacity for work (such as persistent drunkenness) may result in forced resignation. Even when a printer opts for a company retirement scheme – now compulsory in a few cases – his son or a friend may 'see him all right' with a few casual shifts. At the *Sunday Times* in the 1970s, two-thirds of the publishing room (mostly SOGAT regular casuals) were estimated to be over sixty-five.

It is rare for a Fleet Street printer to transfer from one chapel to another, let alone to a chapel owing notional allegiance to another union. The reluctance of the NGA machine minders to accept NATSOPA (now SOGAT '82) assistants into their ranks – although the work is virtually identical – has been the cause of constant unrest in Fleet Street in the 1980s, bringing costly stoppages to the *Observer*, the *Sunday Times* and the *Financial Times*. The one area where movement between chapels is traditional is in the composing room, for instance from timehand to piece-case worker. The latter make up the headlines on piece rates and can earn considerably more as a result. It is a promotion tolerated largely because it dates back to Benjamin Franklin's day, though the promotion is rigidly controlled by the companionship.

As a result, the Fleet Street printer has little hope of career advancement. His prospects are circumscribed by the confines of the companionship. He may do the same work on another newspaper, but he is unlikely to acquire other skills or have any opportunity to improve those he has (prior to new technology). He therefore becomes acutely aware of comparisons with workers elsewhere in the production cycle. He sees how much effort is required of them to do their work and how much they earn. He learns of their price structures and overtime rates, their devices and fiddles. He develops a fraternity with those doing the same work on other newspapers, and is part of a grapevine of information on pay and differentials running through the late-night cafés and bars of Fleet Street. When newspaper deadlines alter or paginations go up or down with circulation or advertising volume, so the differentials will be changing and must be protected. The modern Fleet Street FOC needs a calculator always at the ready.

The printer is paid by a pricing system that has guaranteed his place among the richest workers in Britain since the Middle Ages. By the late eighteenth century, type compositors were earning on average 50 per cent more than equivalent skills in other trades. During the Napoleonic inflation, printers' wages still kept well ahead of the field. Compositors working on newspapers regularly received up to 20 per cent more than those in other areas of printing. This was achieved by exploiting their bargaining position in an industry that depended on swift production for its profit. There is little evidence of overt militancy since militancy was seldom required. When John Walter took on extra apprentices in 1786 to increase productivity, he defied his own journeymen, who wanted more money for the work themselves, by advertising for boys in his own paper. His workers succeeded in stopping the advertisement appearing in any rival journal.

Compositors' earnings are based on a combination of piece rates – payment for a job done – for some workers and time rates for others. Those who actually set the type either on the Linotype machines or at the headline cases (piece-case hands) have traditionally been paid per line of type according to the *London Scale of Prices*. This was first drawn up in 1785 when Walter introduced his Logographic system for setting whole words on fixed slugs to speed the composing process. It has been a typesetter's bible ever since. It was revised in 1810 and 1891, when the coming of Linotype necessitated a further revision, and again by the London Typographical Society in 1956 before the NGA existed. It is an extraordinary document. For morning papers, the charge was set at 12.075d per 1,000 ens (a printing width roughly the size of the letter n). This basic rate was then embroidered to fill a book which lies on every hot-metal office shelf, dog-eared and scarcely legible with additions and amendments.

Extra charges are levied, often running to eight decimal places of a penny, for small type or large type, for corrections, alterations, lists and boxes. 'Bad copy or manuscript' is charged one-third extra; 'other than ordinary English' is charged one-half extra; Greek is charged at the rate of one line per word. Charges are made for white space at the ends of lines when set narrow measure – lest the compositor should lose out by such a designer's conceit. The original scale laid down charges for pulling extra proofs, for case-hands moving copy round the composing room and for that eternal printers' fallback, 'for extra trouble occasioned'. Charges are even made for work that might have been done but for some reason is not: for a stoppage elsewhere in the plant, for advertisement copy set outside the building, for anything passing through the composing room that might have been charged for had it been set in the normal way. Such charges are rightly known as fat.

In theory, the *London Scale of Prices* is objective. What makes it less so is the 'custom and practice' that has built up round it in different houses. Thus, particular jobs are charged at 'four-to-one' or 'six-to-one' against the scale. At the *Sun*, the shortage of actual words in the paper led compositors to demand enhancement of their rates to such an extent that they were, in 1981, earning £100 a week more than their equivalents on the high-setting *Financial Times*. At the time of the closure of Bouverie Street in 1986, they reportedly still were. Indeed, it was *Sun* printers who first broke through the £1,000 a week barrier. Actual earnings are calculated by a checker who counts every line set by each operator on a galley proof marked with his name and specially set aside for the purpose. The checkers' spike is a sacred corner of the composing room. Yet so complex are the payments that checking is often dispensed with. The compositor simply submits his own 'docket' to the chapel, which claims on his behalf.

Most piecework schemes are criticized, by both management and unions, for setting worker against worker in a bid for earnings. Fleet Street compositors avoid such a source of potential discord by collectively converting piecework earnings back into a time rate. All earnings are paid into a 'companionship pool', from which chapel members draw their share pro rata with the number of days they have worked each week. An operator has a formal right to remain outside the pool, but matters are so organized that he is unlikely to benefit as a result. The authority of the chapel is thus further enhanced: it monitors individual earnings; it levies the additional charges on management for special work; it regulates rotas and holidays and arranges for sickness cover. Although each production worker has a normal employment contract with the management – useful (and lucrative) should redundancy beckon – he is effectively employed and paid by his chapel. Such arrangements are convenient for management – recruitment, training, administration and discipline can all be left to chapel committees – but the price of this convenience has soared. Pieceworkers may, in theory, earn less when papers are small and more when they are big. However, the growth in newspaper size over the past twenty years has led to Linotype operators earning large, even fabulous, incomes. In 1961 they were still ranked third in print earnings behind piece-case workers (to which operators had traditionally graduated) and stereotypers, working in the foundry. By 1970 they were top and by a wide margin.* By the early 1980s they were regularly receiving over £400 on high-setting papers (such as the *Daily Telegraph*) for a four-day week, often compressed into just three nights. Such earnings were swiftly transmitted to low-setting papers (such as the *Daily Mirror*), where chapels would make claims to match. At one house, the Linotype operators' chapel felt it had fallen so far behind it simply added a 50 per cent mark-up to the rates charged on its dockets. The management duly paid.

Men with such earnings live well, spend heavily and will

*Sisson gives an analysis of printers' incomes. See bibliography.

naturally fight to maintain their positions. A modern compositor owns his home, with possibly a second by the sea. He will have moved out of London's traditional print districts, Hoxton and Elephant and Castle, to the suburbs of Epping, Romford and Chislehurst. He probably takes at least one foreign holiday a year, likes eating out and spends lavishly on golf or racing. His middle-class status has been achieved with no burden of executive responsibility and with a skill which, the printer will grudgingly admit, is possessed by the average copy typist. He will also accept that there is little stimulus in the work. Since most printers nowadays assume it will not last indefinitely, many have invested in their own businesses, including minicabs, building and decorating, pubs, jobbing printing and picture framing. As proprietors have diversified out of newspapers, so too have those working for them. Few claim to want their children to enter the trade.

At the start of 1986 there were probably fewer than 1,000 Linotype operators in Fleet Street earning very large incomes from piece rates as such, yet they set the tone for other skilled workers, especially hourly paid timehands whose job is to compose the columns and headlines of type into metal chases for proofing and moulding. Traditionally these men enjoyed a rough-and-ready differential with the pieceworkers. Just as Linotype chapels evened out individual differentials by pooling, so from the 1950s 'imperial' composing room chapels evened out divergences between piece and time rates by 'allocation'. This was a straight cross-subsidy from the pieceworkers' pool to the timehands' pool, designed to maintain an accepted differential between their respective earnings.

Such an example of mutual self-help across skill boundaries had intriguing implications. During periods of statutory pay restraint, pieceworkers were able to manipulate their rates upwards and transfer some of the money through the pool to enhance the legally capped time rates. Allocation was thus a convenient mechanism through which management could soothe pay rivalry within composing rooms without having to break pay policy. Yet it did little to satisfy non-composing staff, and it meant that managements were under constant pressure to match the latest device accepted by their rivals anywhere in the industry. As a chapel official remarked during *The Times* dispute in 1978:

> Because this management have not made any under-the-counter deals in breach of Government pay policy, our members at *The Times* over the last three years have fallen from the top rung of the wages scale in Fleet Street . . . there is no way that I or anyone else can persuade them this is just and fair [quoted by Jacobs].

The distortion of differentials enshrined in custom and practice for up to a century underlay much of Fleet Street's earnings chaos in the 1960s and 1970s. The scale of the chaos is hard to exaggerate. Just as pieceworkers found it expedient to convert their payment-by-result into what were effectively hourly earnings, so the hourly paid workers sought every way of injecting a 'piece' element into the calculation of their rates. The piece elements began with the timehands in the composing room and have worked through into every corner of the newspaper office, affecting even journalists. These 'special payments' are among the most exotic blooms in Britain's industrial glasshouse. As one manager said to the 1962 Royal Commission, 'We pay the basic rates to get the men to come to the office. Then we have to pay them for everything they do there.'

The extra payments reflect the special charges that have been levied in composing rooms since the eighteenth century under the *London Scale of Prices*. The most common is related to the size of the paper each day and has the advantage that it is not, theoretically, open to argument – though much debate will surround whose fault it is when the size is not what it might have been. Other payments may relate to extra additions required by the editor, late running to cover special stories, the number of rules or boxes put round stories, the balance of pictures and text. The payments may take the form of overtime to existing staff or extra 'shifts'. Thus an agreed manning level for a twenty-eight-page paper might be 200 shifts in the machine room, 220 for a thirty-two-page paper, 240 for a thirty-six-page paper and so on. These extra shifts are seldom composed of real people since not all departments are involved in extra work as newspaper size increases. They simply require more money to be paid by management into existing chapel pools. The most bizarre payments are those already mentioned as fat. The growth of photogravure for colour pages, often with whole sections of a paper being printed outside London and shipped in for collation, has led to huge fat money going to the chapels. Charges are made for not setting, not handling, not casting, not printing, just as if the work had been done 'in house'. Other charges are made for any divergence from custom and practice; for allowing a chapel to cross into another's traditional preserve; for any special task requested by management.

Down among the printing presses and binding machines, far from the rarefied air of the composing rooms, the special payments become even more fantastic. To insiders, they are merely 'old Spanish customs' – a genteel phrase for what amounts to a fraud on the company and its shareholders. The favourite method of increasing earnings in the machine and publishing departments is to manipulate what are called 'blows' and 'cuts'. Newspapers have always allowed generous periods, called blow time, during the working day for resting from the occasionally arduous job of production. Similarly, if an edition goes out before the end of a shift, workers on that shift can be permitted to leave early – known as a cut. As time passes, blows and cuts become established custom and practice. They are not taken flexibly as the needs of production allow, but are built into agreements: a 'one-hour cut' becomes accepted. If the time is subsequently required after all, a special payment must be made or extra men taken on to cover. Blows and cuts can mean men working for only a fraction of a shift, often while working similarly fractional shifts on other papers. In the casual world of Saturday night production, men may sign on at one paper, take a cut and walk round to sign on for a later shift at another. The *Sunday Telegraph* and the *News of the World* were well known for this double banking.

At the apex of this abuse stand the ghost shifts. These are

shifts notionally built into a negotiated manning level on the assumption of a high level of production but not normally required. When they are required, the chapel either works a bit harder or, more often, declares itself understaffed and demands 'more men'. This can make it prohibitively expensive for most newspapers suddenly or temporarily to increase circulation. When *The Times* needed an extra 50,000 copies as a result of its Portfolio bingo in 1985, the machine chapels demanded (and got) seventy extra 'men'; other chapels demanded parallel payments since these men simply implied more money paid to the machine room.

In due course, a number of ghost shifts per task became regarded as an entitlement, paid into the chapel pool and shared round the members. At the *Financial Times*, such shifts were docketed in blue and became known as blue shifts. At the *Daily Telegraph* in the early 1960s, the manning level in the machine room for a twenty-eight-page paper was agreed at 306. Of these shifts, only 252 were known individuals who turned up for work, the rest being ghost wage packets shared between them.* Attrition meant that whenever a worker resigned from a chapel, there was more money for the survivors and an incentive not to take on new recruits. Hence the contradiction that as Fleet Street numbers fell in this period many offices were not overmanned but increasingly undermanned. In 1978 the Linotype chapel at the *Evening Standard* had seventy-two operators on its books. Less than half that number might be in the building at any one time, with rows of machines lying idle at peak production time.

In the 'regular casual' sections of publishing departments especially, men would sign on two or three times lest it appear that agreed numbers were not being supplied by the chapels. This was known as biffing. Two famous names among casuals were (and presumably still are) 'Gordon Richards of Tattenham Corner' and 'M. Mouse of Sunset Boulevard'. Others would sign the name of the relevant proprietor. At the end of a Saturday night there are usually

*Cleverley, see bibliography.

unclaimed wage packets from men who literally forgot that they had signed on, or forgot the names they had used. These are not considered abuses – except by the Inland Revenue – since the relevant number of shifts has been agreed with the management. By the late 1970s, blows, cuts and ghosts could account for over half the negotiated manning levels on some newspapers.

The question is often asked, why have managements not taken a tougher line against these practices? The basic answer is that most have some sort of vested interest in the chapel system, or at least in not offending it. The cost of each concession is usually small while the price of resisting a claim can be astronomical. There are roughly 100 distinct operations required to get an (old-technology) newspaper on to the street. A stoppage to debate even a minor variation to an agreement can cost minutes. Trains can be missed, sales lost. As proprietors constantly point out to Royal Commissions, the press is a production industry with the disciplines of a service industry. A copy lost for just a few minutes is lost for ever, and with it sales and advertising revenue and the good-will of the reader. The need for speed demands total management flexibility, yet flexibility is the one thing a precise agreement rarely yields. Any request to bend a rule and the chapel official will pounce: 'Of course we can do it, boss, but there'll be a payment.' Even if there is no payment, the incident will involve 'goodwill' or its inverse, 'bad blood'.

Goodwill can be as valuable to a chapel negotiator as real money, since it can be traded in some future bargain or withdrawn to enforce some new claim. Rarely do Fleet Street chapels flagrantly breach agreements: the charging system for their labour is so inappropriate to the needs of flexible newspaper production that agreements are breached every night through sheer necessity. A page is faulty and must be urgently remade. A correction has come through not covered by an existing payment. Bad weather means trains running early and pages rushed through ahead of time. Each breaks the brittle structure of an agreement and stores up trouble.* Even

*This is why many old Fleet Street hands are sceptical of the current fashion for 'legally binding contracts'.

where a procedure is technically broken by the chapel, management will be reluctant to invoke a formal dispute. Invoking may mean a withdrawal of goodwill and the submission of a host of counter-claims kept by the chapel 'against a rainy day'. Existing concessions will be revealed for other chapels to see and imitate. Executives may see their past weaknesses revealed to colleagues. In a negotiated settlement someone further up the hierarchy pays.

To be fair to managements, they have on occasions sought to order this chaos. The amalgamation of print unions in the mid-1960s, the advent of a Labour Government and subsequent wage control, led some to feel the time had come for reform, in particular to the archaic payments systems and overmanning. The result was a movement towards 'comprehensive house agreements'. In essence, these were intended to consolidate earnings into standard rates. Deals would be struck with individual chapels, which the chapels would then police. It was a *de facto* recognition of the power of chapels as labour-only sub-contractors to each newspaper. The hope was that they would deliver more flexible work methods and accept a measure of responsibility for performing the contract.

The agreements spread across the industry throughout the 1960s. They were a success with the chapels but a disaster for management. When I arrived in Fleet Street in 1966, hourly paid workers still punched a card to clock in and out each day and management at least knew how much of the day each man had spent officially at work. The agreements ended even this discipline. Responsibility for seeing that men came to work devolved on to the chapel, although, legally, the company still employed them. The chapels were now wholly in charge of labour supply in each department. Not only was managerial control lost, so too was quality control. Despite having had no hire and fire power, each manager had previously been able to exert some authority over production through overseers, graced with historic titles such as The Printer, The Publisher, The Works Manager. These men, usually promoted from the ranks, were kings of their domains. The Printer especially was a central personality in a newspaper's culture. He would lord it over mere journalists when they visited his composing room.

The comprehensive agreements stripped overseers of such authority. On most old-technology papers, the FOC became responsible for allocating staff to tasks within his department, previously a crucial function of the overseer. Since the FOC's prime concern is to maintain group earnings, quality of performance is not uppermost in his mind. While in theory the agreements laid down a clean sub-contract between overseer and chapel, in practice they reinforced the worst aspects of chapel freedom without adding any sanction on performance. To take what may seem a trivial example, compositors after lunch or in the evening are occasionally drunk. Previously, a head printer would ensure that a drunk man was not allocated to a 'late' page requiring fast work. When allocation became a chapel responsibility, few FOCs regarded sobriety as a matter for their concern: tasks would be allocated on rota with fair shares for all – or for favourites. Many a transposed line can be attributed to this problem. (There are, I should add, exceptions to this accusation.)

Under comprehensive agreements, the paraphernalia of blow time, fat and ghost shifts ran out of hand. Managements knew how much a job was costing them, but not how many men were actually doing it. They lost control over speed of performance and over the individual earnings of their employees. In 1979, in an evocative metaphor, the then editor of *The Times*, Sir William Rees-Mogg, likened it to playing a row of rusting fruit machines on a windswept pier. The manager has to get 'three strawberries on each of the fruit machines at the same time . . . Some reject the coin that is put in – however large – while one has a lemon and another a raspberry permanently in place.'* Managements accepted all the obligations of a normal employer for taxation, insurance, sickness and redundancy, while down on the shop floor a chapel of just twelve men could have one fully occupied, on the firm's time, working out rotas and payments. Offices would be crowded with huddles of men calculating their

---

*Speech to Engineering Employers Federation, February 1979.

hours and earnings on scraps of paper, frequently exploding into internal arguments that disrupted production.

Most of Fleet Street hailed comprehensive agreements as a 'victory for common sense', and they did at least end the situation of hundreds of men hanging about drinking tea and playing cards. As Keith Sisson has shown, most papers saw a fall in staff in the late 1960s. Some even saw a fall in total production wages. Yet the overall consequence was twofold. First, the earnings of those who came to work soared – since comprehensive agreements were more public than fragmented bargaining, the knock-on effect of each settlement was more severe. Second, chapels were now freed to let natural wastage and restricted recruitment reduce actual numbers, whatever manning level had supposedly been negotiated for a task. The leeway was taken up by ghosting. This gave them a hugely comfortable cushion against subsequent job losses. By the late 1970s as many as half the unskilled shifts in some Fleet Street offices were ghosts, effectively doubling the notional incomes of those actually at work. In retrospect, Fleet Street executives seem to have been startlingly ignorant of the practices rife in their own plants. Even as astute an observer as Graham Cleverley admits that in five years of working as a manager at the *Sunday Telegraph* he never realized that, for instance, its wire room was staffed by more ghosts than real people. He quotes evidence given by the Telegraph group to the 1962 Royal Commission on payments in the paper's process department: 'In this department we pay a House Extra of £5.10s a week, but we are far from clear why.'

Most newspapers carelessly assumed national union officers would reflect chapels' views. These officers were naturally concerned to protect Fleet Street employment overall, to maintain membership and thus subscriptions. To newspaper managers this seemed excellent leverage. A threat to lay off staff would be a threat the unions could not ignore. As we have seen, the chapels had, if anything, an opposite incentive. Falling numbers meant rising individual earnings through the manipulation of comprehensive agreements. As Sisson points out, in successive so-called productivity deals in the late 1960s, chapels 'sold jobs with little regard . . . for casuals who had no fixed pattern of working or for those members of the printing industry who wished to get jobs in Fleet Street'. The process was similar to that experienced in the docks, where, as employment declined, new entry was restricted to 'sons and nephews' and sometimes stopped altogether. Labour shortages were generated in some companionships 'against a rainy day'. It was an effective form of work rationing, and newspapers were its victims. An economist would say chapels were maintaining the price of their labour by carefully reducing its supply. The surprise is that few managers realized this.

By the 1970s most Fleet Street printers understood that computerized technology would be as traumatic to their craft as the Linotype machine a century before. Their behaviour duly adjusted to this: they determined that, as with the Linotype, they would obtain maximum control over new technology wherever it was introduced. They would seek to splice the old piecework customs on to the computer keyboard. They would seek lineage payments and fat and would endeavour to prevent other chapels from gaining access to the terminals. Above all, they would have agreements; they would maintain control. Until that revolution came, they would strive to postpone it and squeeze the old agreements for all they were worth, especially printers who decided that they would take redundancy and leave the industry for good. The companionship thus became a lucrative but wasting personal asset. As redundancy and 'cost-cutting' schemes were introduced at the end of the 1970s, chapels had lists of members ready, indeed eager, to inflate their savings with up to £40,000 of buy-out money. Every productivity crisis led to a procession of printers leaving the industry with golden handshakes – some even returning as casuals.

This shifted the negotiating balance of power substantially in the chapels' favour. It increased their capacity to absorb surplus labour in emergencies, notably during strikes or lock-outs on other titles. It was well worth a *Financial Times* machine assistant sharing some of his ghost shifts with a temporarily unemployed colleague rather then see that colleague concede the principle of reduced manning elsewhere. Hence the bitterness of the fight over reduced manning levels to 'save' the *Observer* in 1975. The men concerned were mostly Saturday night casuals. The *Observer* management asked them to concede a principle that would threaten the earnings of equivalent chapels across Fleet Street: that machines could be operated with 25 per cent fewer men. After the cuts had been conceded, the chapels found it was not the paper but the Astor proprietorship they had been asked to save. The salvation failed and the paper was transferred to a wealthy buyer (ARCO, see page 60). The chapels felt that they had been victim of a bluff and the *Observer* machine room was the scene of continual disruption as chapels struggled to re-establish former manning levels.

The changed balance of power also made it harder for proprietors to threaten total closure as a discipline on their workforce. As *The Times* found in 1978, closure may be regarded by chapels as preferable to allowing a proprietor to set a precedent of drastic demanning. *The Times*' executives failed to comprehend that a chapel member's first loyalty is horizontal, within his skill group, not vertical to the survival of any one title. It is better to lose fifty shifts for good at the *Sunday Times* than accept the principle of a twenty-shift reduction that might snowball across Fleet Street. The NGA's chapels spent £700,000 in strike pay during *The Times*' stoppage and considered it money well spent to maintain the principle of uniform, industry-wide manning agreements.

Indeed, by 1985 threats of closure from the boardrooms of Fleet Street had lost their force. Managers who through the 1970s had claimed there were 'too many titles in Fleet Street' were seen to have cried wolf. There were fewer printers, but they were vastly richer than they had been a decade earlier. The names of the proprietors had changed, but to the printers that was of no account. I remember a chapel official listening patiently as a manager hurled abuse at him for threatening the future of his paper with an exorbitant demand. He replied, 'Don't worry, boss. If you don't want to pay, there's plenty more out there happy to take your place.' He was right. Of the eighteen daily, Sunday and evening titles published in London at the end of 1985, fourteen had changed hands in the previous sixteen years, some more than once and most after empty threats of closure from their departing proprietors.

As the new owners arrived, they had little idea of what they were taking on. They entered their new offices and visited their plants as Roy Thomson had done in 1959. They smiled patronizingly at the Linotype machines and foundry casters and great printing presses spitting oil. They said the time had come to send them all to a museum. No such fate awaited their industrial relations. Under new proprietors as under old ones, ghosts and blows, cutting and biffing, allocations and old Spanish customs flourished unchecked.

# 5

## PAPER TIGERS

When daily newspapers became a national industry at the turn of the century, proprietors adopted – though rarely adapted – existing Fleet Street practices. Plant which was appropriate for small-circulation London newspapers was expanded. New rotary presses and Linotype machines were installed and, as we have seen, chapel 'custom and practice' was taken as read. The impact on the cost of starting a newspaper likely to cover its costs was impressive. When Alfred Harmsworth launched the *Daily Mail*, he had to spend £500,000 on the necessary composing and printing equipment. So immediate was his success and so large his profit that he could treat his production costs with indulgence. He proved an editorial innovator but he was certainly not an industrial one.

The great proprietors were impresarios: Northcliffe and Beaverbrook were Conservatives who derided the cheese-paring habits of provincial, mostly Liberal, capitalists. Northcliffe believed his workers should be the wealthiest in the land. He told them to support their unions, and even paid their union dues for them. As early as 1920 he said that every printer should be rich enough to own a car. Delicately poised negotiations were wrecked by last-minute Northcliffe concessions. Low wages, he said, might drive good printers to emigrate to America. (Many were indeed leaving to work in New York, taking their restrictive practices with them.)

When Alfred's brother Harold called his attention to some of the firm's extravagant methods, the former would laugh: 'There's my brother moaning about money again.'

Northcliffe believed printers should share in the profits of growth, and he would chide others in the industry – many of them struggling with loss-making products – for their meanness. 'As soon as the newspaper owners were hit by the war,' he said in 1918 in reply to a NATSOPA claim, 'they doubled and in some cases trebled the price of their product. I have not yet heard that they doubled or trebled the wages of their workers, whose cost of living has in many cases doubled *and* trebled.' When proprietors, in common with other employers, sought to combine to hold down printers' wages, he would have none of it: 'I am not likely to join combinations of rich men for grinding down poor men,' he said. He would sometimes make a show of a fight in particular cases. He once called a disgruntled worker at his Paris newspaper, the *Continental Daily Mail*, an 'ungrateful swine' and hurled him bodily from the room. But that was in Paris and such incidents were mostly bravado. Northcliffe's managers were left in no doubt that their duty was to get the papers out on time, with no argument or disruption.

Beaverbrook shared Northcliffe's views. Both had a rocky, at times non-existent, relationship with the owners who formed the Newspaper Proprietors' Association in 1906 to negotiate joint agreements with unions and distributors. (This hesitant combine never achieved a strong bargaining position.) Like a benevolent landowner boasting of a contented tenantry, Beaverbrook was proud of the fact that *Daily Express* workers were regarded as the best-paid in Fleet Street. His parsimony in trivial matters – like his insistence on the re-use of old envelopes – rarely extended to the printers' wage packets. He was anti-socialist but never anti-union. He would give lavishly to printers' charities and told his editors to excoriate those who did not: 'Look with hatred and contempt on those rich men who cut down on their private expenditure and public benefactions. Cover the wealthy niggards with ridicule. Pour scorn on the stingy.' During the 1926 General Strike, Beaverbrook wanted to continue publishing even when the unions demanded the right to censor copy. 'I should have been perfectly prepared to go on publishing at almost any cost,' he later declared, 'even though the actual editing of the *Evening Standard* was interfered with by the fathers of the chapels.'* It was Churchill who prevailed upon him to close down.

The benevolent attitude of the two men who at one point controlled three-quarters of Britain's national press output infected the whole industry. Other proprietors could not pay their printers less and collective efforts to cut wages during the 1930s foundered on Beaverbrook's opposition. His rivals had to acquiesce. If high wages reduced profit at least they increased pressure on rivals and were a barrier against new entrants. When rising costs were pushing the *Daily Herald* and *Daily Mirror* towards price increases in 1948, Beaverbrook ordered his general manager to 'refuse to increase your selling price, tighten your belt and let the suffering and misery descend upon the wretches who supported the Socialists in the last election'. Such were the attitudes conditioning Fleet Street's industrial performance.

This climate, not surprisingly, did nothing to motivate line managers. Most newspapers were family firms in which senior members took a personal interest in decisions. It was not easy for a managerial class to develop and, where delegation took place, it was mostly to editors rather than to other executives: at the *Observer*, J. L. Garvin was known as 'editor and manager'. Proprietors preferred to delegate to men from similar backgrounds to their own, whether or not they possessed management skills. Such crucial figures in controlling costs or promoting revenues as the head printer, the publisher, the office manager were often promoted from the shop floor. They might be highly respected by the family, yet still regarded as a trusty butler or land agent, with total discretion 'below stairs' provided no hint of trouble was ever noticeable above.

The 1940s and 1950s reinforced this traditionalism by emphasizing the role of the editor in the salvation of a paper.

*Quoted from Taylor, see bibliography.

When a Bartholomew or a Christiansen could transform a balance sheet by efforts entirely directed towards raising revenue, why accord status to those who, however hard they worked, could not cut production costs by more than a small fraction of those borne by their rivals? Few Fleet Street titles developed anything like a normal management hierarchy, let alone one capable of meeting the need to innovate from the 1960s onwards. Line management in Fleet Street was concerned with one thing: badgering the chapels to produce a paper on time. So all-consuming did this task become that executives had no scope for normal business management, for product development or for considering new systems. By the mid-1970s the Royal Commission was hearing that 80 per cent of a newspaper management's time was spent on what was essentially industrial relations.

The production executive of a newspaper is the man who must resolve the twin forces of chapel pressure and proprietorial motivation. Faced with a chapel demand for an extra payment, this manager will be asked by the head printer what he should do. The manager will know that resistance could mean trouble, possibly a stoppage. He may put up a show of a fight, but any delay in the next print run will bring his chief executive and even the proprietor on the phone, demanding to know the whereabouts of the paper. The manager may explain that an unreasonable claim is being resisted. He will be asked how much is involved. His reply will usually be that the sum is small but the principle crucial and the knock-on effect severe. His boss may indicate that a certain 'flexibility' may be in order this time to get the paper out, but that he should hold firm on the knock-on claims. How soon can you restart the presses? will be the final question. Chastened, the manager does a deal with the offending chapel and waits for that day's knock-on claim to become the next day's crisis. One manager has compared his job to that of a provincial governor during the Indian Mutiny: 'One's whole time is taken up suppressing the latest revolt and predicting where the next one is going to flare up – apart from the time spent convincing one's superiors that all is under control.'

It is even worse when a manager is told by his boss, in a bout of toughness, to 'resist all claims, however small'. The chapel will immediately demand to 'see the chief', under threat of industrial action. Few proprietors faced with the loss of an edition of their paper refuse to see a chapel, indeed most never meet their workers except in such extraordinary circumstances. The proprietor discovers that the men have at least some legitimate grievance – as we saw in chapter four, a grievance is always to hand for such occasions. After much shouting and banging of tables, he negotiates a statesmanlike compromise and blames the subordinate executive for allowing the situation to arise. The latter's authority is undermined. The most blatant recent instance of such intervention was by Tiny Rowland at the *Observer* in the summer of 1984 (see pages 170–2). Production chapels have repeatedly appealed successfully over the heads of line management. The manager always has the cards stacked against him and is thus under pressure to forestall humiliation at the hands of his boss by making the concession himself. Until recently chapels referred to Fleet Street managers as 'jelly babies', yet the managers only reflected the wobbling inclinations of their proprietors.

How far proprietors have really been short-sighted in their behaviour is open to question. It is not a wholly misguided tactic to seek to sustain circulation and advertising revenue where freedom of manoeuvre over labour costs is limited. A stoppage certainly costs a newspaper much more than it costs a chapel. The collectivity of chapels across Fleet Street has been such that no management could step out of industrial line for long. Any who tried, as most titles did occasionally and *The Times* did systematically in 1978, usually went down to costly defeat. The proprietors who appeared to accept the fact of their weak bargaining position, notably Lord Rothermere at the *Daily Mail* and Lord Hartwell at the *Daily Telegraph*, rarely found themselves losing production and saved accordingly. Their costs were not noticeably higher than their more belligerent rivals, the *Daily Express* and *The Times*. Until 1986 few companies were able to gain a substantial, long-term advantage over rivals by attacking their own labour costs – though they could certainly gain in the short term.

On the whole, it has not been labour costs that have affected the negotiating position of a manager but the amount a particular chapel has received to do a particular job elsewhere in the industry. Keith Sisson found in 1975 that though overall labour costs might vary widely between titles at any one time – given the extreme unreliability of statistics on this subject – there were remarkable similarities between rates paid for specific skills in comparable newspapers. In 1961 timehands on two quality papers were earning £24.15 and £24.62 a week respectively. While an oiler on one London evening paper was getting £30, his counterpart on the other received £30.40. This suggests that wages, though in theory under a measure of management control, were almost as much a fixed cost as newsprint. Up to 1973, production (over half of it printers' wages) absorbed about 40 per cent of the budgets of most popular titles, with newsprint taking about 30 per cent. The threefold rise in newsprint prices in the aftermath of the oil crisis of that year pushed newsprint up, above 40 per cent in many cases. A substantial proportion of total costs thus seemed beyond managerial control, certainly as long as chapels colluded to hold up their wages – and as long as proprietors would not collude to force them down.

Under the circumstances newspaper boards and their chairmen would turn in despair from their costs and find solace instead in revenue, especially from circulation. They were supported in this by the unique and influential inquiry into Fleet Street management conducted in 1965–6 by The Economist Intelligence Unit (EIU). This affirmed that costs, though too high, were not the industry's major problem, which was inadequate revenue. Here, the challenge lay in moving from an overdependence on advertising revenue to a greater emphasis on sales. The EIU researchers appeared to believe that the existing number of titles was for some reason democratically bespoke and that a paper with high sales revenue was a purer product than one with high advertising. This curious thesis made a deep impact on the 1977 Royal

Commission and was music to Fleet Street's ears. Circulation has always been the score-card of success, a daily general election of proprietorial potency. The *Daily Express* versus the *Daily Mail*, the *Daily Mirror* versus the *Sun*, *The Times* versus the *Daily Telegraph* are dynastic battles that have obsessed newspaper managers since the turn of the century. 'Going for sales' is a strategy that involves the heart of the paper, its editorial staff. It means spending money, not saving it. Especially when morale is low, it can be a live-or-die crusade, with every department donning armour, recruiting spies in the enemy camp and swearing death to the rest of Fleet Street. Little thought is given to marketing cost-effectiveness or rates of return.

To the Fleet Street manager, higher circulation is the most objective performance indicator. Ask him his 'sales figure' and he will reply not, as in most industries, with a sum of money but with copies sold. He knows that it is this figure by which he and his colleagues are judged. When the *Daily Express* was selling more than 4 million copies in the 1950s, it carried the fact on its front page. Audit Bureau of Circulation figures are always front-page news, suitably doctored to the paper's advantage. The *UK Press Gazette* analyses sales in meticulous detail. Yet no paper ever trumpets its balance sheet. Provided, as Beaverbrook insisted, a paper is 'secure in reserves' (and even if it is not) the quantity of its readers is what matters.

Almost every Fleet Street title has at some time been brought close to ruin by its proprietor's obsession with circulation unrelated to costs. As *The Times* sank from glory in the 1900s, its manager, Moberly Bell, sought one means after another to increase sales, including a subscription discount scheme and a cheap book club. This halted the decline and sales 'triumphantly' topped 40,000 in 1906 for the first time in fifteen years. Yet each extra copy, priced at 3d, was costing 6d to produce. The strategy could have succeeded only with an inconceivably large increase in advertising rates. It failed. Bell had to sell the paper's shares portfolio to pay his newsprint bills. Two years later *The Times* went into receivership and was sold to Harmsworth.

No lesson was learned. Throughout the circulation war of the 1930s, the popular press dissipated what should have been – and in most cases were – large profits on fruitless sales campaigns. The *Daily Herald* was losing money when acquired by Odhams in 1930 with a circulation of 250,000. It was relaunched to sell 1 million, regarded by Julius Elias, on the basis of no evidence, as the 'minimum for viability'. It reached 1 million and lost more money than ever. Elias decided he had to sell 2 million. His canvassers, in a frenzy of activity, were spending £1 on free gifts to buy 5s worth of subscription. The *Daily Herald* was the first paper in Fleet Street to 'sell' 2 million. Yet it was not being sold but given away. Readers took it free with their books, teasets, clothes and insurance policies.

To Francis Williams, such gimmicks were necessary because of the need to attract advertising to compete with the Conservative rivals. To him, the 2 million figure was 'a remarkable achievement and one which Elias felt justified everything: he had increased the *Herald*'s circulation eight-fold and brought it from nowhere to first place'. But to what purpose? The fact was that not enough readers wanted to buy the paper for its editorial content in competition with the *Daily Mirror* or the *Daily Express*. Extra readers could be 'bought' but they were not loyal ones, and advertisers were naturally sceptical of their real interest in reading what was inside it. Given its costs, the *Daily Herald* appears to have been unviable at any level of sale. The Elias saga merely suggested that it was more viable at a lower sale than at 2 million.

Run-on costs, including promotion, seem to have been higher than marginal revenue throughout the struggles of the 1930s. But as long as the *Daily Herald* was buying sales, none of the other titles had the courage unilaterally to desist. After the war, the end of newsprint rationing coincided with growing competition from television in the 1950s. Proprietors, now mostly of the second generation, found themselves drawn back to their fathers' ways. The latter had entered the battle at the head of their troops, as editors-in-chief or self-taught marketing executives. The new generation fought through the mercenaries of the advertising industry. They gloried not in the newspaper as it was but in an idealized version of it, presented through the haze of a West End 'presentation'. Fleet Street marketing, in the 1950s and 1960s, became psychotherapy for jaded managers. It offered victory for no more than the price of one more advertising campaign. The concept of the 'relaunch', which came to consume the energies of, for instance, the *Daily Mirror* and *Daily Express*, was created by marketing demands. A convincing new editorial appeal was rarely established to keep new readers at a sensible cost after the impact of the promotion wore off.

Even if most Fleet Street marketing since the Second World War was a waste of money, this did not justify the intense hostility marketing men encountered from those whose work they were trying to promote – the editorial staff. Journalists were and are second only to printers in the awe they accord to their chosen calling and in the jealousy with which they mark out their preserve. The employment of outsiders to help 'sell' journalism was treated as a criticism of its inability to sell itself. This attitude was doubly odd since most agencies, if only to win the account, tended to apply a glowing cosmetic to a newspaper's self-image. The intention was not to change but to 'communicate' the spirit of a paper, in order to reach those eager for it yet, for some reason, reluctant to buy it. Few advertising agencies dared tell a proprietor his paper was rubbish. Marketing thus became not just a diversion from production troubles and a weapon in an ancestral war but an excuse for avoiding painful editorial decisions. Journalists engaged in ridiculous battles with marketing men. When Lord Thomson took over *The Times* in 1966 (with his publicists pretending he would not interfere with editorial decisions), marketing consultants flooded the organization. Journalists viewed them as the enemy, to the extent of laying childish traps for them: I recall one falling backwards off a doctored chair at a meeting of *The Times* supplements to gales of laughter from the journalists present. Graham Cleverley points out that marketing departments were relevant to editorial promotion if to anything. Yet such was the hostility towards them that on most papers they had to be put under the protective wing of the chief executive, 'independent of the editorial function which misunderstands, misapplies or simply ignores them'.

If proprietors could not increase their revenue from higher sales, they could at least take part of the EIU/Royal Commission message to heart and increase their revenue from cover price. After a long period of stagnation, the cover prices of national papers doubled in real terms between 1961 and 1984. They appear to have been grossly underpriced before. Harry Henry's exhaustive study of the subject (*The Dynamics of the British Press*, see bibliography) was hard put to find much correlation between price rises and circulation decline. Indeed, in the 1970s when quality newspaper prices were actually increasing in real terms, total circulation increased as well, attributed by Henry to the rising popularity of quality papers as against tabloid ones, despite their rising price. This, together with the apparent lack of other easy ways of raising revenue (advertising being more market sensitive), left proprietors ready to milk their readers as the least painful way of feeding their printers.

Perhaps the most startling fact about the British newspaper market since the Second World War is that, for all the circulation battles and fluctuations in price, it has been so stable. National morning sales declined gently from 16 million in the mid-1940s to near 14 million in the recession of the mid-1970s (see appendix). They picked up almost to 16 million again by the end of 1984 (with help from bingo) and then settled at just over 15 million. Sunday papers have fallen faster, largely through popular titles losing out to burgeoning weekly magazines. In this static market Fleet Street's fixation on circulation could be justified only in strictly limited circumstances. Spoiling the market for the *News Chronicle*, *Daily Herald* and *Daily Sketch* was a plausible tactic for the *Daily Express*, *Daily Mail* and *Daily Mirror* in the 1950s. Again, in the 1970s, much effort at the *Daily Express* and *Daily Mail* was devoted to forcing the other to sue for a disadvantageous merger – as happened eventually with their respective evening titles. Proprietorial machismo forestalled any merger of the main titles. Although the *Daily Mail* gained steadily on the *Daily Express* over the decade, the latter found two new owners who were prepared to continue the fight rather than give an inch to Lord Rothermere.

Once new proprietorial blood was flowing into Fleet Street from the mid-1960s onwards, failing titles were sold and relaunched rather than closed. In these circumstances, a paper was usually foolish to spend money on promoting circulation with the intention of forcing a rival to the wall. It merely secured for its enemy a new cash injection. Extra circulation can be justified commercially only where a new increase in revenue exceeds the cost of achieving it. Given the high cost of newsprint and the structure of payments in the printing departments, these run-on costs can be very high. Add to them the promotional costs of a circulation drive and it is rare for there to be real extra money in the bank from a sales drive. Only tabloid newspapers – whose cover price yields roughly 70 per cent of total revenue – can be relatively certain of securing such a return from rising sales and then only if they can avoid heavy promotional spending. The bingo war of the early 1980s saw millions squandered on what became essentially a defensive operation, each title against the others.

Quality newspapers normally base their case for a high-sales strategy on their ability to raise their advertising rates. In contrast to the tabloids, advertising contributes up to 75 per cent of their revenues. In theory the strategy is perfectly sound, though a paper normally needs a prolonged and audited rise in sales before it can attempt an increase in rates. Certainly, a falling circulation may undermine the rate card and force salesmen to offer discounts, but even a rising sale may not increase advertising revenue if the new readers are not in the socio-economic category that advertisers want to reach. No paper better exemplified this than (yet again) *The Times* in the 1960s. The paper's managers repeated precisely the mistakes made by their predecessors in 1906. In the six months following the change to front-page news and a major promotional drive, the paper's circulation rose by 20 per cent. It thus took 'a big step away from the concept of a small élite readership and towards a newer, better-educated democracy', say Woods and Bishop, with evident satisfaction. The increase was the main target for the editor, William Haley, 'to which his editorship has been largely dedicated'.

The promotion cost so much that the Astors, like the Walters before them, ran out of money and had to sell. By 1968 with a new owner (Lord Thomson) but the same strategy, the sale was 50 per cent higher, boosted by student discounts, advertising campaigns and wider distribution. Advertising volume was 70 per cent higher. As sales reached the 400,000 mark in 1968, there was much talk of breaking through to the 'magic half-million'. This figure was not so much magic as necromancy: each extra copy was costing the company 2s to produce and distribute, with 6d coming back from the public.

*The Times*' traditional advertisers were unimpressed by the new, 'non-élite' readers – most of them students – and predictably resisted any attempt to increase advertising rates. Since advertising had to cover 75 per cent of the expense of printing *The Times*, a gap swiftly widened between a largely static revenue source and rising run-on costs. The chapels demanded extra money for 'extra work', and were given it. The effect on profitability was devastating. *The Times* had been losing roughly £250,000 a year before the relaunch. It lost Thomson £5 million in his first three years of ownership. Eventually, the management reversed the policy of going for sales. The circulation, and the losses, began to fall, *The Times*' sales dropping 50,000 in 1970-1 alone. The same policy was adopted, for the third time, in 1985 under Rupert Murdoch when he launched Portfolio bingo. The exorbitant production cost of acquiring an extra 50,000 sales was one of the factors that precipitated the move to Wapping.

Any examination of the Fleet Street story during the 1960s and 1970s must conclude that there was little connection between high spending on promotion and increased sales, and even less between increased sales and commercial prosperity. The EIU report concluded that 'sharp changes in publicity expenditure have little or no effect on circulation trends'. Readers certainly respond when given something for nothing, as the gyrations of the bingo wars showed. They also responded when one paper held back a price rise rather than following the oligopolistic collusion (since broken) whereby all papers in a section of the market increased their cover prices together. Yet British newspaper readers are creatures of remarkable habit: the true phenomenon of the market is its resistance to circulation-boosting blandishments – at least those unconnected with the editorial character of the product.

The papers that appeared to be most successful in circulation terms during the 1960s and 1970s were the five that presented a clear personality to their chosen audience. After a chaotic period, the *Daily Mail* in 1971 contrived to find stability on insecure ground midway between the tabloid and quality markets. The *Sunday Times* likewise recast its character under Lord Thomson, leaving the *Daily Telegraph* readers whom Hartwell was courting, and offering a 'middle-brow mix' of a preoccupation with consumer durables and sensational investigative reporting. The success of the *Sun* was based on the exploitation of an old editorial formula (that of the *News of the World*) with new flair. It doubled its own sales in four years and spawned an imitator, the *Daily Star*,* which built up a sale of over 1 million. The *Guardian* saw its sales climb steadily from 160,000 in 1956 to overtake *The Times* at 360,000 in 1974. It did so through identifying and appealing to a new market – those passing through (and often staying in) the booming tertiary education industry of the 1960s. It was a market for intelligent, progressive journalism, long deserted by the *News Chronicle* and the *Daily Herald*. Lastly, the *Financial Times* developed from a specialist paper to cover the arts, leisure and general news, quietly doubling its circulation over two decades.

All five titles were regarded as Fleet Street success stories and of them, only the *Sunday Times* has changed hands in the past fifteen years. Most, but not all, increased their circulation at the expense of market rivals, yet only three of the five made profits, with the *Daily Mail* and the *Guardian*

*Its name was changed to the *Star* in mid-1985.

losing money persistently during the period. The *Sunday Times*, the *Sun* and the *Financial Times* suffered some of the worst industrial relations in Fleet Street. But they possessed what their proprietors expected them to possess: public recognition and an editorial self-confidence that communicated itself easily to their readers.

A concern for sales volume is clearly important to any business. The most successful of the new proprietors, Rupert Murdoch, made it his guiding star. Since the *Sun* and the *News of the World* were peculiarly susceptible to high marginal returns, he was right to do so. When he turned the same techniques on *The Times* he encountered the bind familiar to the rest of Fleet Street: chapel-determined production costs that can eliminate the gains from higher sales. Consideration of one could not be divorced from consideration of the other. It was a bind that Murdoch finally resolved in a drastic way. The purpose of this chapter is not to deride sales growth as a commercial ambition: it is to point out how far its appeal dazzled new owners as much as it had old ones. It was the mark of success in the market for glory. It consequently occupied a disproportionate share of management time. It aided the chapels in bidding up their earnings and it diverted attention from the more pressing issue of cheaper and more flexible production.

# 6

# THE FOUR MEDICIS

Newspapermen require that those who rule Fleet Street are big men – big in good and big in evil. The sons of the great proprietors had failed this test. They were mostly weak, unworthy of the gossip, myth and notoriety that had enveloped their fathers. The new proprietors to whom they sold out were of a different stamp. They were seen as company men, their position achieved by commercial acumen not by the accident of birth. Their eyes would be on the balance sheet, it was thought, not on the guest list. They would deal unsentimentally with papers that fell beneath an exacting standard of profitability. Above all, by virtue of their success and experience outside Fleet Street, often in some overseas financial jungle, they would confront the chapels. With computerized technology widely available from the early 1960s onwards, an industrial transformation was at hand, greater even than that produced by the Linotype machine a century before.

No new proprietor seemed initially to meet this stereotype more exactly than the first to appear on the scene: Roy Herbert Thomson. Over the course of forty years in Canadian business, he had built a successful empire mainly composed of newspapers and radio stations. In 1952, at the age of fifty-eight, he decided the time had come to move on to politics, standing as Progressive Conservative party candidate for the Riding of York Centre in Toronto. He pumped hands and knocked on doors. He moved house into the constituency and promised his audiences that 'When I get to Ottawa I won't be a backbencher with nothing to say.' As an established millionaire and one of the leading figures of the Canadian media, he could reasonably anticipate a prominent second career. He even hinted that the Ministry of Finance might be within his capabilities. It was not to be. Thomson was beaten by a strong Liberal candidate and afterwards made little attempt to conceal his indignation at the humiliation. When he met the party leader, George Drew, after the election, he bluntly told him, 'As far as I'm concerned, you're a wonderful leader. But the public doesn't think so – so you'll have to go.' It was Thomson who went.

The reverse at York Centre was the end of what Thomson had planned as the summit of his career. His wife Edna had died the previous year and he decided to turn his back on Canada and prepare for retirement elsewhere. He told his family that he wished to spend his remaining years quietly running a newspaper in his ancestral homeland, Scotland. He would no longer expend his energies bidding for profit, but would be content with prestige. He would declare this ambition to anyone who cared to ask: 'What I want more than anything else in the world is a knighthood.'

In 1953 Thomson purchased the august *Scotsman* newspaper (together with the *Edinburgh Evening Dispatch*). It appeared to fulfil his dream. He delighted in its Scottishness. He reorganized its management, failed to make it profitable but was not over-worried by its losses. This was not enough for the restless Torontonian. The *Scotsman* proved a useful bargaining counter in his securing the franchise for Scottish commercial television, his 'licence to print money'. Then, in 1959 came the acquisition of the *Sunday Times*. Thomson revelled in the purchase. He proudly recorded

My diary for the last months of the year had dates in it to attend a reception at No. 10 and meet the prime minister, to dine with Lord Beaverbrook and then with Lord and Lady Rosebery, to appear on (BBC) Panorama, to lunch with Cecil King, to lunch with the German ambassador and meet Chancellor Adenauer, to go to a reception at the Gaitskells, to visit the famed Marquis of Salisbury . . .

In 1962 he travelled to Russia to promote his new *Sunday Times Magazine* and was delighted to be invited to discuss East–West relations with Nikita Khrushchev. He acted as *de facto* ambassador on his well-publicized return. Such glories would never have been visited on the MP for York Centre, Toronto, however rich. Two years later he was created a hereditary peer by Harold Macmillan, the last before the hereditary principle was discontinued (to be resumed in 1983 by Margaret Thatcher). He had been particularly keen on a hereditary title, pointing out it was the best way of ensuring that his descendants viewed the British press with the same reverence that he did.

Not even this was to equal Thomson's delight in his acquisition of *The Times*. Dismayed at the slow and often humiliating grind of the Monopolies Commission, he was at least gratified by the outcome. He had passed the Establishment's initiation ceremony and not been found wanting. The most remarkable feature of the deal was Thomson's treatment of the paper's losses not as a challenge to his commercial ingenuity but as the opposite, a badge of honour to be borne as token of his good intentions. He told *The Times*' readers that the paper's 'special position throughout the world will now be safeguarded for all time'. He added that the editor-in-chief had been 'guaranteed absolute freedom from interference. He will direct the paper *in the best interests of the country*' [my italics]. He proudly admitted that his purchase was

> something beyond the limits of normal business . . . we were setting no limit to the money we were prepared to put into it and we were asking no guarantees about ever getting it back. To save *The Times* we must put the kind of money into it that would carry it through without any strings attached or restrictions applied and my son has agreed with me.

Thomson even secured his son Kenneth's agreement to live in Britain after he was dead. He professed himself 'greatly moved that my son . . . wholeheartedly agreed with me in pouring away all those millions to save an ideal'. It was, he admitted, 'an impulse of generosity'. It was also 'perhaps the oddest deal I ever made'.

Lord Thomson's main claim to fame among journalists then and since was his widely trumpeted belief that editors should be left to express their own opinions without interference from him. Given his past political aspirations, this was true abstinence. When he ran for mayor in North Bay, Ontario, there was no talk of independence for his local radio station. As far as his British papers were concerned, though, he felt a deference to the politics of his adopted land. A rarity among proprietors, he had 'passed through' his political phase before reaching Fleet Street. Though by no means politically naïve, he regarded editorial opinions as best left to editors. He certainly expressed private worries at what he regarded as the 'urban guerrillas' on the *Sunday Times* staff, and was upset by that paper's attacks on Macmillan just as he was confidently expecting a peerage. But he wrote that he would have 'bitten my tongue off' rather than reprimand the editor concerned.

To this extent, Lord Thomson understood what Rupert Murdoch never has, that the British Establishment (which obsessed them both when they arrived in Fleet Street) will forgive any vulgarity provided the shibboleth of editorial independence is respected. Thomson's jolly face and thick-lensed glasses were well suited to his image of sugar daddy to the quality newspaper-reading classes. He might tease his staff by his fascination for column inches of advertising – even taking out a ruler and measuring them in *Pravda* on his Moscow visit. He enjoyed the (apocryphal) attribution to him of the saying that editorial material was something 'to separate the ads with'. Whatever recklessness might be perpetrated on the editorial floor, he appeared to smile indulgently and sign another cheque. To journalists, such proprietors are made in heaven.

Yet just as Thomson's early reputation as a crude profiteer evaporated as it approached the bright lights and high costs of Fleet Street, so his non-interventionism also evaporated. He could hardly buy so distinguished a product and not leave some mark of himself on it. Thomson might well have rejected Haley's Operation Breakthrough, with its para-phernalia of front-page news, cartoons, women's-interest features and higher circulation. Instead, he could have led the paper back to being once more the 'Establishment's tribal noticeboard'. Since he wanted *The Times* neither for profit nor for political influence but for the prestige of owning one of the world's most famous newspapers, why not glory in subsidizing its existing reputation?

Thomson's impact on *The Times* in 1966–8 was remarkably similar to that of Northcliffe in the early years of the latter's proprietorship. Thomson wanted the world to know he had owned and 'improved' *The Times*, and the one mark of such improvement recognized by Fleet Street was rising sales; hence the bid for the 'magic half-million'. Denis Hamilton was brought from the *Sunday Times* to achieve it. Special supplements were added. The cover price was held down. Thomson may not have interfered with the content of the leading articles, but the leader column is only part of a paper's being. The circulation target affected every corner of *The Times*. In 1971 some writers were so depressed by the ensuing popularization that they wrote a round robin of criticism to the editor, William Rees-Mogg (known as the White Swan letter from the pub in which it was composed). Resignations were frequent. The older guard on the staff felt that Thomson's 'quali-pop' policy was by no means honour-ing his commitment to the paper's tradition.

As the circulation continued to rise, so too did the losses: from £250,000 before Lord Thomson's purchase to £1 million plus, two years later. Despair spread through the paper's management. Working in the building at the time, I well remember the helplessness with which each month's figures were greeted and the absence of any alternative strategy for dealing with the cost spiral. Even at *The Times*, going for sales was the only technique in which Fleet Street managers had been schooled. Yet the chapels continued unconcernedly to make their claims. Each crisis merely served to impress on them his lordship's wealth and generosity. Thomson event-ually stopped congratulating his staff on the rising sales and accepted that a retrenchment was called for. As we saw in the last chapter, *The Times*' losses duly fell, parallel with its circulation. The paper had cost Thomson £8 million of his private fortune by the time of his death in 1976. None the less, his pride in his acquisition remained undiminished. Unlike most new proprietors, he knew the burden he had accepted on entering Fleet Street and continued to bear it with fortitude. If anything, it heightened the 'great sense of responsibility' that he felt proprietorship entailed.

Lord Thomson did not usher in a new age of tough and realistic management. He bruised *The Times* editorially, yet confirmed the chapels in their conviction that proprietorial geese lay golden eggs. Fleet Street's next new proprietor offered a contrast in style. Rupert Murdoch arrived in Fleet Street three years after Thomson had bought *The Times*, just when the latter's strategy was on the verge of collapse. Unlike Thomson, Murdoch came not to crown a successful career 'in the colonies', but to find a bigger challenge for his ambition than Australia could supply. His father, Sir Keith Murdoch, had been manager of the *Melbourne Herald* and proprietor of a chain of newspapers across Australia. He saw his son to Oxford but, unlike Fleet Street's earlier grandees, not into the Guards or a Conservative seat. The young Murdoch gained his further education on the sub-editorial desk of the *Daily Express* and with the proprietorship of the *Adelaide News* at the age of twenty-two (a similar beginning to Hearst, with whom Murdoch has more in common than with any English proprietor).

Sir Keith Murdoch was a friend and admirer of Lord Northcliffe whom he described as 'the biggest influence and the biggest force' in his life. He received lengthy advice from Northcliffe on how to increase the sale of the *Melbourne Herald*, all of it sound, and he later revelled in the nickname, 'Lord Southcliffe'. His son stepped naturally into these shoes. Independent of his father's estate, he swiftly acquired his own network of local papers across Australia and founded the country's first national, the *Australian*. He was not a writing journalist and his sub-editorial and managerial upbringing bred in him an early – and lasting – scepticism of the writer's craft. Like Bartholomew, he believed most people looked at newspapers rather than read them.

Rupert Murdoch inherited to the full his father's assumption of the status of proprietor-as-public-figure. His launch and continued support of the loss-making *Australian* was a risky business proposition. His treatment of its staff was cavalier and he frequently despaired of its dull seriousness, tearing it and its senior staff apart. Yet for all the criticism heaped on him as a result, Murdoch continued to back the paper. His support was not commercial but was, he plausibly claimed, rooted in a desire to be considered a distinguished Australian, not just a publisher of sensational newspapers. He defended himself before the Australian Broadcasting Tribunal in 1979 by asking, 'Who else has risked everything to start a national newspaper which goes across the length and breadth of this country? I started the *Australian* fifteen years ago as a dream. Nearly $A13 million has gone into making that dream a reality.' Even after Murdoch left Australia for Europe and then America, he took a continuing interest in its politics. He immersed himself in both the advancement and the toppling of Labour Prime Minister Gough Whitlam, developing a relationship with him similar to that of Northcliffe with Lloyd George. The involvement cost him dear when his empire began to push against the limits of monopoly regulation. A subtle proprietor lowers his political profile as his circulation rises: subtlety has never been Murdoch's style.

In 1969, still in his thirties and hyperactive, Murdoch threw himself at Fleet Street like a raucous gatecrasher. Not for him Lord Thomson's nervous waiting for an invitation. At the *News of the World* he was uncomfortable in being forced first to woo, then dissemble to the Carr family as a prelude to their removal from the scene. He later protested that he was only doing what the ever-obliging City of London told him to do. He was further embittered when Fleet Street, which had regarded the *News of the World* as quaintly acceptable in the hands of the Carrs, treated Murdoch's interest in it as squalid. Cecil King asked in his diary why anyone should want to be owner of the *News of the World*. His sarcastic answer was that in the case of Murdoch, 'apparently it will give him greater standing in Australia'.

Murdoch, never one to pour oil on troubled waters, responded to criticism of his treatment of the Carrs by purchasing and publishing, within a month of taking control, a tawdry, updated version of the Christine Keeler memoirs. Many Fleet Street revelations have been as disreputable as the Keeler serialization; few have been so excoriated by politicians and journalists. Fleet Street had far outdone Murdoch in its obsession with the affair six years earlier, but he was rubbing sore its guilt. That he was recently arrived from Australia made it the more unacceptable. He was battered by criticism and reacted with excuses that played into his critics' hands. He claimed variously that the attacks on him had been 'whipped up by members of the Establishment'; that he was only doing business; that the memoirs were not sleazy but a 'cautionary tale'; and that it was all 'going to sell newspapers'. It was the apologia of the populist publisher down the ages.

Murdoch was scarred by the Keeler affair and the resulting personal criticism. It made him incautious in his dealings with his enemies. He threatened to get his own back on the *Observer* and on London Weekend Television (LWT), whose David Frost programme had shown him no mercy. He bore grudges. Having recently settled in London with his young family, he felt socially contaminated. As Michael Leapman remarks, 'In public he affected a swaggering disregard for such matters. But to his friends it was clear that it did matter . . . He was being ostracized for a quite legitimate piece of journalistic enterprise and he hated it.'

Still he ploughed on. The formula for the new *Sun*, launched months later in 1969, was in direct line of descent from Pulitzer and Hearst through Northcliffe to his father. Its blend of raciness and conservatism had been tested in the weekly market by the *News of the World*. Murdoch's chief good fortune lay in the parlous state of his competitors. The *Daily Mirror* under Cecil King and then Hugh Cudlipp had assumed the pomposity of many radical papers which choose to 'educate' their readers rather than amuse them. Its

Mirrorscope and Inside Page features on issues of the day delighted politicians but left it vulnerable to less worthy rivals. Murdoch took the view that working-class taste in newspapers was much the same the world over: except when a big story is breaking, it wants sex, entertainment and sport.

Key to the *Sun*'s success was an identity of view between Murdoch and his editor, Larry Lamb, as to what the paper should be and how it should look. There were few wrangles between them over who was the boss. The first issue of the new *Sun* carried a statement signed by Murdoch and couched in traditional proprietorial banalities: 'The *Sun* is a paper that cares, passionately, about truth and beauty and justice.' Initially at least, there was no sign of Murdoch being any less susceptible than most proprietors to the political access that came with the job. He was courted by Prime Minister Harold Wilson. He visited Chequers and threw the *Sun*'s opinion columns behind Labour at the 1970 general election. Only after Edward Heath emerged the winner did the paper move steadily rightwards.

Politics, however, was never to be an important part of the *Sun*'s appeal. Murdoch was, according to *Fortune* magazine, 'happiest with a first edition spread out on his desk, slashing red lines through unsatisfactory pictures and snapping over the telephone at subordinates'. Within two years he had undermined the self-confidence of the British popular press. He forced one rival, the *Daily Sketch*, into closure and another, the *Daily Mirror*, into an often ludicrous self-doubt. Its chairman, Hugh Cudlipp, was quoted as saying, 'Someone will always be found to scrape the bottom of the barrel.' (An odd judgement from a student of Bartholomew and one which Cudlipp later graciously retracted.) Most embarrassing was the *Daily Mirror*'s decision to imitate the *Sun* by showing naked breasts, qualified by the promise that breasts would appear only 'where relevant'.

Murdoch shared with every previous proprietor a fatalism towards industrial relations in Fleet Street. He had obtained the paper only after the chapels had rejected Robert Maxwell's bid involving a 50 per cent cut in staffing. In moving the *Sun* to Bouverie Street, he was able to negotiate some manning reductions. The machine room was cut initially by 25 per cent, though Murdoch was not able to extend to the *Sun* the *News of the World*'s Victorian eccentricity of having no NGA minders on its printing presses.

Trouble began when the *Sun*'s sales started to rise. Far from helping to rescue an ailing title, the chapels realized they were helping a new one to grow at the expense of an old one. A newspaper extends its print run by increasing the number or running time of a sequence of linked presses, known as folders. An agreement for these machines must be renegotiated whenever such an increase is required. As the *Sun*'s output increased, the chapels carefully set limits on how much they would print before requesting new agreements. There were still close links between the *Sun* and *Daily Mirror* chapels and more than a suspicion that the *Sun*'s production was being deliberately held back to protect the *Daily Mirror* – and to protect its chapels' earnings. Where the *Sun* increased its sales, the 'damaging' level of its productivity became subject of heated inter-chapel controversy.

The tension between the two titles was too great for peace to last. Battle was eventually joined between Murdoch and the *Sun*'s machine-room NATSOPA chapel in 1973. A substantial claim for more shifts (that is, more cash to the chapels to distribute to existing staff) was met head on, with Murdoch threatening to stop the paper and invoke a Newspaper Publishers' Association (NPA) protocol whereby all publishers would agree to close if one were hit by industrial action. In a rare act of collective will, the NPA initially agreed to shut down Fleet Street until such time as the *Sun*'s NATSOPA chapel relented. This was no small achievement, since costs were under severe pressure and Murdoch's emerging market strength was affecting tabloid sales across the board. The deal proved too much for Beaverbrook Newspapers' Sir Max Aitken, who could not bring himself to shut the *Daily Express* for the sake of the *Sun*. The collective stand was immediately abandoned. One observer recalled, 'The *Sun* representatives stormed out of the building and immediately conceded NATSOPA's claim. Murdoch never trusted Fleet Street to stand together against the unions again.' He was right.

1. Viscount Northcliffe
(*Press Association Ltd*)

2. 1st Viscount Rothermere
(*BBC Hulton Picture Library*)

3. Lord Beaverbrook
(*Press Association Ltd*)

4. 1st Baron Astor of Hever
(*BBC Hulton Picture Library*)

5. Lord Thomson
(*Press Association Ltd*)

6. Cecil King
(*Press Association Ltd*)

7. Lord Hartwell
(*Press Association Ltd*)

8. Sir Max Aitken
(*BBC Hulton Picture Library*)

9. Rupert Murdoch
(*Press Association Ltd*)

10. Lord Matthews
(*Press Association Ltd*)

11. Tiny Rowland
(*Press Association Ltd*)

12. 3rd Viscount Rothermere
(*Press Association Ltd*)

13. Robert Maxwell
(*Paul Armiger, Camera Press, London*)

14. Conrad Black
(*John Mahler, Camera Press, London*)

15. David Stevens
(*Press Association Ltd*)

16. Eddy Shah
(*Press Association Ltd*)

The affair reinforced Murdoch's sense of isolation from the Fleet Street, and British, Establishment. As far as newspaper costs were concerned, he reverted to Beaverbrook's old maxim: let the other 'miserable wretches' feel the strain. By 1973 the *Sun* and the *News of the World* were making a substantial profit, to the discomfort of both Reed's Mirror group and Beaverbrook Newspapers. While their chapels negotiated earnings ever upwards to become some of the best paid in Fleet Street, they never produced run-on costs that were higher than the additional revenue. Murdoch's titles thus achieved a rare state of Fleet Street grace; they could actually profit from rising sales.

Murdoch's restlessness led him to diversify. He bought into television, acquiring, for a time, effective control of LWT. He also bought an expanded chain of provincial titles. Yet he found England stifling and snobbish. He had been the object of extraordinary public contempt. In an interview to the New York *Village Voice* three years later, he recalled, 'Maybe I just have an inferiority complex about being an Australian.' He could not see that he was doing anything different from populist proprietors down the ages, yet 'just as we were being invited round to places we'd catch Lord Lambton in bed or something and then we'd be barred from everything'. He admitted that it was 'very difficult not at some point to be sucked into the Establishment. But the last thing I wanted to be was a bloody press lord.'

Murdoch rejected the traditional blandishments Fleet Street offers its proprietors. He had come to live in London, yet did not go to the clubs and dinners at which senior newspapermen gathered, slapped each other on the back and swapped horror stories about their chapels. He was one of nature's predators. Despite his sensitivity to criticism, he seemed always to be courting more. His desire for respectability sat ill alongside his papers' intrusions into the private lives of others. He seemed to deflect sympathy like a repelling magnet. But for all this, the ostracism of Rupert Murdoch was Fleet Street at its most hypocritical. At the end of 1973 he decided to leave London 'in disgust' and try his hand in America. He promptly acquired two papers in San

Antonio and three years later launched himself on to New York with his purchase of the *New York Post*. Here his zest for down-market journalism was indulged to the full, with garish presentation, the hysterical pursuit of the 'Son of Sam' killer in 1977 and the boosting of Ed Koch for mayor in the same year.

Murdoch did not turn the *New York Post* into a money-spinner: in 1978, a city-wide machine room claim saw him forced to confront his unions in an almost identical dispute to that which had plagued him in London. He was thrust into the leadership of the New York Publishers' Association, a post he regarded as having more than industrial significance. 'Aside from the temptation of flattery,' he told *The New Yorker*, 'I knew I would be a lightning rod. There was a chance to be seen arguing a case other than Son of Sam or some dumb headline in the *Post*.' Yet he undid any such benefit to his reputation by deserting his fellow proprietors and doing a deal with the union on his own, an inversion of the treatment meted out to him by the NPA in London. The attacks on his behaviour now equalled those of 1973 in London. He became involved in a public slanging match with the distinguished dean of the Columbia School of Journalism, Osborn Elliott. He found himself once again the newspaperman the Establishment loved to hate. A. M. Rosenthal of the *New York Times* castigated him as 'a bad element, practising mean, ugly, violent journalism'.

Rupert Murdoch remained an enigma to the public. He had not come to terms with his egocentricity as had Lord Thomson. He was neither corporate executive nor idiosyncratic businessman. He was essentially a gambler, seeking to prove himself with ever more reckless bets, yet without a gambler's flamboyance. And still Fleet Street seemed the most appealing casino. Within three years of leaving for New York, Murdoch was back. In 1976 he was asked by the board of the *Observer* to be the paper's saviour, only to suffer the humiliation of rejection when news leaked to the staff and an alternative buyer was discovered. The same year he acquired 32 per cent of the non-voting stock in Beaverbrook Newspapers. He was direct in his ambitions. When asked what he

intended to do with the titles, he said he would change the
*Daily Express* but not the *Evening Standard*. 'I like the
*Standard* the way it is,' he said. 'It will give me respectability.'* Again, he was pipped at the post in favour of a less
radical suitor; again, he felt himself victim of an 'Establishment shut-out'; and yet again he had proved his own worst
enemy. At both the *Observer* and the *Daily Express*, a
crucial element in Murdoch's defeat was the antipathy
toward him of key players: Donald Trelford, editor of the
*Observer*, and Jocelyn Stevens, chief executive of Beaverbrook Newspapers. Murdoch signalled to both that their
days were numbered if he won. He could never play poker
with a straight face.

The *Observer*'s deliverance from Murdoch came through the
intervention of ARCO. Few Fleet Street take-overs have
displayed so obviously uncommercial a motivation. The
American company's chairman, Robert Anderson, was glor-
ified by the British media. David Astor described him as 'the
last of the true Medicis'. Mr Anderson's prior acquaintance
with the *Observer* was small. None the less, he felt moved to
declare, 'It must be preserved as an independent and vigorous voice in Great Britain and abroad. I believe that its
future can be as long and illustrious as its past.' When
Anderson arrived in Britain to inspect his new purchase, he
was fêted with a visit to 10 Downing Street and dinner at
High Table at University College, Oxford. Lord Goodman,
former chairman of the *Observer* and architect of the take-
over, was the host. The guest speaker was the Prime Minister, Harold Wilson, who sang the praises of the bemused and
delighted Anderson. The latter announced the setting up by
the *Observer* of 'an advisory council to extend its international reach, including outstanding representatives from a
number of countries'. *Observer* executives would fly each
year to his foundation in Colorado for a 'think-in'. It was a
source of great pride to him, he said, to be 'joining the
*Observer* partnership'. It was proprietorship as apotheosis.

*Conversation with the author.

In a sardonic comment on Anderson's acquisition, the *Washington Post* remarked that 'he is not seeking a profitable asset for his company's growing domain.' This was to prove an understatement. At the time of the purchase (for a nominal £1), the company had made no more than a nod in the direction of viability. It said casually that the paper had been 'a profitable company for most of its 185-year history and we see no reason to believe that it cannot continue strong and viable'. No indication was given as to how this was to be achieved. In the event, ARCO spent some $20 million on the *Observer* in just over four years. Much of this was to pay for higher circulation resulting from the closure of the *Sunday Times* in 1978–9, when the sale almost doubled from its previous 670,000. Gradually, however, the glamour wore thin, if not for Anderson at least for his shareholders. Although there was talk of the acquisition helping ARCO with the British Government in possible North Sea oil ventures, few believed it was other than a public-spirited foible on the chairman's part. Anderson had omitted to follow Lord Thomson's example and charge his paper to his personal fortune.

ARCO's period of ownership was a blessed respite for the *Observer*, as if its journalism had been touched with a wand and turned to gold. But it was only a respite. The partnership to which Anderson referred proved to be chiefly between his company's cash flow and the capacious pockets of the *Observer*'s printers. What resounded round chapel meetings was David Astor's reference to the Medicis. Those who a year earlier had been induced by threats of bankruptcy to concede lower manning levels now wanted the Medicis to restore them.

Within two years, the *Observer*'s twenty-eight-strong NGA machine minders' chapel put in a bid to increase the number of shifts back to near their former level. The excuse was in part the increased demand due to the *Sunday Times* closure. The chapel threatened strike action and, for once, the intervention of the NGA's national executive forced the chapel to back down. However, the chapel returned with a further claim in 1980. ARCO played the closure card and issued notices to all 500 staff at the paper. Once again the NGA backed off under pressure from its national officers, though in this case the crucial factor appears to have been a belief that NATSOPA machine assistants might break ranks and operate the machines without NGA minders. This possibility has always been the one threat seriously to worry Fleet Street's toughest mafia, the 'Saturday night minders'. The secretary of SOGAT, William Keys, went so far as to accuse the NGA of acting like 'kamikaze pilots' in the affair. After a month of cliff-hanging confrontation, in which the paper's fate seemed daily before the nation's eyes, the *Observer* minders at last accepted the management's 'final' offer (of close to £100 for a single night's work). The NGA's journal, *Print*, acknowledged that 'the jobs of other NGA members and members of other unions would be lost if the paper ceased publication'. This assumption of impending closure, threatened as often by national unions as by proprietors, had been untrue of the *Observer* in 1975. It was to prove untrue within a year.

For ARCO, the dispute was the last straw. Within six months Anderson accepted the view of his board that it could not operate a recalcitrant company thousands of miles from its Los Angeles headquarters. A proprietorship born in the glow of institutional glory ended under a cloud of differentials and ghost shifts. In February 1981 a secret deal was struck between Anderson and Tiny Rowland to transfer the paper to Lonrho's Scottish publishing company, Outrams. A graveside eulogy on Anderson's proprietorship was given by his Los Angeles spokesman: 'We have never envisioned [sic] ourselves as being newspaper publishers. We got into the *Observer* in the first place because of the newspaper's plight. It seemed a worthy thing to do, a philanthropic move.' The paper, by implication, had been saved for four years from Rupert Murdoch. Now it was someone else's turn.

ARCO's purchase of the *Observer* in 1976 seemed at first a throwback to the nineteenth century, to the Fleet Street of Newnes' *Westminster Gazette* or the Cadburys' *Daily News*. Yet within a year, the idea that this might be an exception to a more sombre new era in proprietorship was allayed by happenings at Beaverbrook Newspapers. An early front-runner in bidding for the group, Sir James Goldsmith, said, 'I want to get into newspapers because I am a politician *manqué*. I want to do exciting things with them, develop them, use them to play a part in public affairs.'\* Goldsmith secretly invited Beaverbrook Newspapers' union officials to his leather-lined offices in Leadenhall Street. He plied them with Havana cigars and assured them of his co-operation in return for theirs. It was hardly surprising that the unions felt under no pressure to discard a lifetime's lucrative 'custom and practice' when tycoons seemed so eager to subsidize it.

On the surface, Trafalgar House, the eventual winner in the race for Beaverbrook Newspapers, was made of sterner stuff. The company had been created by a young property developer, Nigel Broackes, through a series of quick-footed deals in the West End in the early 1960s. Broackes survived the 1970s property recession by having diversified carefully when the market was at its peak. He acquired Cementation and Trollope & Colls, and in 1964 took Victor Matthews, a builder fifteen years his senior, into partnership. To outsiders, the Stowe-educated Broackes provided the strategic brains, the *élan* and the ability to move fast through financially complex deals while Matthews, schooled in the business of construction sites, was the managerial brawn – the unusual combination fascinated the City. Recovery opportunities constantly came their way, companies down on their luck or, more often, down on their management. They rescued such institutions as the Ritz Hotel and the Cunard shipping line, with its flagship, the *Queen Elizabeth II*. By 1977 Trafalgar House was turning over £587 million.

The Beaverbrook Newspapers deal was presented to the public as of the same character. The *Daily Express* was a 'great institution'. Trafalgar House committed itself to retain the existing management – a key factor in the success of its bid – and to make redundancies 'only after full consultation with trade union representatives'. Yet Broackes's pro-

*Conversation with the author.

126

prietorship was full of curiosities. He was highly conscious of his image and was already a benefactor of such charities as the Tate Gallery and The Royal Opera, Covent Garden. His company was one of the largest corporate contributors to Conservative Party funds. Newspapers are more prominent, and certainly more political, institutions than ships or hotels and it would have been natural for Broackes, on acquiring the *Daily Express*, to have immersed himself in Fleet Street. Instead, he delegated to Matthews the job of chairman and chief executive of the renamed Express Newspapers group, with a clear remit to make its three titles profitable in three years. There was to be no injection of new management from Trafalgar House. Given this hands-off approach by the top man at Trafalgar House, there was talk of an asset-stripping operation, perhaps with Broackes resurrecting the deal with Associated Newspapers and taking a profit on the property at the end. This, however, was denied by both Broackes and Matthews, and plausibly so. No new proprietor has ever bought into Fleet Street to close titles and realize property – however comforting the property assets might seem when the financial going gets rough. To have closed the *Daily Express* promptly would have been dreadful public relations for Trafalgar House. Although Broackes was not forthcoming on the subject, he implies in his autobiography that he saw the move of Matthews as a way of relieving the somewhat strained relations between the two men, and in a direction that exploited Matthews's managerial skills. At the same time, he failed to predict the attention that would be directed at his subordinate as publisher of the *Daily Express*. Nor did he realize how far Matthews would assume the status of traditional proprietor – and have it accepted at face value by Fleet Street. The rival *Daily Mail* derided the purchase as a 'fun stock for the ruling duo at Trafalgar'. Nigel Broackes, in the negotiations prior to the take-over, had indicated that he would be at least an equal party to this fun. He appears to have misjudged the industry into which he was buying.

Matthews heard that Trafalgar House was the preferred bidder in his Berkeley Street office at lunchtime on 30 June 1977. He immediately rushed to his Rolls-Royce, sweeping with him a BBC Television crew, to drive round to Fleet Street. An interviewer asked him not how would he put the *Daily Express* back on its feet but whether he felt any affinity with Lord Beaverbrook. 'Oh, yes, very much so,' replied Matthews. 'Very keenly, I believe in the things he believed in, otherwise I don't feel one could do this.' Matthews never pretended to be anything other than a modest businessman by occupation – one of his more attractive qualities – yet on the pavement outside the Express building he was bombarded with questions more appropriate for a party leader after an election victory. What was his political philosophy? What was his view of Britain's place in the world? Whom would he support in government? Struggling for the appropriate cliché, he murmured, 'I believe in Britain and want to help make her great again.' That night, the *Daily Express* declared, 'Your *Express*: A New Horizon,' alongside Matthews's portrait. It was the first time his picture had made the front page. That of Nigel Broackes was nowhere to be seen.

Matthews was transformed by the experience of Fleet Street. Before the above scene took place, when I first discussed with him his approach to newspaper management, he admitted that his eyes rarely strayed from the racing section of most papers. He did not read the quality press. Apart from an aversion to socialism, he disclaimed any interest in politics or in editorializing on the subject. After assuming the chairmanship of Express Newspapers, Matthews did not lose this simplicity or take on a phoney sophistication, but he revelled in his sudden fame. Within days, he told his 'political people' that he would appreciate an invitation to Downing Street. The flattery of proprietors has long been a sport of prime ministers and an invitation duly came.

The *Daily Express* became a reflection of the eccentricities of its proprietor to an extent hardly seen even in Beaverbrook's day. Matthews involved himself daily in the editorial affairs of the paper. He was available for comment to any journalist who rang him up with a stream of political maxims: 'We have not got an Empire any more, but we have got Britain'; 'The Left wants to change our life. I do not believe in levelling down. I want to level up'; 'If believing in Britain means being Conservative then that's what we will be'; 'Porn is the easy way; that is not for us'; and his most celebrated: 'By and large the editors will have complete freedom as long as they agree with the policy I have laid down.' The editors of the *Daily Express* – who proceeded to change under Matthews as often as they had under Aitken – had to endure lengthy political discourses from the proprietor, usually at the busiest time of the day. These would often have to be re-created by a journalist in the form of an editorial. He would discuss in detail the main front-page headline, and hold hour-long post mortems. (I had to plead against the *Evening Standard* being expected to call for a nuclear first strike on Moscow, 'to rid the world of communism, just like that'.)

Matthews soon began to suffer from the occupational disease of proprietorship: a susceptibility to comments about his papers at the functions to which he was now constantly invited. Beaverbrook Newspapers' once robust attitude to the royal family was changed to one of adulation. Matthews thought of stopping the William Hickey gossip column, such was the embarrassment it caused him. Following discreet lobbying at Downing Street by a member of the Trafalgar House board, he achieved the summit of proprietorial ambition when Mrs Thatcher ennobled him in 1980. Nigel Broackes, according to friends, was stunned. He not unreasonably thought it was he who had saved the *Daily Express*. Yet Fleet Street tradition had enabled Matthews to trump his ace. (Broackes was later knighted for his chairmanship of the London Docklands Development Corporation.)

Lord Matthews's fascination with the trappings of his new role was inevitably a distraction from the central task that Trafalgar House had set itself, that of restoring the group to profitability. His naïvety was at first a virtue. He was splendidly blunt. At his first meeting with the production chapels, he was subjected to a litany of complaints about broken agreements and eroded differentials from self-righteous officials. Such ingratitude from those whose jobs he had rescued genuinely mystified Matthews. He said he could not see why he should listen to such stuff from an unprofitable company and threatened to take himself and his money off to the Bahamas instead. His audience gasped at the remark. Many of his listeners could themselves afford a Caribbean retirement – though only if men such as Matthews stayed put. Certainly it promised a novel approach to industrial relations.

Within two months Trafalgar House was put to the test. Differentials between Linotype operators and the hourly paid chapels were, as in all Fleet Street houses in the late 1970s, under particular strain. In September 1977 the skilled maintenance engineers (allegedly 161 of them) were the first to strike, demanding parity with the 'highest-paid workers' in the plant. The claim was backed by disruptive action. Matthews claimed they had dismissed themselves and the London production of the *Daily Express* stopped immediately. Following sabotage in the works and the calling in of the police, Matthews was adamant that he would not take those responsible back on to the payroll.

Matthews was lucky in his opponents. Print engineers, like electricians, are a small and exclusive Fleet Street fraternity. Their claim was exorbitant and they were unlikely to secure sympathy from printing chapels. They were also subject to stronger national union discipline in the person of the print engineers' leader, Reg Birch. After a week of stoppage, the chapel was induced to put its claim to negotiation and the papers reopened. It agreed to end a variety of restrictive practices and behave more flexibly under its house agreement. In practice, the dispute merely resurrected some of the long-abused features of the old 'comprehensive' package. Matthews was forced to reinstate the wreckers: Reg Birch told him such sackings were unacceptable to the union, nor would he allow Matthews to carry out his threat to transfer printing of the Express group's national distribution to its Manchester plant. 'I am glad we are now back to a little order,' Birch reflected afterwards. The order was that of the status quo.

An important lesson of Fleet Street industrial relations is that victory is seen to go to whoever claims it most loudly. Matthews and his chief executive, Jocelyn Stevens, immediately hailed the settlement as 'a new style of newspaper management in Fleet Street'. Stevens added that 'chapel meetings would no longer interfere with production. No one else in Fleet Street has got this in an agreement. What we now have is management able to manage.' It was a hollow boast. An outrageous claim had certainly been resisted, but no new chapter in the industry's history was inaugurated. Matthews was hailed as a hero, but rather than capitalize on his supposed triumph to reduce costs elsewhere in his plant, he turned instead to the proprietor's oldest hobby – attempting to increase the volume of his output.

'Bottoming out' the fall in *Daily Express* sales by tearing it apart editorially consumed Matthews's attention. The latest editor, Roy Wright, was replaced with Derek Jameson, brought in from the *Daily Mirror*. He was told to leave the *Daily Mail* market alone and attack that occupied by his former employer. The *Daily Express* was again relaunched with new typography, pictures of girls and an aggressively down-market image. Serials, special offers and competitions – a Jameson speciality – proliferated. The paper's circulation rallied encouragingly in 1978 in response to £5 million a year of Trafalgar House money being pumped into it at this time. It then continued its slide. By the start of 1979, it was down to 2.4 million, 250,000 less than when Trafalgar House had bought it.

Not a week passed without some new project being tossed at a hard-pressed management team. One, two, or even three new titles were mooted. At one point it seemed that the *Daily Express* might join the *Daily Mirror* in a complete photocomposition programme. Instead, Matthews opted for a new title, the *Daily Star*. It was to be launched to compete with the *Sun* primarily in the north of England, where the latter did not have a printing plant. The paper would be down-market and left of centre, so as not to attack directly the 'bottom end' of the *Daily Express* readership. The concept was a case of making do with second best: if costs could not be reduced, at least find a way to spread overheads across higher output. The essential proviso was that promotional and run-on costs did not exceed the additional revenue. It was hoped that by printing the new paper in Manchester this danger might be avoided.

For the unions, the *Daily Star* threatened a crucial principle: by producing a paper in Manchester that had nationwide distribution, Matthews was undermining the status of Fleet Street as the national printing capital. Earnings on the Manchester editions of national newspapers were below those prevalent in London. As the Advisory, Conciliation & Arbitration Service (ACAS) had said in its report to the Royal Commission in 1976, 'The casual system of employment is better regulated in Manchester; the management/union relationships are superior; production is more efficient; and inter-union links are closer and less turbulent.' Not surprisingly, 'the Manchester option' became the subject of speculation throughout management circles in the late 1970s.

Aware of this danger, chapels on the *Daily Star* sought to ensure that its manning levels corresponded not to those prevailing in other Manchester offices but to what they would have been had the paper been printed in London. It was essential to deter other proprietors from considering a move north for their southern editions. As a result, from the moment of the paper's launch in November 1978, the *Daily Star*'s chapels struggled to export London costs northwards. To the fury of other publishing houses, they were mostly successful.

The journalists were first past the post. Learning tricks from their manual colleagues, *Daily Star* journalists (many of them transferred from elsewhere in the *Express* group) demanded more to work on the paper in Manchester than they would have got in London. *Daily Express* journalists in Manchester had to be paid likewise. Their London colleagues demanded more money. *Daily Mail* staff in Manchester demanded comparability with their new rivals – for the 'increased effort' of competing with it. *Daily Mail* staff in London joined the bandwagon. Early in 1979 Manchester was seething with comparability claims in every department. *Daily Mirror* machine minders went on strike for parity with the much higher night-time payments now being made to minders on the *Daily Star*. The *Daily Mirror*, already hit by the *Daily Star*'s costly sales drive in the north, regarded Matthews's interpretation of the Manchester option as a disaster. Needless to say, virtually all these claims were conceded.

Despite an initial sale of well over 1 million copies, the *Daily Star* was not a commercial success. It fell to 500,000 within six months, not helped, in Stevens's view, by Matthews's insistence that the paper stop attacking the Prime Minister, Margaret Thatcher, (who had just ennobled him) and switch its support to the Conservatives.* For years its losses added to the burden on the *Daily Express*, its proprietor taking comfort in the fact that at least its sales began rising again, to top 1 million in 1980 and to continue up (with help from bingo) until 1985. By then, the *Star* (as it had now been renamed) had enabled the Express Newspapers group to increase its share of the daily market from 17 per cent to 22 per cent. The appropriate proprietorial honour was thus satisfied.

Matthews was adamant that he was not an 'old-style' proprietor, but an executive protecting the interests of his shareholders. The claim did not ring true to his journalists. However, in 1982 Trafalgar House decided to float the group away into a separate public company, Fleet Holdings, with Matthews as chairman and a separate public shareholding. Despite denials, the severance reflected the view of a number of Trafalgar House board members that Matthews was indeed behaving as proprietor. The Express Newspapers titles were still losing money – £1.6 million in the first nine months under the new Fleet Holdings – and their total valuation was just over £13 million. The group had in no sense repaid Trafalgar House for the cost of five years' support. It had brought Broackes and his board no profit and little pleasure. Even Matthews had had his fair share of misery from the experience, though he at least had a peerage to show for it. Broackes was clearly happy to see him go.

The direction of the *Daily Express* continued to parody itself. Derek Jameson was sacked as editor. Jocelyn Stevens,

* Article in *UK Press Gazette*, 28 October 1986.

one of Fleet Street's more colourful survivors, was sacked as chief executive. Jameson's successor, Christopher Ward, also acquired from the *Daily Mirror*, was sacked to be followed by Sir Larry Lamb. The circulation went steadily down, dropping below 2 million in 1983. It appeared at one point that the *Daily Mail* might even overtake the *Daily Express* – an epochal event only forestalled by aggressive and costly bingo promotion (see page 164). Matthews was cast into gloom by this mark of Cain on his proprietorship. He had thrown five editors at the *Daily Express*, he said, and still it had not worked. It was as if editors were First World War subalterns.

Yet the losses were falling as well. By 1985 Matthews could reasonably claim to have put the Express Newspapers group into respectable financial shape. He was a shrewd enthusiast for the flotation of Reuters shares (see page 157). In 1984 he watched the old Beaverbrook apportionment of these shares climb from an initial valuation of £56 million to almost double that. He did what the Aitkens had never dared do, and diversified into other media activities, including a purchase of 31 per cent of the TV-am television company. In 1980 he reached terms with Associated Newspapers, finally rationalizing both groups' loss-making evening papers with printing at the *Daily Express* for a joint *Standard–News* product. A subsidiary company was established, owned half by each group, with the paper remaining at the Express building and under the *Evening Standard* flag (though later renamed the London *Standard*). Rothermere was given the satisfaction of seeing his own man, Louis Kirby, take over the editorship, recompense for his humiliation during merger talks three years earlier. Matthews thus converted a heavy loss on the *Evening Standard* into a developable property in Shoe Lane and a £4-million printing contract at his Fleet Street plant for the merged title. Fleet Holdings' pre-tax profits (including the Morgan Grampian magazines) rose in the three years after its formation from £3 million to £28 million – though only some £7 million was from the daily and Sunday titles.

Matthews was more of a Fleet Street innovator than his

critics expected. He founded the first genuinely new daily paper in Britain since Northcliffe (apart from the abortive *New Daily* of 1960), thus showing that new markets could be carved out of old. He pioneered the use of the law against the print unions. His frequent injunctions against the print unions under the Conservative Government's new legislation may have had little impact on his costs, but it carried a torch for other employers at a time when many believed the legislation might be a dead letter. Finally, in October 1985, Matthews's managing director, Ian Irving, reported the signature of a new technology deal with the NGA, transferring all the Express Newspapers titles to photocomposition. It was the culmination of a decade-long process within the group.

As the Aitkens had learned, such innovations often come too little and too late. The Reuters-led increase in the value of Fleet Holdings perversely made it more attractive to predators. In the bid fever of 1985, these included the Australian Robert Holmes a' Court, the Egyptian Dr Ashraf Marwan (believed to have links with Lonrho) and the ambitious chairman of the provincial United Newspapers group, David Stevens. In January Stevens had bought Robert Maxwell's 15 per cent share in Fleet Holdings. He began a whispering campaign against Matthews's leadership, designed to undermine the confidence of Fleet Holdings' institutional shareholders. Matthews belligerently refused to have him on the Fleet Holdings board and watched his share price climb, it was thought, well out of Stevens's reach.

In October, however, Stevens made what proved an immaculately timed assault, winning control with a bid of £317 million, some £70 million more than the market value of his own company. It was a remarkable *coup* and left Matthews in a state of dejection. In a sad comment on his past radicalism, he accused Stevens of promising manning reductions (20 per cent of the 6,000 workforce) that would result in 'mayhem' and damage the company's profits. After his defeat, he withdrew from the scene as swiftly as he had come. He later retired as chairman of the *Standard* company, jointly owned with Associated Newspapers. Rothermere then bought out the other half-share (still owned by Trafalgar House) and saw fifteen years of patient effort at last rewarded. He now enjoyed the London evening paper monopoly he had long coveted, though within a year it was to be threatened by Robert Maxwell.

Thomson, Murdoch, Anderson and Matthews were the first 'new' proprietors to arrive in Fleet Street after the war. Each had a different personality and enjoyed different relationships with their respective titles. Although only Thomson and Murdoch had personal control of their companies while Anderson and Matthews were answerable to conglomerate boards, all displayed customary 'proprietorial' characteristics. Murdoch and Matthews intervened regularly in matters of editorial content. Thomson's impact on his editorial staff was at one remove, through goading his managers to find ways of selling more copies. Anderson treated the *Observer* as journalism's equivalent of the Crown Jewels. Both Thomson and Matthews craved an honour, and got one. Even Murdoch, the most undazzled of the four, was hurt by the low status of the *Sun* and returned to Fleet Street again and again to bid for titles which, however costly, might give him respectability.

All appeared to possess a conviction that Fleet Street titles had a significance transcending the corporate balance sheet. With the possible exception of Murdoch at the *Sun*, they saw themselves as custodians of institutions with a central function in British public life. Their achievement would lie first in increasing their circulation and dominance over their traditional rivals and, only second, in making money out of them. None sought seriously to reorder the industry's labour relations. None confronted head-on its production costs. All fostered in the chapels a belief that the Medici millions would go on for ever.

# 7

# FALSE STARTS

Fleet Street never does anything by half. The recession of the mid-1970s increased fuel and newsprint costs and drove many proprietors, both old and new, to the brink of panic. One of the first acts of the 1974 Labour Government was to set up another Royal Commission to investigate the economic plight of the press and the impact this might have on the public's choice of titles, the third such Commission since the Second World War. Fleet Street was collectively opposed to the idea, seeing behind it a socialist desire to regulate, and possibly subsidize, competition for the predominantly Conservative press. By the autumn of 1975, however, alarm at rising costs was so great that the proprietors collectively pleaded with the Commission to produce an interim report. They said they now faced 'a crisis of unprecedented dimensions and dangers'. The interim report was published in the spring of 1976 and discovered that in 1974 only three dailies and three Sundays made profits; in 1975 only four dailies and one Sunday did so. 'In particular,' the Commission added in tones heavy with doom, 'the publishers of quality newspapers, even after taking account of their other publishing activities, made losses in 1975 totalling over £4 million.'

The industry's habit of lumping its annual losses together to make the total seem as grim as possible – like a court reporter accumulating the sentences on a gang of convicts – is wholly meaningless. It takes no account of the different reactions to a loss on the part of different companies, or of the size or motivation of a cross-subsidy. It also leads to false conclusions. Hence the Royal Commission decided that, for British newspapers, the 'only means of improving their prospects of survival is substantial savings in cost as quickly as possible'. The Commission made no mention of how this might be achieved beyond a proposal, redolent of the 1960s, to establish 'a national joint body as forum for industry level discussion'. Events over the next decade indicated that, at least for the chapels, a less tortuous alternative did exist: a series of transfers of ownership followed by injections of new cash. The Commission had chosen to ignore the message of *The Times* and *Observer* purchases, that production and other costs were in rough-and-ready equilibrium with a buoyant demand for newspaper ownership, however much existing owners might be shocked by the sudden price rises for fuel and newsprint.

The recession had one salutary effect: it concentrated the minds of the national print unions (though not their chapels) on the coming of new technology to Fleet Street. The NGA's general secretary, Joe Wade, admitted that 'there is no way in which we can avoid grasping the nettle of overmanning'. Similar pious hopes emanated from his colleagues in SOGAT and NATSOPA. The union leaders came together with the proprietors under a 'joint standing committee' to discuss the implications of computerized technology for Fleet Street. For the first time in newspaper history, a complete range of issues was on the table for discussion, including manning levels in the machine and publishing rooms, training and redundancy terms and the growing indiscipline of chapels. But at heart the committee was concerned with Fleet Street's archaic composing rooms, which were, in the 1970s, still using Linotype machines for almost all their work. These machines were wearing out and replacements were hard to find. The recession had seen a fall in piecework earnings and many compositors were taking their substantial profits to begin alternative careers elsewhere. To chapels, this was a natural response to market circumstances:

numbers were being held down to maintain earnings. To the unions, however, it meant lost members and lost subscription income. The latter therefore had at last an incentive to promote reform.

From the early 1970s, machinery to replace 'hot-metal' Linotypes with 'cold-type' keyboards and computer screens was widely available and in use on most provincial papers. The computer produced type on paper which was then cut and pasted on to a page for photographing. The bromide could then be etched straight on to a printing plate. It was neat, clean and, at least in theory, fast. The NGA was the union most threatened by this innovation, since journalists and advertising staff could type their own material straight into the computers, and sub-editors could paste it up thereafter. Compositors were as superfluous as hand type-setters had been after the introduction of Linotypes. The NGA therefore sought to ensure, as in the nineteenth century, that it could retain control of the new technology. It did this by insisting, both in the provinces and in Fleet Street, that access to the computers was the preserve of its members. Everything that appeared in a paper had to have been set on screen by an NGA printer. This insistence was to be the catalyst for the battles of the 1980s. For the moment, no Fleet Street manager (nor most of his provincial counter-parts) could contemplate direct access to typesetting computers by non-NGA staff.

In 1976 the joint standing committee produced its Programme for Action. It was blessed by every representative body in the industry, union executives, publishers, even the Royal Commission itself. The document proposed flexibility on demanning and innovation from the union side in return for new pension and redundancy arrangements from the employers, with no compulsory redundancy. In each plant, a joint house committee would be established to further industrial and technological innovation, though its role would be consultative and it would not interfere with individual chapel negotiations. Other proposals reflected the prevailing collaborative spirit of the Bullock committee on industrial democracy. (The report reads in retrospect like

*139*

that of a disarmament conference at which all mention of guns, bombs and missiles has been forbidden.)

The Programme for Action was put to a ballot of the Fleet Street and Manchester chapels in the spring of 1977. Each union leader recommended acceptance. Owen O'Brien of NATSOPA assured his members, ominously, that it did not 'undermine union rights in any way'. Joe Wade declared that 'Rejection . . . can lead only to the death of two or three national newspapers.' He and the newspaper managements might have believed this, but his chapels no longer regarded such threats as credible. Nor were they convinced that the time had yet arrived for them to surrender their lucrative negotiating practices, whether for computerized printing or not. The NGA members rejected the proposals over-whelmingly – the London chapels by 82 per cent – and SOGAT and NATSOPA by narrower margins. This humili-ation of the union leaders received almost no publicity from the disillusioned publishers. It demonstrated how far a decade of plant bargaining under comprehensive agreements had divorced the chapels from the influence and authority of those who purported to speak on their behalf.

The rejection of the Programme for Action came at a time when successive government pay policies were eroding Fleet Street's ever-shaky industrial discipline. Productivity loop-holes, vetted by inexperienced civil servants, brought a fan-tasy quality to negotiations. Necessity became the mother of extraordinary invention. Even journalists began fabricating 'piece' supplements to their pay. Writers on the *Daily Mirror* claimed payment for 'flexibility' in being telephoned at home. Chapel officials dreamed up productivity even during cuts, blows and ghost shifts. Management and chapels had to form alliances to outwit government inspectors. Papers found they were running as many as a dozen disputes at any one time.

By 1977 the industry was beginning to recover from reces-sion. The advent of Trafalgar House as owner of the *Daily Express* brought hope of new money and new rivalry among proprietors. More advertising increased pagination and this in turn pushed up piecework earnings and eroded differentials.

Occasional displays of resolution, as at the *Daily Express* and the *Observer*, ended in settlements that spokesmen struggled to present as 'victories for common sense'. Yet the queue of potential proprietors lengthened and chapel power increased accordingly. It was a bad time to expect the industry to discipline itself under threat of extinction.

Significantly the three groups that did most in the late 1970s to press for innovation in Fleet Street all lacked any dominant proprietorial figure. Each had seen the emergence of vigorous executives ready to force the pace of industrial change. The first was the *Financial Times*, run since 1957 by a subsidiary company of the far-flung Pearson group. It was housed away from Fleet Street in Bracken House in the shadow of St Paul's Cathedral where its corridors evoked an atmosphere of a cultured and well-bred family concern. The paper's chairmen during the 1970s were Lord Drogheda, Lord Gibson (married to a Pearson) and Alan Hare (related to a Pearson by marriage). Drogheda was chairman of the Royal Opera, Covent Garden, and Gibson of both the Arts Council and the National Trust. Under its editor, Sir Gordon Newton, the *Financial Times* had expanded from being a largely financial journal to become a rounded quality newspaper with sales capable of challenging *The Times* (190,000 in 1975). Its small, specialized market together with large corporate reserves made it an ideal standard bearer for a new age of Fleet Street management. In 1975, when Gibson took over the chair, it appointed Justin Dukes, an enthusiastic Fleet Street reformer, as joint managing director.

That year, the *Financial Times* decided on a development plan for demanning and a swift conversion to new typesetting technology, with generous safeguards and redundancy payments for production staff. The plan required an end to the traditional demarcation lines between tasks and chapels, thus permitting a measure of direct inputting by non-NGA staff.* It carefully sought to maintain 'net earnings'. The proposals

---

*Direct inputting is the term customarily given to the process of typing material directly into a computer via a keyboard – either by journalists or advertising clerks.

were discussed with national union officials – at the time of the Programme for Action discussions – but not in any detail with the chapels. The management appeared to be relying on the national leadership to sell, or support the management in selling, the proposals to its workforce. Such discussion behind the backs of the chapels was risky. It took at face value what was regarded as a new dawn in Fleet Street labour relations: the establishment of union authority over chapel autonomy. Yet such a dawn never took place. The result, as Roderick Martin points out, was to maximize confusion and minimize information. 'Management could only guess at shop floor reactions, and the shop floor could only suspect the worst of management.'*

Only after negotiations had been conducted at a national level were they started with the chapels and immediately slowed to a crawl. The management's tactics began to alter. Equipment difficulties suggested there might be a loss of production in the course of the changeover. The plan was adjusted to allow for a more gradual introduction of computerization, starting with the survey pages alone. This failed. The journalists on the staff, accustomed to castigating British management for its incompetence and inertia, attacked the paper's own board for the same faults. By 1977, still with no substantive progress towards implementing the plan, the *Financial Times* found its profit beginning to recover and the original sense of urgency evaporated. The paper abandoned its proposals and decided instead on the easier and more familiar course: going for an expansion in sales. The first European edition of the *Financial Times* was printed in Frankfurt in 1979. When the paper finally began partial computer typesetting in 1981, it was on the basis of normal demarcation, with terminals reserved for NGA members. A decade after the 1975 plan had been put forward, Linotype machines were still lucratively clattering away in Bracken House, a breakthrough not being finally achieved until the traumatic year of 1986.

*Martin (see bibliography) gives a detailed account of Fleet Street's struggle to innovate in this period.

Since the noisy departure of Cecil King from the Mirror building in 1968, IPC had passed through hard times. The rise of the *Sun* had ended its pre-eminence in working-class journalism. In 1970 a merger took place with the Reed group to form Reed International. Its chairman, Sir Don (now Lord) Ryder, a former editor of the *Stock Exchange Gazette*, lacked proprietorial enthusiasm or charisma. He seemed embarrassed by his product as it contorted itself to compete with the paper Cudlipp had virtually given to Murdoch. The *Daily Mirror* lost money for the first time since the Second World War in 1973–4 and its circulation moved steadily downward. When Ryder left for the National Enterprise Board in 1975, there were rumours that Reed might put the paper up for sale.

It was not sold. The chief executive at the time was the enterprising and ebullient Percy Roberts, who had long resisted the view of King and Cudlipp that a manager's first job was simply to bring out the paper each night. He was eager for innovative leadership and found it in the form of Ryder's successor, (now Sir) Alex Jarratt, a most unbureaucratic former civil servant working in Reed International's newspaper division. Jarratt presented himself as a symbol of Fleet Street's new, reformist mood. He told the *Financial Times*

> There has always been something slightly mystical about news – but only slightly mystical. The product is different and the people are different . . . but the industry has been very profligate in the past, in its bonanza years, and allowed all sorts of practices to develop which we will have to change. We need much more professional management.

The *Daily Mirror*'s development plan was produced in 1975 under the title 'Programme for Survival', such hyperbole being *de rigueur* in new-technology presentations. It was less radical than that produced the same year by the *Financial Times* in that it did not attempt to end the NGA monopoly of typesetting and was scrupulously discussed with the chapels. It estimated that savings of £5 million annually could be made in the composing room. Negotiations proceeded for two years amid constant disruption and acrimony from the chapels, but an agreement was eventually signed in November 1977, following half-hearted intervention by national union leaders. It established a joint composing room chapel to cover all operators working the new computer terminals, an end to the *London Scale of Prices* (at a 'buy-out' per man averaging £6,000) and the usual promises to adhere to disputes procedures.

Compositors at the *Daily Mirror* have since proved that the cool environment of the computer room is just as fertile ground for enhancing earnings as was the hot-metal composing room. The deal proved extremely expensive: compositors were to be paid £174 a week rising to £230 over three years. But a disastrous mixture of chapel militancy and technical trouble with the equipment led to the promised manning reductions not being achieved. Pagination and other piecework devices began to flourish and the customary glance over the shoulder at earnings on the *Sun* kept *Daily Mirror* printers well up in the front rank. The paper's journalists struck next for increases equivalent to those granted to compositors for working new technology, despite the embarrassing fact that journalists had no access to the equipment. The management was having to pay as if it had direct input, although it could not benefit from it. Knock-on claims spread like a disease throughout the building.

By 1979 whole pages of the *Daily Mirror* were being set in cold type, a Fleet Street breakthrough. But to most other proprietors, and to many of the paper's staff, the victory was pyrrhic. Far from yielding savings on composing, the innovation involved the *Daily Mirror* in additional composing costs of between £750,000 and an astronomical £3 million (according to Roderick Martin). This outcome, not surprisingly, did more to slow the pace of change in Fleet Street than did the agonies through which Percy Roberts had gone to achieve it. The NGA chapels had been allowed to make a crucial point: they had shown the rest of the industry that its 'state-of-the-art' industrial relations could still make investment in state-of-the-art technology not worth the money and effort involved. Roberts retired early, a martyr to managerial activism.

Half a mile up Grays Inn Road at Times Newspapers, management felt it was on stronger ground. On Lord Thomson's death in 1976, the custodianship of *The Times* passed to his son Kenneth in Toronto. Unlike the London-based off-spring of former proprietors, he was impervious to the magnetism that had drawn his father to Fleet Street. He now told *The Times'* management that he expected the losses borne by his family to end. He did not move to live in England, as his father had promised he would. He declared that as soon as the titles were collectively in profit – predicted for the first time in 1977 – they would be transferred into the Thomson Organisation and away from any family liability. The new Lord Thomson took the view that a decade of ownership had expunged his father's commitment to maintain the papers. The family guarantee to the Monopolies Commission in 1966 was a purely 'moral' one and, he told a Canadian interviewer, 'It is certainly not one that legally we are obliged to discharge.' The statement, though true, was at variance with the letter and spirit of his father's commitment.

The effect of these declarations was to galvanize the Thomson Organisation in Britain and the management of its subsidiary, Times Newspapers. The two companies were under the command of Gordon Brunton and 'Duke' Hussey respectively, both veterans of the London publishing scene, Brunton from Odhams and Hussey from Associated Newspapers. Hussey's key assistant for development was Dugal Nisbet-Smith, who had been responsible for bringing new technology to the Mirror group in Scotland. Though observers were later to deride this team – and particularly Hussey's Guards-officer manner – as inept and old-fashioned, it was the most able and experienced group yet assembled to assault the fortress of chapel power.

The initial Times Newspapers plan for new technology was introduced as 'Opportunity for Success' in 1976. The language was brisk and the prospect glorious, 'to introduce in the most practical and precisely phased way a computerized photocomposition system'. The plan involved direct inputting by journalists as well as manning cuts in all departments and new disputes procedures. Installation would begin in January 1977. The plans came at a time when the commercial position of the group, even as it emerged from recession, was dire. It lost money from 1974–6, with losses even recorded by the normally profitable *Sunday Times*. 1977 was expected to be better – circulation had fallen slightly after a 50 per cent rise – and an overall profit was optimistically anticipated for 1978. It was a good time to go for a change, and with the collapse of the industry-wide Programme for Action initiative, in which Hussey had led the management side, the company realized it had to go it alone. *The Times*, by implication, was still the greatest paper in Fleet Street and as such should lead the way.

The Thomson Organisation now agreed to forgo any profit from Times Newspapers for five years to enable Opportunity for Success to be implemented. This act of corporate generosity proved an empty one. (By then the Thomson family had lost an estimated £16 million on the papers.) As 1977 progressed, industrial disruption, particularly on the *Sunday Times*, worsened. Chapels found their differentials buffeted by Government pay policy and by a desire on the part of each of them to establish a strong position in advance of new-technology negotiations. Times Newspapers' management, virtually alone in Fleet Street, decided to enforce pay policy rigorously. Production of the *Sunday Times* was hit every weekend. Development plan deadlines were missed. As at the *Financial Times*, the momentum for change was lost.

Brunton and Hussey did not give up. In April 1978 the board of the Thomson Organisation agreed to support the Times Newspapers management in what came to be called the 'big bang' approach: agreements with all sixty-five chapels on the original package and on a wide range of other productivity issues, or the papers would close. The strategy would be backed by the full financial resources of a corporation then rich in North Sea oil. The board was encouraged by the success of the *New York Times* in 1974, in enduring a long closure to achieve computerized setting and reduce manning levels. Nor were there to be any *Daily Mirror*-style half measures. The plan was essentially un-negotiable, in particular the insistence that journalists and classified advertisement clerks should have direct access to the computer terminals, which the NGA was claiming as its own.

The proposals were put in outline to the national union leaders at a meeting in Birmingham. Increasingly irritated by indiscipline among their Fleet Street members, these leaders were inclined to sympathize with the management. An instructive account of one trade unionist's view is given by Eric Jacobs: 'What is happening in Fleet Street is anarchic and has to be stopped; we think you are the company most likely to act decisively; if you do, we will support you; the very worst thing you could do is start and then draw back; if you do that, we will wash our hands of your affairs.' Duke Hussey duly issued his ultimatum to his chapels: agree by November or 'publication of all our newspapers will be suspended'. Considerable bitterness surrounded what was seen as an excessively brief seven-month deadline for negotiation. The management team was too small to cope with the vast range of issues thrown up by the ultimatum, many of which involved negotiating the demise of whole chapels. Despite frantic work on all sides, agreement was reached with only two chapels even after the deadline was extended into December.

On that date, without further ado, the titles were shut down. It was a remarkable event in Fleet Street history: a proprietor effectively pushing his management not just to the brink of closure but over the edge. *The Times*' editorial staff could not believe their fate was bound up in anything as mundane as a productivity dispute. In a valedictory leader, its editor, William Rees-Mogg, was moved to regard his plight as 'a symbol of a national crisis'. The paper was now caught up in 'major historic themes': the future of trade unionism and the struggle for higher real, 'not phoney', wages. If the democratic status of the press had formerly been used to justify keeping the presses rolling come what may in the production departments, now it could be used to justify their silence.

The course of Times Newspapers' stoppage was unpleasant and, especially for management, disillusioning. Other publishers were torn between capitalizing on a suddenly increased market share and having to bear the soaring, probably temporary, on-cost of doing so. Nor were they able to stop their own chapels cross-subsidizing the dispute by offering spare shifts to many of the estimated 4,000 workers laid off at Times Newspapers. The NGA levied all its members and paid those involved in the dispute £70–80 a week throughout the closure. The company lost £10 million within six months and was expecting to lose £30 million by the end of the first year's stoppage. Not surprisingly under these pressures, management resolve began to weaken and differences emerged between directors. In June 1979 Lord Thomson arrived from Canada and, in an intervention worthy of Lord Northcliffe, decided the time had come to climb down from his management's insistence on direct inputting to the typesetting computers. To save face it was stipulated that direct inputting would indeed occur, but would be negotiated within a fixed period after the titles had reopened. (Like most such promises, this proved a dead letter.)

The national unions insisted that staff would be reinstated at a rate 20 per cent above that on which they had left the previous year – a customarily generous way of burying the Fleet Street hatchet. This may have satisfied the national unions, but there then ensued a drawn-out fight over the precise terms on which each chapel would return to work. Having lost the essence of its development plan, the management still wanted cuts of 20–30 per cent in its manning levels, especially in the printing and publishing departments. As we have seen, such arguments are rarely about actual numbers employed, but about the lump-sum cost to management of a particular task. NATSOPA's machine assistants' leader, Reg Brady, had long fought to bring his members' earnings (as he saw it) up to the Fleet Street average. He was reluctant to relinquish these advances. His rival for office within NATSOPA, Barry Fitzpatrick of Times Newspapers' clerical workers, felt much the same way. Both held out to the end and were able to claim victory as a result. Last to settle were the NGA machine minders, villains of many a Fleet Street piece, sustaining a differentials claim until late on the night of reopening, 13 November 1979. They returned only on the promise of arbitration.

The management laid down a heavy barrage of public relations to prove they had won '70 per cent' of what they had originally demanded. This was absurd. Direct inputting, core issue of the big bang principle, had been effectively abandoned. The use of computerized equipment was agreed, but on similar terms to those offered by the NGA and implemented at the *Daily Mirror*. Labour costs were reportedly cut by 20 per cent – no mean feat – though much of this gain was eaten up by increases granted after reinstatement. To rub salt into the wound, the £3-million-worth of computerized typesetting equipment was regarded as obsolete. Times Newspapers was a hot metal publisher for the duration of Lord Thomson's ownership. Nor were new disciplines established to ensure continuous production of the papers. Indeed, performance on the *Sunday Times* worsened as chapels struggled to regain such earnings as they had been forced to concede. A year after reopening, even *The Times*' journalists found themselves striking. Given the long history of disrupted procedures in Fleet Street, assurances of 'continuous production' were no more than a fig leaf to conceal a management defeat. Without legal sanctions, they carried no credibility.

In August 1980 it was calculated (by the *Financial Times*) that Times Newspapers had lost £40 million on the stoppage. The Thomson Organisation expected to lose £15 million that year on its national titles and possibly even more in 1981. The chief cause was admitted by the company to be 'the failure to implement agreements on the resumption of publication'. Nor had the stoppage helped the rest of Fleet Street. Roderick Martin records that 'paradoxically in the medium term, the *Guardian* and the *Observer* were the major losers from the suspension of *The Times*, since their expansion and subsequent contraction led to considerable financial and industrial relations difficulties'. The higher earnings on titles which occupied the markets vacated by *The Times* and *Sunday Times* soon spread round Fleet Street, and eventually found their way back to Grays Inn Road after the resumption of work.

The Thomson Organisation had had enough. It announced

in October 1980 that 'more than £70 million has been advanced from Thomson sources and used for investment, working capital and losses incurred . . . if the present situation is allowed to continue it will threaten the development of the Organisation as a whole'. The company offered to sell the titles to a new owner, precisely the salvation it said it would never permit during the closure. Bids had to be in by the end of December. If no buyer could be found, the papers would be closed down in March 1981. A prospectus of sale was drawn up. This optimistically predicted that the losses could be reduced from £13 million to £4.3 million, since a new buyer would get the manning cuts which had so expensively eluded the Thomson Organisation. In 1982 an £8-million profit was suggested. It was an extraordinary claim.

The market place once again filled with buyers. Journalists derided the 'seven dwarfs' who usually stepped forward whenever a paper was for sale: Rupert Murdoch, Robert Maxwell, Lord Rothermere, Tiny Rowland, Sir James Goldsmith, Lord Matthews and Lord Barnetson (of the provincial United Newspapers, shortly to be succeeded by David Stevens). Others soon declared an interest, including the anglophile American shipping magnate James Sherwood, the Aga Khan, the Australian Robert Holmes a' Court, and even ARCO, despite its continuing troubles at the *Observer*. Murdoch declared his interest by ironically remarking the year before that 'to buy *The Times* would be a highly irresponsible thing to do to your shareholders'. Bids were also prepared from consortia of journalists on both papers. During the 1979 closure, a journalists' co-operative had been formed, uncomfortably named 'Journalists of *The Times*'. One of its options was to produce *The Times* without union labour on a 'green-field' site outside the reach of Fleet Street. This idea was now revived, though with inadequate research or financial backing. Its time had not yet come.

The transfer of power was conventional. Lord Thomson's one concession to his inheritance was to insist that the two titles be sold together in order to ensure a continued cross-subsidy to *The Times* from the *Sunday Times*. This undermined any prospect of the *Sunday Times* establishing itself as an independent concern, whether as a co-operative or not. Gordon Brunton favoured Murdoch as the proprietor most likely to keep both titles in being and most likely to win some of the battles that he, Brunton, had lost. The most serious alternative, Associated Newspapers, was clearly eager for a Sunday title to put on its *Daily Mail* presses but seemed less committed to keeping *The Times* in being. (It is hard to believe Rothermere would have closed it: his bid suffered from his being out of the country at the time.)

Times had changed *The Times*. A year of closure and another of strikes and disruption had cost it its dignity. Less was now heard of its status as a national institution. Resilience and toughness seemed the qualities most needed in a new proprietor, qualities that Murdoch possessed in abundance. The *Sunday Times*' journalists declared that Murdoch was their preferred buyer. The unions told Brunton the same (a more ominous assurance). At a cosmetic interview before the independent directors of Times Newspapers, Murdoch swore the proprietorial Hippocratic oath, guaranteeing he would not interfere with editorial freedom. Few felt such promises were worth arguing over – they had the same credibility as promises of continuous production from the chapels. The Government played its part by refusing to refer the deal to the Monopolies Commission, despite the drastic expansion it meant to Murdoch's Fleet Street market share. That much had changed from the first Lord Thomson's day.

Murdoch could not conceal his delight. He trotted round the Times building, met the journalistic staff and referred to his forthcoming proprietorship as his 'greatest-ever challenge'. For Murdoch as for Thomson, *The Times* was still the prize of Fleet Street. The problems confronting him were considerable and his performance in the early years of his ownership suggested he had little strategy for dealing with them. The acquisition was, like the purchase of the *New York Post*, a gamble. Yet Murdoch clearly regarded the prestige as worth the struggle. After ten years of being insulted to his face and behind his back, he could now read in the once-fearless *Sunday Times* a eulogy to 'his energy, his

directness, his publishing flair and above all, the commit-
ments he has given on editorial independence'. It was a sweet
revenge.

Blame for the three defeats examined in this chapter cannot
be laid wholly at the doors of the companies concerned. Each
was a brave attempt to bring innovation to Fleet Street. Each
was initiated by managers earnestly seeking a breakthrough
to new manning levels. Traditional proprietors had implicitly
accepted Fleet Street's industrial traditions until such time as
they could no longer afford them. They then sold out to
others, most of whom arrived with an enthusiasm to publish
newspapers, not reform an industry. By contrast, at the
*Financial Times*, the *Daily Mirror* and *The Times*, managers
were able to see their determination backed by board support, both in the form of money and in (albeit temporary)
protection from corporate sabotage should the going get
tough. It was a brief foretaste of a phenomenon we shall see
in later chapters: proprietorial status derived from business
machismo rather than editorial or circulation success.

In the case of two of the papers, the *Financial Times* and
*The Times*, 'proprietorialism' reasserted itself when it was
clear that victory was not in sight. Family interests declared
that enough was enough. Famous newspapers had better
continue in being, at whatever cost to management prestige.
The *Financial Times* beat its retreat before even attempting
closure. At the *Daily Mirror*, the introduction of new technology was achieved, but at a price so high as to make it seem
a step backwards rather than forwards. The cost of the
conflict made certain the eventual sale of the paper, as it did
at *The Times*.

The cause of defeat was the same in all three cases: managers overestimated their leverage in Fleet Street's balance
of industrial power. A Fleet Street newspaper is not what it
may seem, a small and compact organization, with a few
thousand staff engaged in a common daily endeavour. It is a
congeries of such organizations, each enjoying an implicit
contractual relation with the others. The editorial and
management staff have little real knowledge of their produc-

tion chapels, and even less of how strong the power of those chapels is to forestall change. In all three examples, managers gave too much weight to the influence of national union officials, with whom they were on good terms, and too little to their FOCs. The national officials had a vested interest in change: it would help secure future membership and end the blight of chapel independence. The chapels had no such interest and few managements ever tried to persuade them otherwise. They could see little sense, and certainly little urgency, in negotiating away past rights and privileges and the lucrative payment structures that depended on them. They knew implicitly – sometimes explicitly – that the money to sustain these structures was still forthcoming, if not from existing owners then from new ones.

The issue was pushed furthest at *The Times*, yet even here, with 4,000 staff on the streets for almost a year, the balance of power was more in the chapels' favour at the end than at the beginning. As long as Times Newspapers was intending to publish with the existing staff at Grays Inn Road, then it would have to pay the 'going rate' to the monopoly supplier of print labour. The concept of a chapel sub-contract was not an *ad hoc* one that proprietors or even chapels might determine at will – Murdoch had learned this at the *Sun* in the early 1970s. It was, in essence, a collective contract, covering the industry as a whole and apparently adjustable only in that wider industrial context. Duke Hussey and his team were not fighting a difficult but winnable war at Grays Inn Road: they were making a public display of their impotence before yet another bout of chapel negotiation. Talks with chapels became real only after the announcement of a date for reopening. They were then no more than a haggle at the margin of the going rate.

Managers of Times Newspapers, reflecting on their defeat, remarked that 'someone had to take on the unions sooner or later'. After the failure of the Programme of Action, it seemed that any joint effort across the industry would fail. A big and wealthy owner had to make the first move. This was true, but a more realistic assessment of the balance of power would have led the management – indeed all managements –

to see that a drastic increase in their fire-power was needed to give a confrontation strategy any hope of success. At various stages in both the *Daily Mirror* and *The Times* disputes, managers contemplated ways of circumventing the chapel monopoly on Fleet Street production by seeking alternative printing locations. The *Daily Mirror* pondered moving its printing to Manchester or to the suburbs of London. *The Times* explored printing in Frankfurt – though only as a stopgap measure and its journalists considered using a non-union plant at Nottingham. In all these cases it was felt that the unions would prevent distribution of the papers, even assuming workers could be found brave enough to cross picket lines to print them. No one put the strategy to the test.

The failure at *The Times* in 1979 cast a lethargic gloom over Fleet Street. Many print workers could hardly believe their victory. They read jeremiads in the press on their irresponsibility and suicidal tendencies. Yet that same year, Linotype operators were earning as much as £400 a week on piecework, having rejected roughly £250 under new-technology, time-rate agreements. Any system that granted such largesse to its workers was probably beyond hope of negotiated reform, at least without a catalytic trauma. Most printers knew it had to end one day, but they were able to take huge earnings out of the industry to insure against that day and could negotiate large 'buy-out' or redundancy payments when it came. The designers and operators of this long-standing cornucopia were also its beneficiaries. They were unlikely to assist in its demise.

# 8

# MUDDLING THROUGH
# THE 1980s

Newspapers love self-imagery. Fleet Street is the Fourth
Estate, the Handmaid of Democracy, the Voice of the
People. To those who work in it, its ranks are mutinous, its
unions lemmings, its rats continually jumping ship. Its managers suffer from paralysis, schizophrenia and myopia. Its
prose is yellow or grey or purple. Beaverbrook, always a
master image-monger, used to demand as his presses roared
through the night, 'Who's in charge of the clattering train?'
He was apparently ignorant of the actual line, 'Death is in
charge of the rattling train.'

A metaphor rarely used, perhaps because it is too near the
mark, is that of show business: a paper *is* a show, a series of
episodes, rewritten and restaged each night for the same
audience. It must contain heroes and villains, stereotypes
and novelty, weighty messages and light relief. Above all,
the show must go on. As the public cries for more, a nightly
struggle takes place backstage over money and schedules and
scene changes. Will the curtain rise? Will the backer like the
show? Will he make money out of it, and if not, will he
regard his loss as money well spent? (He may, of course, be
its director.)

Two themes should have emerged so far in this book. The
first is that Fleet Street yields its proprietors a complex of
mostly non-pecuniary rewards. The second is that despite
this, the laws of economics are no less applicable to Fleet

Street for being thus distorted. As in business, someone has to pay when a product makes a loss. As in business, the market clearing price for labour will find equilibrium where marginal utilities are in the balance. As in business, groups will exploit monopolies and resist competition until someone stops them.

Fleet Street spokesmen often refer to the fate of the American newspaper industry as a warning. They usually read the lesson wrong. In 1963 the city of New York had a choice of twelve morning and evening newspapers, all printed by methods still prevalent in London twenty years later. Their unions were strong and their wages high. Fifteen years later there were just three papers (plus the Long Island *Newsday*). Fast-rising costs and outdated technology had forced the rest to close or amalgamate. How, Fleet Street asked, could the unions be so foolish as to kill off such a lucrative industry? And why did the British unions not realize that the same might happen in London?

We have already seen that chapels do not exist to manage an industry but to guard the short-term earnings of their members. In New York, control over craft entry and continuing wastage (subsidized by redundancy payments) meant that the unions could keep the earnings of survivors rising even as job opportunities for newcomers fell. In 1974 the severely depleted ranks of the New York compositors struck against the *New York Times* and the *Daily News* who were seeking to introduce photocomposition. The fact that previous newspapers had closed was of no concern to those compositors and they did well out of the strike: the management offered them all job security for life.

Despite this strike, both papers together with the *New York Post* then had to fight – and lose – the same battle with their machine room staff four years later. Rupert Murdoch was losing money on the *New York Post* then, and he has been ever since. Yet the printers knew he wanted to go on publishing and knew that he would find the money to do so. If he should tire, they were faced with a variety of options: someone else could buy the paper and pay their rates; the paper could close and they could take redundancy; or they could arrange a job, at the same high rates, on a surviving title as and when natural wastage offered one. Each was considered preferable to conceding management's demand and undermining machine room rates across New York as a whole.

In London, the closure option has not been a credible threat, at least since the early 1960s. The apocalyptic Royal Commission report of 1976 predicted that without a drastic cutting of costs, many papers would soon disappear. It assumed that Fleet Street was an ordinary product line and ignored its magnetism for new capital. The industry responded defiantly to the Royal Commission by launching two new titles, the *Star* and *The Mail on Sunday*, both on the basis of customary chapel agreements. In the 1980s a similar gloom descended on Fleet Street, although in the harsher climate of Thatcherism there was no suggestion that this merited yet another public inquiry into its finances. In one of its sweeping announcements, the NPA declared that in the four years 1981–5, the industry as a whole made only £27 million on a turnover of £5 billion. However meaningful such totals – few titles give details of profit or losses, let alone cross-subsidy – it is reasonable to conclude that respectable profits were being earned only by the *Sun* and occasionally the *Sunday Times* and *Financial Times*.

Despite this predicament, the recession that accompanied Margaret Thatcher's first administration saw little talk of closure, more of expansion in the newspaper industry. In the early 1980s Fleet Street appeared to have lost none of its vitality. For all its heavy losses, printers' earnings continued high, new capital was plentiful, investment was unprecedented. One reason for this, though only one, was that in May 1982 an event occurred which dramatically relieved the financial burden of proprietorship: Reuters news agency announced from its Lutyens palace in Fleet Street that it was declaring its first profit for forty-one years.

Reuters had long been a backwater of British journalism. It was owned in trust, mostly by other newspaper groups, to protect its independence in supplying British and foreign papers with overseas news. Its deadpan reports from around the world would land on foreign news desks like embassy telegrams in a Foreign Office in-tray. They made no money for the company. But Reuters' newly established financial intelligence service, Monitor, was a different matter. By 1982 it was making more profit than the group could sensibly consume. The directors duly decided to give £1.9 million to their shareholders.

Some shareholders soon realized the assets this implied were the shares to be placed on the open market. Here was money to relieve the conglomerate pressure on hard-pressed chairmen, notably Lord Matthews of Express Newspapers and Alan Hare of the *Financial Times*, both of whom were prime movers in the Reuters flotation. For once, Fleet Street was presented with an 'in-house' cross-subsidy. The industry reacted with unprecedented speed. A new two-tier ownership structure was agreed. Under a revised constitution, voting power would remain with the original shareholders, supposedly to safeguard Reuters' editorial independence. The flotation was announced, with Reuters appearing on the stock market two years later. It had an initial valuation of over £800 million, a figure that later almost trebled.

Reuters offered a crock of gold to men who, in the opinion of some, ill-deserved it. Fleet Holdings, whose Express Newspapers was limping between profit and loss, was richer by £56 million overnight. Associated Newspapers, whose *Daily Mail* was losing heavily, found itself with the same amount. The *Guardian*'s shares were worth £28 million, those of the *Daily Telegraph* £26 million. Following an agreement that large stakes would not be sold immediately for fear of depressing the price, most groups sold small numbers of shares each year as and when they needed the money. Some, such as the *Daily Express*, used it as proof of sound management in trying (unsuccessfully) to fight off take-over bids. Reed International hoped to use it to float the Mirror group titles into a separate company, though they eventually sold to Robert Maxwell instead. A number of staff and directors of Reuters who had held small quantities of shares became millionaires. Those groups who did not sell saw their holdings soar in value over the next three years. Reuters itself made profits of £4 million in 1980, £53 million in 1983 and nearly £90 million in 1985.

Newspapers took the opportunity to resurrect development plans that had lain on the shelf since the 1970s. The Reuters bounty enabled most titles to contemplate a mass escape from the cramped streets of Fleet Street into the open spaces, and investment tax havens, of Docklands in the East End of London. For the *Sun* and the *Daily Mail*, outgrowing antiquated plant south of Fleet Street, a move was needed to meet growing circulations. For others such as the *Guardian* and the *Daily Telegraph*, it would be cheaper than continuing to own or rent inefficient capacity in central London. (The *Daily Telegraph* had first drawn up its plans, like many other papers, in 1975, but they had never been implemented.) Such a move also offered the chance of a once-for-all change in manning agreements and cost structure. Away from the pubs and call offices of Fleet Street, chapel collaboration would surely weaken and management be at last able to reassert itself. The 'Docklands option' became an elixir of proprietorial vigour.

Rupert Murdoch acted first. His chief executive, Bert Hardy, desperate for extra capacity to print the *Sun*, persuaded an initially reluctant Murdoch that a new plant would have to be built. Such radicalism had not, in the past, been Murdoch's style. After abandoning a scheme to move to King's Cross, Hardy negotiated with Tower Hamlets' council to build a works on the old London Docks site in Wapping, just beyond the Tower of London. It involved destroying the finest group of Georgian warehouses in Britain, and would have been stopped had the planning minister at the time, Peter Shore, not also been the local MP. In view of later events, it was ironic that the local Labour party was enthusiastic about Murdoch's move. It was proud that he would demolish the high Georgian dock walls, which had symbolized the exclusion of dockers from their place of work. (He had to put up razor wire in their place, to defend his plant against, among others, that same Labour party!)

Where Murdoch led, others followed. Four miles to the east on the Isle of Dogs, a large printing plant was set up for the *Daily Telegraph* and another for the *Guardian*. From the summit of the old dock Mudshoot, now eerily occupied by an urban farm, the two buildings rise like high-tech monsters marooned in the landscape. To the south of the Thames, the *Daily Mail* booked space in the Surrey Docks for a works due to be completed in 1990 (since brought forward by two years). The Mirror group also said it had 'booked' space in Docklands, though no location was mentioned; so too did the *Financial Times*. These schemes were expensive to build and equip. All were intended purely as printing plants, with typesetting continuing in central London and made-up pages transmitted electronically down a line. This implied total photocomposition in Fleet Street's composing rooms.

As far as typesetting was concerned, the composing chapels were naturally reluctant to agree terms less favour-able than those in operation at titles, such as the *Daily Mirror*, that already had photocomposition. The deals reached at the *Daily Mirror* in 1975 and at *The Times* in 1979 thus cast their shadows forward. Few Fleet Street managers, as late as 1985, expected to obtain appreciably better deals with their composing chapels than those in operation for the past decade – for instance, no one expected to have non-NGA access to the computer terminals. None the less, composing room chapels were resigned to the new era and were, anyway, not moving to Docklands.

It was the machine room agreements that were regarded as crucial. Here the chapels faced removal to the bleak wastes of the East End and the certainty of fierce pressure to cut back on shift payments. Yet their technology was not chang-ing and they could not see why they should accept lower manning levels for what was, in effect, the same output. Even where new manning agreements were to be conceded, they would not concede on the principle of task demarcation and chapel autonomy. It was this principle, as we have seen, that underpinned the chapels' ability to force up earnings, in the future as much as in the past.

Managers waited nervously to see who would sign the first deal. Murdoch was the first to complete his plant – it was ready in 1984 – but his negotiators refused to accede to chapel demands that would effectively transport Bouverie Street practices to Wapping. The result was stalemate. The *Daily Mail* held fire, but the *Daily Telegraph* could not afford to do so. Its management had £60-million-worth of new plant coming on stream on the Isle of Dogs and in Manchester in 1986. Interest payments were rising and Lord Hartwell badly needed the £20 million that he optimistically hoped the plant would save him each year. His executives duly sought a package of measures, including £40 million set aside to buy out existing (mostly composing room) agreements. A deal was reached in Manchester on the basis of existing demarcation. None had been signed for the Isle of Dogs when the effort proved too costly and Hartwell's grip on proprietorship slipped away. Other managements viewed the *Daily Telegraph* negotiations with dismay, fearing a repeat of the *Daily Star*'s costly launch in Manchester. Yet no one else stepped forward to meet the challenge.

The importance of the Docklands option lay in the fact that the machine room chapels were the chief source of conflict in Fleet Street in the early 1980s. The prospect of a move reopened old sores between the NGA machine minders and the SOGAT assistants on the printing presses. Each began jockeying for position, the minders knowing that the assistants might take their jobs should the issue ever be forced. It was the worst context in which to be approaching a new industrial era.

In the early 1980s the *Financial Times* joined the *Observer* as host to the annual NGA/SOGAT '82 machine room skirmish. Each summer was now punctuated by news of ructions at Bracken House, lending added force to its advertising slogan, 'No *FT*, No Comment'. In 1983 the paper was off the streets for nine weeks, including during the general election campaign. Each time, the paper's mild-mannered chairman, Alan Hare, would peer into the same abyss as had faced Duke Hussey at *The Times* in 1978, and turn hesitantly back. His machine minders seemed formidably powerful. Each time, the management would concede the chapel's demand, with a little held back for 'face'. The 1983 stoppage was referred to by Hare as 'one of the most unrewarding in the annals of Fleet Street'.* It cost the company £10 million but was less unrewarding for the twenty-four minders, many of whom also worked elsewhere. The minders hit the paper again in 1984 and 1985, when finally the company took injunctions against them, this time with some effect. Their leader, Charlie Miller, who also worked at the *Sunday Times*, became something of a legend among the journalists at Bracken House. His members' every wage packet turned to gold.

Alan Hare at least had company in his misfortune. Rupert Murdoch, within months of taking over Times Newspapers in 1981, found himself facing a machine room differential dispute between the same two chapels that were afflicting the *Observer* and the *Financial Times*. He too faced the prospect of closing down his recently acquired papers. Each year he would arrive in London from New York breathing fire and demanding manning cuts at Grays Inn Road. Each year he would back off, finding himself up against more implacable rough-house tacticians than he was himself. For long months, usually in the summer (when holiday pay and smaller papers play havoc with agreements), the *Sunday Times* would never complete its Saturday night production run. For Murdoch, it was a frustrating experience. As his delight at being proprietor of *The Times* faded, so his determination not to risk his corporate cash flow increased. Times Newspapers became a running sore.

The NGA machine minders were unnecessary. They were an appendix in Fleet Street industrial relations, as irrelevant as a 'fireman' on a diesel locomotive. At the *Observer*, the *Financial Times* and the *Sunday Times*, the option of asking the machine assistants to run the presses without minders was often floated in the course of negotiations. Many assistants (and their national leaders) expected to be 'put to the test' on this issue sooner or later. Few doubted that, at least under the pressure of closure, assistants would have defied traditional trade union solidarity and worked the machines without the NGA present. Had this challenge been made, it

*_____

*Financial Times*, 9 August 1983.

is probable that NGA machine minding would have crumbled. The minders enjoyed little sympathy from their NGA brothers in the composing room, and little from branch or national headquarters. Officials such as Charlie Miller of the *Financial Times* or Pat Phelan of the *Observer*, colourful characters though they might be, were thorns in the side of their national leadership. Yet no management ever dared push the issue. There was, to the best of my knowledge, no attempt at collusion with other managements and this despite the significance a breakthrough would imply for manning the Docklands plants.

Confronting such issues has never been part of Fleet Street's proprietorial culture. In 1982 Murdoch turned away from his defeats and restored his reputation for proprietorial vigour by firing one of his editors, Harold Evans, brought in a year earlier to galvanize *The Times*. Evans retreated to write a searing attack on Murdoch, a man who evokes strong emotions in his ex-editors. (The incident gave rise to a naïve comedy called *Pravda* at the National Theatre, which succeeded only in glorifying Murdoch at the expense of his caricatured employees. It was immensely popular.)

Other proprietors found equally traditional ways of putting production costs out of sight and mind. For once it was not Murdoch but another tabloid proprietor, Lord Matthews, who stood accused of taking the industry downmarket in a spurious bid for sales. The circulation war that consumed the attention of the tabloid press from 1981 to 1985 began in an attempt to boost the sales of Matthews's flagging *Daily Star*. This time it was not life insurance, silverware or bound volumes of Dickens but the crudest of all selling gimmicks, betting on numbers through bingo. As analysts were quick to point out, it was not real bingo but a system whereby a more-or-less controlled handful of readers was given a large cash prize. Cards, produced for most bingo papers by the Blackburn firm Europrint, were distributed to newsagents throughout the country, up to 12 million a week for each paper. Readers ticked off on their card the numbers printed in the paper each day. If and when the card was full, they could claim their winnings. Petrol stations use much the

same technique with lucky number cards to promote custo-
mer loyalty.

The key to a successful bingo promotion was to secure one
big winner each week, not hundreds of small ones. This was
achieved by ensuring that almost all cards contained 'eliminator' numbers which would never appear in the paper. At the
start of each game, plenty of 'filler' numbers would give the
player a feeling he or she was in with a chance. Only at the
end of the period, usually a Saturday when sales need a fillip,
would a flurry of winning numbers appear, applicable to only
a few cards. The newspaper would hope that one of these
cards was still in use on the final day, to give them a lucky
reader easy to publicize. The winning cards could even be
targeted to different parts of the country each game. Securing just one winner became a fine, and desperate, art during
the millionaire bingo hysteria of the summer of 1984. On one
occasion that year, the *Sun* found itself besieged with 3,000
winners claiming a share in the prize money. An eliminator
number had inadvertently been printed.

The 'bingo war' began in June 1981, when the then editor-
in-chief of the *Daily Star*, Derek Jameson, noticed that a
local West Country newspaper was offering cash prizes for
bingo. The *Daily Star*'s losses were high and the paper clearly
had to grab a share of the *Sun*'s and *Daily Mirror*'s markets,
and hold it without a heavy increase in cost. Jameson started
by offering prizes of £5–10,000. For a tabloid newspaper with
marginal revenue that ought to be greater than run-on costs,
he calculated this might be a cheaper way of buying sales
than a normal advertising campaign. An extra 250,000 copies
of a 10p paper could mean over £7 million a year of extra
revenue, to be split between the paper (and its printers) and
the newsagents. It depended on readers staying hooked and
prizes staying low. Predictably, however, Jameson merely
produced panic among the other tabloids. To them, Matthews's *Daily Star* was moving from being a loss-making
nuisance to being a 'spoiler'. The *Sun* and *Daily Mirror* felt
obliged to produce their own bingo games within weeks, with
prizes substantially higher than the *Daily Star*'s. The *Daily
Express* and the *Daily Mail* followed suit. Bingo certainly

boosted total sales: the tabloid market as a whole rose to 13 million by the end of 1981, a figure not seen since the 1960s. The initial winners were the *Sun* and the *Daily Star*, adding 800,000 between them by the second half of 1981. The *Daily Mirror* lost 200,000.

The boom was almost over as soon as it had begun. Readers realized the odds against winning were astronomical, or at best they took the cards and sneaked a look at the numbers on news-stands without buying a paper. Over the next three years an occasional 'steal' on a rival could be gained with a new idea, such as the *Daily Mail*'s pseudo-respectable Casino. Then, in the summer of 1984 the new proprietor of the *Daily Mirror*, Robert Maxwell, gave the contest a final, and ludicrous, flourish with his 'millionaire bingo'. He cleared his front page for a 'Pledge from Robert Maxwell: I guarantee that one of our readers will win £1 million', together with two pictures of himself. Yet to his chagrin, the *Sun* found a way of giving one of its readers £1 million even before Maxwell did. Fleet Street appeared to be operating a voluntary lottery for the benefit of its readers. It made management protestations of poverty to the chapels wholly incredible.

In September 1984, a month after the start of millionaire bingo, all five tabloids found they had increased their joint sales by 500,000, equally spread between all of them. Yet the additional revenue was swamped by the cost of prize money, promotion and extra payments to chapels. The *Daily Express*, struggling to stay ahead of the *Daily Mail* at any price, promised its readers a 'millionaire a month', beyond anything justifiable in revenue terms. Though total tabloid sales rose, briefly, to touch 13.5 million, they fell back to 12.47 million in the first half of 1985 and to 11.89 million in December of that year. The *Daily Star*, having fired the first shot, ironically fared best, its sales remaining 25 per cent up on its pre-bingo level. The most reckless bingo impresario, Maxwell, saw his circulation fall below 3 million, an experience the *Daily Mirror* had not suffered since the 1940s. The bingo rivalry petered out towards the end of 1985 as more serious forms of competition took over. Cards continued to be distributed but the games were relegated to inside pages and prizes reduced. They became, like strip cartoons, just another way of retaining reader loyalty.

The bingo war left tabloid newspapers more than ever like American television channels, mimicking each other's ideas, stealing each other's staff and avoiding any material that risked boring, or seriously engaging, their audience. It had taken ten years from the advent of Murdoch's *Sun* for its message to permeate Fleet Street: a popular newspaper must yield pride of place to television in communicating instant news. It could not compete; it had to complement. Political or world news was mostly confined to page two, the 'dead' page. Each of the remaining pages would seek to convey just one story, usually enlivened by a picture of a girl, often with a wholly fictional caption. Sub-editors would heavily rewrite mundane 'human-interest' material to give it added excitement. Revelatory memoirs of television actors and sportsmen became a stock in trade. If one paper promised such an exclusive, the others would cobble together similar material from cuttings as a spoiler. Readers were given information on sports and entertainment as a 'glimpse behind the screen', much as movie magazines had done between the wars.

There was little new in this development. Such journalism, and its critics, had been current since the pre-Northcliffe Sunday press, with its mix of fiction, scandal and escapism. What was more remarkable was that the popular press managed to adjust to new market circumstances with so little disruption to its ownership structure. It defied all predictions of its decline. Despite the closure of the *Daily Sketch* and four years of bingo war, its six-monthly total sale has, for fifteen years, fluctuated by no more than 8 per cent around a mean of 12.5 million copies (see appendix).

However, the down-market editorial trend of the popular press at the time of the bingo wars had a more fundamental implication: it risked undermining the enthusiasm of proprietors to own such newspapers. A product with so little political or cultural content, much of which, in Lord Matthews's celebrated words, 'I would not want on my family breakfast table,' was hardly likely to stimulate the proprietorial appetite. Editors and even proprietors of tabloid newspapers often found themselves on the defensive. Sir Larry Lamb had to add up the political items in the *Sun* to 'prove' that it kept readers in touch with current affairs. Lloyd Turner of the *Daily Star* was called to account by an embarrassed Lord Matthews for his intrusions on the royal family. The *Daily Mirror* would carry often baffling 'scoops' by its columnist Paul Foot, as evidence of its left-wing credentials. There were few cheers round the boardroom table at the prospect of owning a stable of 'page three girls' or the exclusive revelations of a snooker star.

Such papers might indeed have to justify their survival on a criterion wholly new to Fleet Street: they might have to make money, pure and simple. In the early 1980s, neither the *Daily Mirror* nor the *Daily Express* was making satisfactory profits or suggesting they could make headway against their major rivals. Clive Thornton, chairman of the Mirror group, and Lord Matthews at Express Newspapers might parade themselves in public as traditional proprietors, but both proved vulnerable to what might be called 'holding company blues'. They might be enjoying Fleet Street personally, but Reed International and Trafalgar House did not see the fun. The historic trade-off between corporate prestige and production costs moved out of equilibrium. Both titles were duly sent to market.

Within a year, in 1984–5, three of Britain's five tabloid newspapers thus changed hands. They were soon snapped up and at handsome, Reuters-inflated prices. But there was little of the public and political hand-wringing that would have accompanied the exchange of such potentially powerful organs of opinion two decades earlier. The *Daily Express*, *Daily Star* and *Daily Mirror* were not the politically significant institutions they once had been. Could it be that at this end of the market at least Fleet Street was losing its historic magnetism?

# 9

# FOUR MUSKETEERS

All four new proprietors who arrived in Fleet Street during the first half of the 1980s were shocked by the state in which they found it. Their surprise was not novel. Earlier arrivals had been equally dismayed at the industry's indiscipline and archaism but had been unable to find any remedy. Thomson, Matthews, Anderson and Murdoch soon diverted their gaze from Fleet Street's costs and concentrated on building up circulation. If the result was a profit, they sighed with relief; if a loss, they bore it until it bored them and then sold out to someone else.

The new generation took on proprietorship at a time when Britain's industrial climate was different. Although they were impelled by a motivation similar to that of their predecessors, they were captains of industry under a new star. Fleet Street might be awash with Reuters money, bingo promotion and 'high-tech' development plans. But the New Realism of Margaret Thatcher's Britain demanded that businessmen apply their minds to the classic concerns of capital. Success lay not just in acting as custodian of a much-loved product, but in flexing managerial muscles, cutting costs, defeating unions and demonstrating some enthusiasm for achieving a commercial return on assets. This was not the Fleet Street of old: the spirit of deregulation and privatization made all industrialists more sensitive to their costs. New trade union laws supplied a weapon to attack these costs. So too, in the case of Fleet Street's Docklands ambitions, did the Government's innovation of enterprise zones with lucrative tax reliefs.

In these circumstances, national newspapers came to offer scope for a new sort of proprietorial glory, not that of the tycoon or the politician *manqué* but of the virile entrepreneur. Where better to clean out a nest of union bandits, mop up a sagging market and turn loss into profit than in the well-publicized realm of the press? In the 1960s and 1970s, 'saving' a national newspaper meant buying it and subsidizing its costs. In the 1980s it meant plans for 30 per cent demanning, threats of closure and late-night confrontations with the unions, conducted beneath arc-lights and television cameras. The reordering of Margaret Thatcher's Britain would take place in the boardrooms of Fleet Street, where everyone could see.

First of the new generation to test his strength was Tiny Rowland, who bought the *Observer* from Robert Anderson in 1981. Rowland's motive in entering Fleet Street was tortuous. His name had been mentioned in almost every newspaper take-over battle of the previous decade. A tall, aloof figure, he never fully recovered his composure after Lonrho's castigation by Edward Heath 'as the unacceptable face of capitalism', a reference to the bizarre tax avoidance methods by which certain of its executives were rewarded. Lonrho was closely involved in Africa, where Rowland specialized in doing business with leaders of one-party states. At home, he was prominent in highly personalized take-over struggles for the Scottish Universal Investment Trust (SUITS) and for Harrods. His desire to enter Fleet Street seems to have been largely personal, to increase Lonrho's visibility and add much-needed lustre to his reputation. His particular enthusiasm for the *Observer*, he once told me and others, was to transform its coverage of southern Africa where he felt its liberalism was abetting the advance of communism.

Rowland's custodianship of the *Observer* was allowed by the Government only after he had accepted 'certain conditions to safeguard editorial independence against potential conflict of interest' with Lonrho's other concerns. These conditions were laid down through the paper's formal articles of association. They stipulated that five independent directors be appointed to resolve disputes between the editor and Lonrho and to give or refuse consent to the appointment or dismissal of the editor. For all the scorn that was poured on them at the time, they were undoubtedly of assistance to the editor – Donald Trelford – in his often tempestuous relations with Rowland.

In the early months of 1984, circumstances induced Rowland to demonstrate a drastic proprietorial intervention in both the paper's editorial direction and its business affairs. In April Trelford published an account (written by himself) of atrocities allegedly committed by Zimbabwean Government troops in Matabeleland. The article could hardly have been more embarrassing for Lonrho, which had substantial interests at risk in Zimbabwe. Rowland wrote to the Prime Minister of Zimbabwe, Robert Mugabe, condemning the piece and dissociating himself and Lonrho from it. He temporarily withdrew Lonrho advertising from the paper and set about seeking to remove Trelford. The independent directors supported him and publicly criticized Rowland for his intervention. Rowland responded by calling them 'troglodytes' and threatened to cut their fees from £4,000 to £1,000. In a strong personal attack on Trelford, he said, 'I am subsidizing the *Observer* and he acts as if he owns and controls it.' He held a much-publicized breakfast with Robert Maxwell, who was still knocking on any Fleet Street door he could find. That prospect alone was calculated to unsettle the *Observer* staff.

The result was stalemate. No weight of independent directors, the *UK Press Gazette* pointed out, could 'compel Lonrho to advertise in the newspaper, underwrite its borrowings or make regular cash injections'. What, it asked, if Lonrho gold were to be available to the paper only if an editor satisfactory to Rowland were in the chair? Aware of this danger, Trelford offered to resign if the financial security of the paper rested on Rowland's confidence in himself as editor. The extent to which a loss-making paper was at the mercy of its owner could hardly have been made more plain.

Yet proprietorship is rarely about such crude plays of power. To have fired Trelford in such circumstances would have destroyed the purpose of Rowland's presence in Fleet Street – the improvement of his public reputation. The proprietor in this case was nothing like as strong as his financial leverage suggested; indeed the more public the dispute, the weaker his position. Rowland backed down. He did not sell to Maxwell. He rejected Trelford's resignation and said it had all been a 'lovers' tiff'.

Despite Rowland's subsequent threat to withdraw subsidy and give the *Observer* 'complete commercial independence', he next turned his attention from its editorship to its management. In March 1984 the paper's NGA machine minders had returned to the familiar battlefield for yet more plunder. In an astonishing claim, they demanded that their pay should be fixed with reference to their hourly paid NGA colleagues in the composing room. This was a wholly new Fleet Street concept. Since the SOGAT '82 assistants in the machine room received 87½ per cent of the minders' rate and since other chapels were bound to seek comparable claims, the management could not possibly give way. With the threat of a strike, the chapel's leader, Pat Phelan, demanded a direct meeting with the proprietor over the head of the paper's management. Rowland, eager to prove he could run the paper better than its managers, fell into the trap. He met Phelan, was won over by the latter's plea to be given a face-saving offer to take back to his members, and granted him a 50p per hour payment 'on the understanding that production would not in future be disrupted'. This brought the minders' pay up to £120 for a night's work. A management memorandum to staff explained coldly that Mr Rowland had 'personally and benevolently helped the machine minders' chapel'.

Relations between Lonrho and the *Observer* management under Roger Harrison from April to June 1984 were a case history of misplaced proprietorial intervention. As the management had predicted, the composing room immediately lodged a counter-claim, with further claims for 'uplift' from other chapels. The cost was estimated at £532,000 in a full year. Harrison demanded from Lonrho to be told 'what you would like the management to do'. Mr Rowland decided to pay off the compositors 'for flexible meal breaks' and naïvely hoped that would be that. It was like pouring petrol on a fire. Phelan's fifty-seven machine minders staged a lightning strike to restore the differential they felt they had negotiated with Rowland earlier, costing the paper an entire edition and another £400,000. Phelan was soon back in Rowland's office, where he was granted yet another rise, communicated on the telephone by Phelan to the management from a pub. In a despairing message, Harrison pleaded that in future Rowland

> only meets general secretaries, and then only to hear their promise of normal working if he will continue the paper. The briefer the meeting the better. A determined response from the owner will strengthen their resolve to deal with their members . . . They will see weakness in any long negotiations.

From the *Observer*'s high point of circulation during the *Sunday Times*' closure, it fell back to 750,000 in 1985, but the losses fell back too. Rowland seemed content to coast along behind the *Sunday Times* and just ahead of the *Sunday Telegraph*. He constrained editorial and promotional costs even if he could not constrain his chapels. By 1986 the *Observer* was no longer a substantial cash drain on the group. Lonrho appeared to have learnt one lesson from Fleet Street's recent history: there is no point in throwing good money at greedy chapels merely to boost circulation and enhance proprietorial prestige. Yet it was hard to see what return – pecuniary or otherwise – Rowland enjoyed from his proprietorship. From 1984 onwards Lonrho had to deny persistent rumours that the newspaper was again for sale.

As Rowland was retreating to lick his wounds in the summer of 1984, the ample figure of Robert Maxwell finally stormed into Fleet Street, bursting with energy after some fifteen years of pent-up frustration. Like Rowland, his name had been associated with Fleet Street take-overs since his first tussle with Murdoch over the *News of the World* in 1969. A loud, extrovert Czech with a gargantuan appetite for work and its rewards, Maxwell contrived at various times to be a Labour MP, book publisher, film producer and owner of Oxford United football team. He was bruised in 1971 when a Government inspector criticized his custodianship of Pergamon Press and implied he was unfit to run a public company. He soon bounced back, though the experience encouraged him to keep his future enterprises under close family control. He recovered his reputation and fortune in 1981 by rescuing the British Printing and Communications Corporation (BPCC) from collapse. A feature of his management technique was constant confrontation with union leaders, usually late at night, and at top volume. In five years of autocratic leadership he succeeded in reorganizing, and in large measure saving, the bulk of Britain's printing industry from the challenge of low-cost European competition.

Like other new proprietors, Maxwell had been victim of often-virulent xenophobia. As with Rupert Murdoch, it seemed to make him crave Fleet Street even more. He would buy any share, telephone any backer, offer any guarantee that he thought might gain him access. He was cheated of the *News of the World*, outmanoeuvred at the *Sun*, spurned by the *Observer*, abused outright at *The Times*, and poised in mid-1984 to bid for Express Newspapers. Each seemed an unlikely object of his affection, yet each offered an admission ticket to Fleet Street. Only the *Daily Mirror* seemed made for Maxwell and he for it. Yet that paper was initially determined to avoid his clutches.

In October 1983 Reed International and its chairman, Sir Alex Jarratt, announced that they were considering the sale of the Mirror group titles the following year. The group was expected to make £5.7 million in 1983–4, down from £8 million the year before. The national papers made only £1.6 million on a turnover of £232 million. The failure of the Mirror group's new-technology initiative to yield anticipated savings and the weak market performance of the titles led Jarratt to conclude that enough was enough. The most Reed International was prepared to concede to the *Daily Mirror*'s noble history was a market flotation with no one buyer receiving more than 15 per cent of the shares. The device was intended to avoid a single bidder, such as Maxwell, being able to take control, at least in the short term.

Maxwell proved more than a match for such a ploy. In July 1984 his Pergamon Press lodged an initial bid of £80 million on condition that the Reed International board withdrew the public flotation. Reed International considered this an inadequate inducement to renege on their commitment to the *Daily Mirror*'s independence. Maxwell then increased his offer to £113.4 million, at least twice what the board had been advised it might get from the restricted flotation. At this point, Reed International felt its obligation to its shareholders outweighed all else. It duly sold the paper and its associated titles to Maxwell, over the heads of a dazed staff and a furious Mirror group chairman, Clive Thornton.

Reed International extracted from Maxwell an undertaking that he would 'maintain the existing editorial independence' of the newspapers and offer shares to the employees on favourable terms 'as soon as practicable'. Maxwell later said the titles would be 'backing Britain' and promptly passed them to a company registered in Liechtenstein. The scene at the Mirror group's ugly red tower in Holborn on the night of Maxwell's triumph was a colourful contrast to Matthews's arrival at the Express building in 1977. With no need of a prompt, Maxwell shouted out his policies for the paper and the world. 'It's a great responsibility to take over these great national newspapers,' he said. He pledged 'the resources that will enable the editors, managers and workforce of these papers to walk eight feet tall'. He promised to overtake the *Sun* in circulation and make the group a £15 million profit by the end of the year. The paper would continue to support the Labour party.

Superficially it seemed the *Daily Mirror* had found an authentic successor to Bartholomew. The latter's portrayal by Francis Williams could be transferred to Maxwell unedited: 'cantankerous, suspicious and jealous of any who withstood his authority . . . a ruthless determination to trample on anyone who got in his way and an occasional odd flash of genial charm. He was also a daemonic fury and a ball of fire.' Yet Bartholomew was at heart a sceptical reporter. Maxwell was at heart a tycoon. His approach to proprietorship was ego-maniacal, not journalistic. The *Daily Mirror* blazoned the doings of the Maxwell family and peddled the opinions of its proprietor without thought for their appeal to the readers. His name would appear regularly in its pages. His exploits – trying to solve the coal strike, travelling the country promoting the paper, flying food to Ethiopia – had to have front-page coverage. Like Matthews, he was delighted to be 'labelled as a Beaverbrook'. His staff at times wondered whether Northcliffe was not a more appropriate model.

Far from overtaking the *Sun*, the *Daily Mirror*'s circulation under Maxwell's command began a remarkable free fall, losing 300,000 within two years. Nor did this fall produce any surge in the paper's financial strength. Millionaire bingo alone cost £6 million. Egocentric though he might be, Maxwell was not a man to avert his eyes from trouble. All new proprietors profess themselves shocked at what they learn about their paper's production costs: Maxwell found they had risen by 70 per cent in five years, supposedly years of labour-saving innovation. In his first six months, the Mirror group's titles made just £241,000 on sales of £140 million and were heading for a year-end loss. He now embarked on a year-long campaign to eliminate 30 per cent of his staff from the group's plants in London, Manchester and Glasgow. The only softening of the blow was the periodic announcement of new projects and publications, some in the north, some in London, some in Ireland. None had actually appeared two years after his arrival in Fleet Street.

For once, the Mirror group's chapels found themselves confronting a proprietor prepared to out-bellow them at any hour of the day or night. This time it was their own officials – rather than senior managers – who were summoned from their beds to conduct instant negotiations. It was they who had to cope with all-night sessions at which a proprietor was dictating the agenda. They complained bitterly that Maxwell did not keep his promises, changed the rules in the course of talks, issued threats and then withdrew them at a moment's notice. Their members were sacked, one, two and three times in a matter of months. Even though reinstatement swiftly followed, chapels were unsettled by being given a taste of their own medicine.

For the first year of his ownership of the *Daily Mirror*, Maxwell tended to come off the worse for his belligerence. A twelve-day closure in August 1985, over the removal of the *Sporting Life*'s printing from the Mirror building to a Maxwell plant in Bermondsey, ended in compromise. The NGA was not prepared to accept that a proprietor could move work round his various London plants at will. The *Sporting Life* was sold instead and Maxwell had to agree to reabsorb its staff in his existing plant. He immediately returned to the attack. A series of demands and renewed threats of closure culminated in his exhausted chapels finally agreeing to staff reductions. In January 1986, Maxwell was able to announce 2,100 redundancies from his 7,000-strong establishment in London and Manchester.

An almost identical operation was then undertaken to cut costs on the group's two Glasgow titles, the *Daily Record* and the *Sunday Mail*. It included court injunctions, the separation of the papers into different companies, a demand for a 30 per cent cut in the 1,050 staff and, finally, a fortnight's closure, complete with guards and barbed wire going up round the buildings. At one point it seemed that Maxwell might 'go green-field' with labour drawn from outside the print unions. Eventually here too, amid a barrage of threats and counter-threats from both sides, he secured his manning cuts.

By the end of 1985, Maxwell was registering substantive advances. The battle was conducted almost single-handed (though with the wily Joe Haines at his side) against a group of chapels long established as among the most entrenched anywhere in Fleet Street. Maxwell separated his printing and publishing into different companies, giving each stage of production a measure of legal protection from industrial action. In Glasgow he employed injunctions and lock-outs as what seemed a standard industrial tactic. This aid would not have been available but for the Conservative Government's industrial relations legislation, a fact that Maxwell readily acknowledged, though it did not diminish his and his papers' continued support of the Labour party. What Maxwell had not done, however, was break the mould. His chapels had been forced to concede manning cuts, but they had not conceded legally binding contracts let alone the removal of the central pillar of their power, the closed shop. The mechanisms for future recovery and earnings drift remained intact. The chapels had lost a battle but been honourably allowed to retain their weapons.

The third new proprietor to pit his wits against his chapels was the man whose path into Fleet Street was eased by Maxwell's share dealings. David Stevens was the most uncharacteristic of the 1980s' intake. A short, assertive man with a house in Belgravia and personalized number plates on his Rolls-Royce, he was a City financier rather than a journalist or entrepreneur. His initial contact with the press was as guardian of Samuel Montagu's 10 per cent stake in the provincial newspaper and magazine chain, United Newspapers. In 1981 he became chairman of that company in succession to Lord Barnetson and immediately embarked on a policy of rapid expansion in Britain and America. His most acclaimed skill was at selling his company's prospects to stock-market analysts. His delight at acquiring the *Daily Express* in 1985 was qualified by the price he was forced to pay for it by Matthews: an exorbitant £317 million. He knew that his shareholders would be watching to see him justify such a gamble with their money.

Of all the new men, Stevens was the most overtly commercial in his behaviour. He realized the key to recovery at the *Daily Express* was a sound management and consistent editorial leadership. The old Matthews team departed but Stevens did not install himself in its place. He hired a new chief executive, Roger Bowes, and left him to push through a staff reduction package more drastic even than Maxwell's at the Mirror group: 2,500 from a total of 6,000. It was not Stevens but Bowes who negotiated with the unions and issued statements to the press. He insisted on a return to five-day working, new agreements and the introduction of

photocomposition within three months. Taking a leaf from
Maxwell's book, Bowes threatened closure in March 1986 if
he did not obtain the support of both the national unions and
the individual chapels. Nothing could have illustrated more
graphically the change that seven years had wrought since
*The Times* conflict – fought over almost identical territory.
Stevens was unlikely to have carried through his threat of
closure; it would have crippled United Newspapers in redundancy payments alone. But by then the chapels were no
longer prepared to take the risk. There were rumours of a
deal between Stevens and Maxwell, possibly involving a
merger of some of their competing titles (still, in mid-1986, a
long-term possibility). The loss of earnings in such a combination would have been enormous. Bowes got his
reductions.

The fourth new arrival faced an even tougher challenge.
The forty-one-year-old Conrad Black might share with the
first Lord Thomson the role of Canadian media tycoon come
to save Fleet Street's dying institutions, but he shared little
else. At home, his reputation was of a short-term asset-
stripper with a predilection for right-wing politics. In the
words of his normally admiring biographer, Peter Newman,
he suffered from a reluctance to 'hang in and operate func-
tioning companies instead of merely trading corporate blocks
. . . that no longer meet his high profits expectations'. However, past performance is seldom a good guide to a proprietor's behaviour when he reaches Fleet Street. An
intelligent enthusiast of European history and politics, Black
was fascinated by newspapers. He had attempted, but failed,
to buy the Toronto *Globe and Mail* and the Southams' publishing chain, but acquired a group of small-town newspapers
in addition to his other business interests. He spoke and
wrote frequently on the state of East–West relations and on
economic and social issues.

Black brought to Fleet Street strong views on proprietorship. A critical profile of him in the British *Director* maga-
zine\* described his regret at the 'demise of resident newspaper

\*Published by the Institute of Directors, March 1986.

proprietors' and recalled his motive in acquiring the *Daily Telegraph*, 'to have access to an authoritative, respected and influential newspaper . . . to ensure the paper continues to be a quality operation, presenting things fairly, and to be able to get things off my chest, though I would do that under my own name'. The *Daily Telegraph* was unlikely to become just another Canadian company ripe for stripping. It is doubtful if any proprietor since Cecil King had such overtly political ambitions for his product. When Black first arrived in Britain after assuming control in 1985, he was rushed to Downing Street to meet Margaret Thatcher before travelling to the Bilderberg conference of world leaders in Scotland.

If Black appeared to be in the mould of Fleet Street's traditional proprietors, he also confronted a traditional Fleet Street problem. By late 1985, the *Daily* and *Sunday Telegraph* were probably running a bigger trading deficit than any other group of titles. The Manchester plant was coming on stream in the new year, with costly chapel agreements already in place. The new Docklands plant was absorbing money. Andrew Knight, Black's chief executive, had not only to formulate a strategy for the new plant but clear out the attic of the Berry proprietorship: inadequate financial controls, no middle management and virtually no information on staff costs. Agreements covering the new plant were urgent since it held the key to staunching the cash outflow, yet the chapels well understood the pressure on Knight to maintain production and could have been forgiven for treating Black as just another foreign sugar daddy come to bail them out.

No sooner had he begun work at the *Daily Telegraph* than Knight found he was working in the shadow of a hurricane. Across Fleet Street, managements and chapels alike were nailing down roofs, lopping loose branches and corralling precious livestock into shelter. Following Maxwell's settlement at the *Daily Mirror* in December 1985, demanning agreements spread round the industry with startling speed. Negotiations on agenda unthinkable two years earlier were urgently proclaimed at the *Financial*

*Times*, the *Guardian* and the *Daily Mail*, in addition to those already noted at the Express and Mirror groups. The *Observer*, still nursing its two-year-old wounds, was the last to decide on drastic action, announcing a move of the editorial offices to Battersea in August 1986, with satellite printing in the provinces.

The reason for this burst of activity was that two men had separately decided the time had come to break down the defences that chapel power had long erected round Fleet Street. Eddy Shah, an outsider, was to be the enthusiastic, if transient, apostle of chapel-free new technology. Rupert Murdoch, whose four-year-old Wapping plant was still lying idle, was the apostle of nothing in particular. He had merely, spectacularly, run out of patience.

# 10

## BATTLE IS JOINED

If one event could be said to have heralded the transformation of the national newspaper industry that took place in 1985–6, it was the physical attack three years earlier by the NGA on a small printing works in the Cheshire town of Warrington. The cause of the trouble seemed trivial. The *Messenger* group of free newspapers, run by thirty-nine-year-old businessman Eddy Shah, had refused a post-entry closed shop to the NGA at two of its works. It had also endured a strike at a third, supported by picketing and secondary action against advertisers. The dispute escalated during 1983 and by November had achieved national prominence as a test of the Government's new trade union laws. Attention was directed in particular at the willingness of the police to give physical protection to employers against secondary action that was reinforced by 'flying pickets'.

The concept of the free newspaper had been imported into Britain from America in the late 1960s to the scorn of 'paid-for' journalism, yet by 1985 it was publishing's fastest growth sector. There were 765 free daily or weekly newspapers in Britain, with a weekly advertising revenue that had risen in ten years from £23 million to £262 million, overtaking that of the paid-for press. It was estimated that 86 per cent of all British homes had a free newspaper of some sort delivered through the door. Some of these publications were thrown together from local advertising interspersed with council handouts and advertisement-related editorial. Some, however, began to rival established titles in editorial content. Most ambitious was the Reed International group, recently shorn of its Fleet Street interests. It planned a chain of 'metro mornings' in ten provincial cities under the general title of the *Daily News*. A Birmingham version launched in 1984 with a circulation of 290,000 was in profit within six months.

Eddy Shah – he spells it with a y – was the son of a cousin of the Aga Khan and an English mother. He had a peripatetic upbringing, went briefly to Gordonstoun School and eventually found work with Granada Television in Manchester. In 1974 his distaste for big organizations led him to try his hand at freesheets in the north-west of England, then one of the industry's wilder frontiers. Shah was a solitary figure, nervous, overweight but blessed with phenomenal energy. He was also prodigiously ambitious. By 1983 he owned five titles distributed in Lancashire and Cheshire. He had married an actress, bought and learned to fly his own plane and adopted the lifestyle of a successful north-country entrepreneur.

Though initially a print union employer, Shah's intolerance of the NGA's rules and restrictions was soon to produce conflict. Whereas most freesheet managers paid the union's 'going rate' and pocketed their still-large profits, Shah turned his frustration into an anti-union crusade. Gradually he introduced non-union labour into his various works. He became a student of the 1980 and 1982 employment laws and separated each of his operations into different companies for protection against secondary action. Eventually, the NGA staff at his Stockport headquarters went on strike to enforce a new union agreement. The strike, a legal one, was followed by illegal secondary action against other plants in the group and against its advertisers. Shah sued the NGA for damages and the union found itself the first to have its funds sequestered under the Government's new laws. The crusade thus captured the attention of the nation. Shah's determination and his exhilaration at being in the public spotlight were those of a classic proprietor in embryo.*

*Goodhart and Wintour give a lively and balanced account of the Shah story. See bibliography.

The NGA decided to raise the temperature by calling out its Fleet Street members, 'spontaneously' so as to avoid a suit for conspiracy. There followed a short-lived lock-out as Fleet Street managers sought guarantees against further disruption. Three 'hard-liners', the Express Newspapers, Mirror and News International groups, felt the moment had come for joint action against the NGA. However unconcerned they might be about Eddy Shah, the important principle of confronting secondary action was at stake. The rest of Fleet Street was not ready to collaborate. After a bitter wrangle at the NPA, one more bid to secure collective proprietorial action collapsed after just a day. The spotlight turned back on to Shah.

As the dispute grew, flying pickets turned up at Shah's Warrington works and the police were compelled to intervene. Printers were supplemented by some 4,000 dockers, miners and assorted activists, the first pitched battle of the new era in industrial law taking place on 29 November 1983. The police were the victors, though this had not been a foregone conclusion. Many critics of the new laws had believed that a union could still place an embargo on a factory in dispute provided it could persuade sufficient numbers to turn up and threaten violence against those entering or leaving the plant. The police could well be reluctant to use the amount and type of force necessary to counteract them. The Government's campaign against the militants could thus be countered by sheer strength of numbers.

Warrington proved this wrong, and the experience influenced police conduct in the 1984–5 miners' strike. The new laws proved effective in another respect as well: the TUC was curtailed in its freedom to offer material assistance to what was an illegal action. Within weeks of the Warrington battle, the NGA was fined £525,000 for its picketing and found the TUC refusing to offer more than moral support. The NGA had to admit defeat and call off its pickets. It was estimated to have lost £2 million in fines and legal fees during the dispute. For the first time in many years, industrial action in the printing industry appeared to have cost a union more than it had cost an employer. Warrington was a sign of a clear shift in the balance of power and it was not lost on the more astute members of the two main print unions.

Shah emerged from the Warrington incident of 1983 a hero of small-scale capitalism. He had humiliated Fleet Street, costing it £20 million in lost production that November and exposing its inability to find common cause against its chapels. Speaking to the provincial Newspaper Society conference the following year, he accused rival publishers of backwardness and remarked that he felt 'as bitter about newspaper managements as I do about the unions'. His initial reaction to his success was to consider a free paper for Manchester, but his gaze was soon directed to higher ambitions. A new-found friend, Andrew Neil, editor of the *Sunday Times*, encouraged him to tackle the challenge of a national paper. Neil pointed out that Fleet Street had long been vulnerable to someone such as Shah, a buccaneer ready to use provincial experience and the latest technology to undercut the exorbitant costs of London printing. Shah was riding high. If he could raise the money, why not have a go?

Shah admits that Neil's prompting was what decided him. His freesheet experience demonstrated that the market for newspapers need not be regarded as stagnant. It showed that the unions were no longer a real obstacle to innovation, provided managements were prepared, in an increasingly hackneyed phrase, 'to manage'. Freesheet owners were used to starting up titles wherever they saw an opening, hiring and firing staff and buying or leasing equipment. They were fast movers who had already made devastating inroads into the established provincial market. Shah had experience at Warrington of computerized typesetting and of operating wholly outside NGA control. Only one big newspaper company enjoyed similar flexibility – including also direct inputting by journalists – T. Bailey Forman's *Nottingham Evening Post*. Its name had been mentioned occasionally in a Fleet Street context, but only as possibly supplying a temporary printing option to strike-hit national newspapers. The unions tolerated it as a 'ring-fenced' exception. One reason for their determination to confront Shah at Warrington was fear of a rash of Nottinghams breaking out all across the freesheet sector.

The NGA had not ignored the imminence of technological change. Its leaders had frequently warned their members that new technology had to be accepted, even to the extent of conceding direct inputting by other unions. Both Joe Wade and his successor, Tony Dubbins, pointed out that NGA compositors had to face an industry that was expanding and fragmenting. They could not hold the line against thousands of back-street print employers. White-collar workers throughout Britain were learning to type direct into a computer through a keyboard. As Wade had told his 1982 annual conference, 'Unless we are prepared to be flexible in our attitudes, we shall be engulfed in a tidal wave of technology which we shall not be able to control.' He was addressing the craftsman's essential concern: not innovation as such but his control over its application. If NGA members rejected new technology, other workers would simply take their places.

Most proprietors, both in the provinces and in Fleet Street, were prepared to take such a promise of flexibility on trust. The NGA reached an agreement with Portsmouth and Sunderland Newspapers for phased direct inputting by journalists and advertisers but battles ensued with two other firms, the Wolverhampton Express and Star and the Kent Messenger groups. Both spent 1985 in conflict with their printers and their journalists. As Mark Kersen, managing director of the *Wolverhamption Express and Star* was reported as saying, 'All the NGA's negotiators ever did was seek ways to preserve the organization, shape and structure of the NGA, in order to preserve their power, authority and control.' It was a clear reflection of Wade's message: within the confines of the closed shop, anything could be discussed and even conceded, but not the fact of the closed shop itself. The closed shop was power.

To Shah, this new flexibility on the part of the NGA was not a sign to return to the negotiating table. It merely suggested that the union was weak and could be more easily bypassed. On the statute book were laws reducing union immunities and prohibiting secondary action. This was more than just a source of intellectual comfort: it shifted the newspaper industry's balance of power. The courts and the police would now have to protect a non-union printer from closed shops, from mass picketing, from any picketing other than at the plant in dispute and from secondary pressure on suppliers or customers. The distribution system for national newspapers, through dispatchers, drivers and railways, was vulnerable to guerrilla action, but a road distribution network might be established to circumvent it. 'Cowboy' lorry networks could be put in place like those that had serviced the electricity and steel industries during the miners' strike. Depots could be set up outside the orbit of wholesalers vulnerable to SOGAT '82 action. What, Shah asked all who met him, could be simpler than to harness all this to the cause of challenging Fleet Street?

Shah's two-year struggle to launch his newspaper was plagued by difficulties. It was novel, risky, and financiers did not like it. Shah was not an organization but a one-man band. He had no track record and few friends in positions to give him references. His one trump card was the fame of his confrontation at Warrington. It was this that brought him the support of a group of right-wing businessmen after orthodox venture capitalists, such as Lloyds Bank International, turned him down. He was eventually backed by Lord Forte, Lord Taylor (of Taylor Woodrow), Norris McWhirter, Lord Cayzer and Sir Richard Storey (of Portsmouth and Sunderland Newspapers). All were Conservatives and most were prominent donors to party funds. As Goodhart and Wintour point out, this group was attracted not by the promise of quick profit but by the romance of a project that represented old-fashioned, free-enterprise virtues: 'To them, Shah is to the national newspaper industry what Mrs Thatcher is to the wider body politic – an invigorating attempt to shake off years of corporate compromise and decline.'

The prospectus for the new paper, prepared in October 1984 by the accountants, Thomson McLintock, was a rosy one. With 500 staff in total and a circulation of 700,000 (half that of the *Daily Mail*, its nearest market rival), the daily and Sunday papers should make £13 million on a turnover of £50 million. This would require £8.5 million of equity and £10 million for presses and equipment. These figures were revised over the two-year planning period, but not so as to suggest the paper would be unviable. So low were its running costs that it should break even at 600,000 sales on cover price alone. With a reasonable expectation of advertising revenue, the break-even circulation could be as low as 400,000. Were it to top the million, the profit should be at least £20 million in the first year, more than covering the expense of the initial launch. Such figures in themselves were astonishing compared with running costs in Fleet Street. Most daily papers needed at least 2,000 staff, not to mention ghost payments for hundreds of non-existent extras. The opportunity needed no emphasis. It depended only on Shah's being able to produce and deliver his product.

Shah took a number of rash steps. He decided not to subcontract his printing but to buy the most advanced colour presses he could find and install them at four centres, one at Heathrow and the rest in the provinces. Pages would be transmitted to them by Mercury cables from the paper's London offices in Vauxhall Bridge Road. The presses were paid for with a loan from the Hungarian Bank, a lively outpost of communism apparently as eager as Shah's other supporters to cock a snook at the City Establishment. Type-setting and page composition would be entirely computerized. A Hastech system enabled journalists' copy to be summoned by an editor on his screen and adjusted to fit any desired page layout. Pictures and headlines could be added at the touch of a button, or at least the flick of an on-screen 'mouse'. Not only did this system dispense with human (NGA) typesetters, it did without the lithography and paste-up staff of conventional photocomposition. It went direct from the page as projected on the sub-editor's screen into the computer for transmission. Shah's confidence in this equipment was to prove a serious miscalculation.

In the year between his announcement of what was to be called *Today* and its launch in March 1986, Shah became a familiar figure on television and on the conference circuit. His message was always that of the aggressive innovator about to teach his elders and betters a lesson. He resisted the temptation to be drawn into editorial specifics, though he and his editor, Brian MacArthur, would slide uneasily into woolly middle-of-the-road jargon when asked what would be the paper's political stance. Despite the Conservative nature of Shah's financial backing, MacArthur dallied with the idea of becoming the first paper overtly to support the Liberal/ SDP Alliance. It would have given the paper a much-needed political identity, and possibly some loyal readers. Though certain of Shah's advisers, including Lord Harris, were prominent Social Democrats and secured him membership of the Reform Club, Shah was a Conservative with an admiration for Margaret Thatcher. He affirmed his paper's political independence and drew up a 'bill of rights' by which its policy would be guided. It was as bland and naïve as the initial manifestos of all new proprietors. *Today* would 'support true democracy and not the false democracy of collectivism' and operate 'not influenced by the intimidation and subterfuge of extremists and their ideologies'. It would not rely on 'scandal, sexual and financial titillation and sensationalism'.

Eddy Shah's politics were as unsophisticated as the man. He would assert vigorously that the editorial side of the paper was for his editors to determine, but no one doubted he would be an interventionist proprietor. He was not an established businessman tiptoeing eagerly, like Lord Matthews, through the haunts of the mighty; he was a radical from the industrial frontier, a restless beginner. He remained living in Cheshire throughout the launch of *Today* and had a provincial scepticism towards London and its enticements. There was a Puritan relish in his determination to attack Fleet Street and its sinful ways. He would soar or crash.

Most of Fleet Street viewed Shah as an exotic. Editorials would admire his 'spirit of enterprise' and consider it time the printers were given a drubbing. Fleet Street managers would treat him indulgently. They felt he was probably biting off more than a simple freesheet operator could chew but with luck he would give the chapels a fright before he went under. But as Shah's planning progressed, he came to seem less of an eccentric and more of a threat. During 1985 there were rumours of collusion between certain managements and SOGAT '82 to deny him his W. H. Smith outlets. Brenda Dean, the new leader of SOGAT '82, wrote to the Hungarian Bank to ask it to withdraw its loan on grounds of socialist solidarity. This bizarre form of secondary action proved abortive. Robert Maxwell used Shah as a regular stick with which to beat his chapels during his year-long war against manning levels on the *Daily Mirror*. He feared Shah could take at least 10 per cent of the *Daily Mirror*'s sale and he spent £60 million on colour presses to be installed in his new Docklands plant. Far from overtaking the *Sun*, he was obsessed, throughout 1985, by having to fight a rearguard action against a provincial upstart.

As we shall see later, Eddy Shah soon failed to live up to his extravagant promises. This, however, should not obscure the impact on the industry of his pre-launch barnstorming. This impact was neither journalistic nor even technological. It was on Fleet Street's most vulnerable spot – its industrial relations. Aware that his printing plants might be the target of militant action, in July 1985 Shah reached a single-union agreement with the Electrical, Electronic Telecommunications and Plumbing Union (EETPU). The deal, for which the initiative came from the union, offered Shah the hope (fully vindicated) that his paper would not be blacked nor his circulation system disrupted. He intended to distribute by van to some eighty franchisees, except in London where he had his own vehicles and in scattered rural areas where W. H. Smith were to be used.

Although he was not relying on the unionized rail network, Shah was clearly at risk from unofficial action, however illegal. To reach a deal with another member of the TUC, even so maverick a union as the EETPU, was some security. The electricians, in return for exclusive negotiating rights, accepted terms that left Fleet Street managers wide-eyed with envy. They included no closed shop, no demarcation, equal status for all staff whether union members or not and a terms-and-conditions board with equal representation of staff and management. There would be no casting vote on this board and disputes would be submitted to pendulum arbitration. Since no existing factory, jobs or titles were involved, the unions felt less able to complain. Shah was still an outsider.

Shah's deal – more properly it should be credited to Eric Hammond, leader of the EETPU – was revolutionary. He and Hammond had swept aside a century and a half of custom and practice in the composing and machine rooms of Fleet Street. As he proffered similar arrangements to Murdoch at Wapping (see below), Hammond was hauled before one TUC committee after another and accused of poaching. It was a charge he, on behalf of his eager members, firmly denied. He regarded new print technology as electricians' work. The equipment was electrical not mechanical, and that was an end to it. The print unions would never keep his members out of an industry that technological change was pushing their way. The real threat to the print unions thus came not from management as such but from a rival labour 'sub-contractor' whose ambitions had been given free rein by management. Shah's agreement with the EETPU would not only be hard to break, it also set a seductive precedent.

Unions that had long taken for granted a common front against such threats now began squabbling with each other. Brenda Dean of SOGAT '82 was exasperated by the NGA's attitude to the various productivity talks then under way both in the provinces and in Fleet Street. She warned that her union could 'not stand by on the sidelines' while the NGA sorted out its attitude towards the new technology and other unions such as the National Union of Journalists (NUJ) and SOGAT '82 itself. She let it be known that she would sign single-union agreements if the NGA did not drag itself into the modern age. In reply, the NGA's Tony Dubbins could only throw up his hands in despair. His Fleet Street chapels were as undisciplined as ever throughout 1985. His London branch officers had long tired of the antics of NGA machine minders. As members of his executive had feared – and some clearly hoped – nemesis seemed to be at hand for the 'fat cat chapels' of Fleet Street.

No one, not even Shah, predicted how soon this nemesis would come. Rupert Murdoch's two new printing works at Wapping and at Kinning Park in Glasgow were begun in 1980 and virtually complete by 1983. Both were intended to print the *Sun* and *News of the World* – Murdoch had not previously printed in Scotland and had to fly copies of the *Sun* north each night. Editorial and typesetting departments would remain at Bouverie Street. Neither Wapping nor Glasgow was regarded initially as a non-union works. As we saw in chapter eight, Murdoch was initially sceptical of the value of a move because of this, and this scepticism was vindicated as negotiations opened in 1981 over the facsimile transmission of pages from London to Glasgow. Brenda Dean, then a SOGAT official in Manchester, opposed the move since it might threaten Manchester's supremacy in the north. Glasgow chapels demanded a full newspaper in Scotland, not one 'faxed' from London. They simply told Murdoch he could not proceed as planned.

In London Murdoch ploughed on. He made a video describing the delights of Wapping to his staff and sent chapel officials to examine new technology in Finland. He was not known as anti-union and his managers had a reputation for talking tough but conceding fast in a dispute. The Bouverie Street workers were among the highest paid in Fleet Street. Murdoch professed himself happy that high earnings should continue to be a feature of Wapping, but wanted lower manning levels and legal, not just verbal, guarantees of continuous production. Talks proceeded slowly throughout 1984 during which chapel officials clearly felt they need concede nothing. Predictable trouble emerged between the NGA and SOGAT '82 over the manning of the machine room (the history of modern Fleet Street could be told in terms of this dispute). Breakdown was finally reached on 19 December, with union negotiators declaring that Wapping would never open – one official allegedly suggesting Murdoch might as well put a match to it.

Credit for persuading Rupert Murdoch to seek a wholly different approach towards Wapping, treating it, if necessary, as a 'green-field' site, should go to his London chief executive – another Australian – Bruce Matthews, though Andrew Neil lent radical encouragement from his editor's chair at the *Sunday Times*. After the breakdown of the 1984 talks Matthews had turned to an EETPU official and remarked that the position was hopeless. The official replied that his union might be able to 'help': some of its districts regularly supplied contractors with temporary labour. Matthews had only to say the word. (Contact thus predated the EETPU's approach to Eddy Shah.)

Reporting on the talks to Murdoch at his American home in January 1985, Matthews pointed out that in three years he had got nowhere. He was tired of banging his head against a wall and then coming over to show his boss the damage. Murdoch asked what alternative he had. Matthews suggested they take a gamble and prepare Wapping and Glasgow for possible non-union operation. The risks were immense, not just to the Wapping investment but to the whole of the Fleet Street business. If the worst came to the worst, not only would the *Sun* and the *News of the World* have to be transferred to Wapping but also *The Times* and the *Sunday Times*. There, they would be at the mercy of whatever staffing and distribution arrangements might be feasible in a context of fierce, probably nationwide, union opposition. The likelihood of at least a temporary collapse in revenue was considerable.

For Murdoch, always reluctant to risk his Fleet Street cash fountain, it was a delicate decision. He was expanding with speed in America – recklessly in the view of many observers. His newspapers there were making little money. His growth had run into monopoly suits in Australia. He was eager to move into television and films and was borrowing heavily to do so. By the end of 1985, his worldwide debt was $2.6 billion. Almost half Murdoch's total profits were earned in Britain, the bulk of them from the *Sun* and the *Sunday Times*. In the year to June 1985, the British News International company contributed £46.8 million to worldwide profits, a cash flow clearly vital to Murdoch's American ambitions.

These considerations alone might have counselled caution. Murdoch was not losing ground in Fleet Street. Economic recovery was boosting advertising revenue. Losses on Times Newspapers had fallen from £15 million when he bought the company in 1981 to £6 million in 1983–4 and turned into a profit of £5 million in 1984–5. The losses on *The Times* itself were reducing. In 1984, his up-market version of bingo, Portfolio, had had an immediate impact on sales, which rose by 100,000 in two months. *The Times* was thus on the brink of overtaking the *Guardian*. The newspapers were neck and neck at 480,000 in December 1985, though the *Guardian* drew away and was first to the 'magic half-million' early in 1986. However, *The Times* found itself caught in the old bind: to print the extra copies, Murdoch's machine room staff demanded an additional seventy 'jobs' at an on-cost of over £1 million a year. Chapels assumed that a management exhilarated by so steep a rise in sales would pay up. They were right, though a knock-on claim from other chapels was resisted after a two-day stoppage in October 1985.

What told against caution was simply Murdoch's – and Matthews's – exasperation at such incidents. They now controlled a third of Fleet Street's total production. Yet it appeared that the unions were determined to stop any further growth. The *News of the World* could not print more copies in Bouverie Street and the *Sunday Times* chapels were preventing expansion at Grays Inn Road, which was disrupted virtually every weekend. At this stage, in early 1985, there was little evidence that the bulk of the chapels would have countenanced any deal giving Murdoch drastic reductions in manning, let alone improved discipline. As he told all who cared to ask, he had had enough. He accepted Matthews' proposal and planning proceeded immediately.

The object of the exercise was to give News International a non-negotiable option in the event of further negotiation failing. This was the crucial departure from Times Newspapers' strategy in 1978, when Lord Thomson finally found himself with no alternative but surrender. Although both Murdoch and Matthews at first more than half-expected that the unions would eventually settle, they wanted to strengthen their hand against failure. They therefore had to be ready to go the whole way to a green-field option, since their existing plants would be vulnerable to industrial action should news of the alternative strategy leak out. Not surprisingly, Matthews called it Operation Impossible.

The strategy pursued between April and December 1985 was two-track. The first assumed the chapels would eventually agree to move at least part of the printing of the *Sun* and the *News of the World* to Wapping. In this case, the spare capacity would be used to produce a new evening paper, the *London Post*. This was scheduled initially for autumn 1985 but later postponed to March 1986. Much controversy surrounded this project, which passed through two editors even before it was due to appear. It was not so much a false scent – as the chapels later claimed – as a double contingency. If the unions continued to delay on the move to Wapping, then the *London Post* might still go ahead there, possibly as a twenty-four-hour non-union newspaper. However, if the chapels became so intransigent as to strike against the whole group because of non-union work at Wapping, then the new paper would be shelved and all Murdoch's production transferred to the new plant. In that case, the *London Post* was useful cover for the installation of the editorial computer terminals. These would be vital to maintain continuous production of the titles that Murdoch had previously stated would continue to be edited in their existing offices.

This last eventuality demanded the most careful planning. It meant a full complement of presses as well as typesetting equipment capable, *in extremis*, of producing two daily and two Sunday newspapers inside Wapping. This required hundreds of Atex terminals (far more than could plausibly be needed by one small London evening paper) installed in total secrecy. Talks began with the Atex Corporation in America as soon as Murdoch and Matthews had made their decision, early in 1985. The company was told not to mention the contact even to its main British office for fear of leaks. Twelve Atex staff were sent over to live in a house in West London and sworn to silence about their work. The company's name was removed from stationery and equipment. The system was assembled away from Wapping and moved in late one night in May. More staff later arrived from America to get the system running. The *Sun* and the *News of the World* journalists could be accommodated in the *London Post* offices, but more space was needed for such copious producers of the written word as *The Times* and the *Sunday Times*. A row of warehouses, all that remained of the old London Docks, was duly converted into a cramped and mostly windowless series of rooms.

Wapping's huge printing and publishing factory could be equipped normally as if for unionized operation. The only deviousness had to surround the training of crews to man the presses. Operating sixty-three units of Goss Headliner presses and an automated publishing room was not a skill acquired overnight. The solution lay in taking up the EETPU offer of the previous year. Matthews had never dealt personally with Eric Hammond, the union's leader, though the latter saw clearly the opportunity Wapping offered his members for breaking through the NGA/SOGAT '82 duopoly in the printing industry. Although he had signed the first single-union agreement for a national paper with Eddy Shah (in July 1985), it was the informal arrangement with Matthews that represented the greater breakthrough.

As far as Wapping was concerned, the EETPU presented itself as a confederation of local labour-only sub-contractors. Its Southampton district office had in the past supplied gangs of casual workers for construction and other projects. Men with specified skills would be supplied for hire on short-term contracts. At Wapping the pay was good, up to £500 a week. The men had to be clear of suspicion of union militancy and likely to keep quiet about the nature of their work. Buses would collect them in Southampton each morning and drive them direct to Wapping. They would be on six-month contracts, later extended to a year. The union hired them, but once inside the plant they were on individual contracts wholly at the disposal of the management. To work at Wapping, even from relatively prosperous Hampshire, was a coveted prize.

It was a risky procedure, since the chance of a potential saboteur, or at least a spy, creeping on to the payroll was clearly high. However, it was an unavoidable risk if the strategy was to succeed. (In the event, the unions gained only a rough idea of what the men were being trained to do.)

Murdoch's lawyers were also active. The Wapping plant was put under a separate company, London Post Printers Ltd, distinct from the Fleet Street operations. Any industrial action against it would thus be secondary and actionable. Meanwhile, News International spokesmen said the workers seen pouring into Wapping each day were merely temporary, preparing the site and its equipment for eventual production, pending union agreements.

More difficult was to acquire, or if necessary establish, a complete alternative distribution system covering the whole country. Christopher Pole-Carew, pioneer of union confrontations as director of T. Bailey Forman in Nottingham, was invited to organize a nationwide lorry network. The Australian transport firm, Thomas Nationwide Transport (TNT), in which Murdoch held a minority stake, had operated in Britain since 1972 and was well placed to challenge British Rail's overnight newspaper monopoly. However, it also had a national closed-shop agreement with the TGWU and was naturally worried that its other business might be jeopardized by a strike-breaking operation. As with the EETPU, the tactic was to combine secrecy with sub-contract. The distribution operation, which required some 800 lorries and vans and up to 2,000 new jobs, was as large and complex as Wapping itself. It was organized apart from TNT's normal depots, with unmarked vehicles and specially recruited drivers. News International agreed to cover the capital cost of the lorries – some £7 million – should the unions settle and distribution revert to the (cheaper) rail system. The deal with TNT was signed in June 1985, and the system was already being tested that summer in the north-east.

There was no hope of the *London Post* – or any other title – appearing from the plant in autumn 1985. Yet the rising tempo of work on the site galvanized the unions. In July Brenda Dean was pressed by her News International chapels to bid for a single-union deal both for the *London Post* and for moving part of the Bouverie Street work to Wapping if the NGA was to continue recalcitrant. Ms Dean was increasingly aware of what was going on behind the walls and was desperate to be part of it, so much so that the concept of a complete machine room without NGA minders appeared at last to be on the Fleet Street horizon. The SOGAT '82 journal poured scorn on its fellow union for 'low level, low intelligence, anti-union abuse'. The union's national executive formally agreed to seek immediate talks on Wapping, as well as with the EETPU on its deal with Shah.

There now ensued one of the most extraordinary six months in Fleet Street history, with SOGAT '82 scrambling to keep its balance as the old certainties heaved and slid from beneath it. By comparison, the NGA appeared to be tumbling out of control. In August respite came with a postponement of the *London Post* to March 1986. In September an initial run of a dummy paper was tested through Wapping with managers and Southampton electricians at the controls. It revealed weaknesses but in no way undermined confidence in the plant's potential. News of the run reached the Fleet Street chapels. They pondered but rejected strike action. They had never before experienced an employer so vigorously taking the initiative. Still the NGA was demanding a presence for its minders in the Wapping machine room. Still SOGAT '82 wanted what management regarded as unrealistic staffing in the publishing area. Neither union could accept the legally binding clauses in the contracts demanded by Matthews.

By now Murdoch and Matthews realized they had to force a crisis. At talks with the unions in September, Murdoch uttered the cry of Fleet Street proprietors down the ages. 'I have strained myself and my senior colleagues physically, emotionally and financially to build this business,' he said, 'and we have met with nothing but cynicism, broken promises and total opposition.' SOGAT '82 demanded to be present at future runs at Wapping. Matthews said no, but reiterated that if agreement could be reached, the *London Post* 'would come second' and printing for the *Sun* and *News of the World* could move to Wapping. By now, it was clear that Matthews and Murdoch were growing in confidence

over their green-field option. They renamed it Operation
Difficult – no longer Impossible. The machinery seemed to
be working and the electricians were in place to man it. A
proprietor was able to conduct negotiations with the luxury
of knowing he might be able to publish behind the back of
the chapels if need be. Probably the last to experience this
sensation had been John Walter when he introduced his
steam presses in 1814 (see page 76).

In October News International prepared and presented to
the unions a document of uncompromising stringency. It was
intended to give management the same flexibility that it
could expect from its existing freelance labour force. It
required total freedom over the allocation of staff at Wapping, an end to the pre-entry and post-entry closed shop,
with managers able to hire whomever they chose, and a
legally binding, no-strike agreement. 'New technology may
be adopted at any time,' it went on, 'with consequential
reductions in manning levels.' Anyone who was involved in
any industrial action during the term of the contract would be
fired without appeal under the disciplinary procedure. It
meant an end to chapel autonomy not only over earnings but
also over recruitment and employment. The potency of the
closed shop would be dead. Direct input to computer terminals was assumed. Agreement was demanded by Christmas, otherwise both sides understood that a deal with the
EETPU would be sought.

In November the chapels showed the first substantive sign
of orderly retreat. The NGA offered a joint package with the
NUJ on direct inputting at Wapping. Though hedged with
conditions, it was the first offered to any Fleet Street house
and would have been a sensation only a year before. However, it left demarcation unresolved with the SOGAT '82
advertising clerks who would also need access to the computers. Nor were the unions able to resolve their old conflicts
in the machine room: they could promise no more than to
help avoid strikes, since the NGA would not tolerate compulsory arbitration. With the exception of a manning agreement offered by the *News of the World* machine assistants
(an eccentric group, as we have noted, since the 1840s), none

of the responses came near to meeting the company's demands, and by Christmas no agreement had been reached.

At this point, the balance of forces was by no means as one-sided as subsequent events might suggest. The unions were confident that while they might be impotent at Wapping, they could inflict sufficient hardship on News International to force Murdoch to compromise. Heavy picketing had been ineffective in the coal industry, but newspapers had only to be disrupted for a few hours to be rendered valueless. Though the unions would be vulnerable to legal action, there were many points along the distribution chain where pressure could be applied. The chapels were convinced that Murdoch could not produce his entire range of papers in Wapping and Glasgow alone. He needed capacity either in Bouverie Street or Grays Inn Road. Maxwell at this time was about to settle, certainly with heavy manning reductions, but with the closed shop intact and no legally binding agreements. Murdoch had compromised in the past. He also had to maintain cash flow since his bid for Metromedia was approaching completion in America. It was Fleet Street's ultimate poker game.

Events moved fast as January approached. Coils of razor wire went up round the Wapping plant, extra guards were employed and tactics discussed with the Tower Hamlets police. Lawyers began preparing the plethora of writs with which Murdoch would afford himself a measure of protection against secondary action. He now ordered both the Wapping and Glasgow plants into a 'state of readiness'. The East End might no longer be the haunt of print workers, but news of happenings in Wapping soon reached the pubs of Fleet Street. The chapels at Bouverie Street put in a desperate bid for a 'jobs for life' deal. This was rejected by the management, who in return served them with a formal six months' notice of the ending of their house agreements pending renegotiation. An advertising supplement for the *Sunday Times* was printed at Wapping on Saturday 18 January, and distributed through the TNT network: the only action Murdoch took in breach of an existing agreement.

The unions now made their final throw. Ballots were held

throughout News International's Fleet Street plants authorizing strike action to enforce the claim for job security. The results proved overwhelmingly in favour. Production on all Murdoch's titles was relatively trouble-free in the week of 20 January as the industry waited to see what he would do next. The TUC's general secretary, Norman Willis, took the initiative, offering what was rightly described as 'the best deal ever offered by any union to any national newspaper employer'. Although it rejected the total discretion required by management, including legally binding contracts, it contained substantial concessions: the right to introduce and manage new technology; demarcation disputes subject to 'binding TUC arbitration'; other industrial disputes also subject to 'ultimately binding arbitration which could be triggered unilaterally by either party'.

Murdoch was no longer interested. The Wapping presses were now warming up for a complete run of the *Sunday Times* the following weekend, with the daily titles planned to move there at the same time. Murdoch decided he would consider a deal only at Bouverie Street and Grays Inn Road, plants that he thought he still might need for full production. Talks finally broke down on the Willis package on 23 January. Murdoch remarked to waiting reporters: 'It's all too late. The Wapping factory, and management's overtures to the unions to work it, was started six years ago . . . If they had come to us with that [deal] two years ago we probably would have been delighted, but not now.' News International said that only a few hundred workers would in future be required at its existing Fleet Street works. For good measure, Murdoch now said he would require legally binding contracts there too.

Murdoch's position was strengthening with each decision made by the unions. Were the unions to sit tight, he would have to pay wages for two entire printing organizations, at least for six months. Had they let the *London Post* go ahead and allowed Wapping into production with Fleet Street still working, they could have inflicted a far more costly blow by striking later in the year. If they struck now, however, Murdoch could immediately dismiss them and relieve himself of redundancy obligations of up to £40 million, a point made to him in a leaked letter from his legal adviser. It was something the unions knew as well as he did. (The only legal restriction was that he should not re-employ any portion of the same staff within three months, thereby victimizing the others.) The unions complained that Murdoch had trapped them into a strike so as to be able to deprive them of redundancy money. Certainly he had raised the stakes with each round in the poker game. But the unions too could choose: either to work at Wapping on Murdoch's terms, or to accept a new deal at Bouverie Street and Grays Inn Road, or to sit tight and demand redundancy. The choices were harsh ones, but chapel officials had spent a profitable lifetime offering proprietors just such harsh choices. Now the balance of negotiating advantage had shifted against them.

The chapels rejected these options. All were an offence to the history of chapel potency in which they had been schooled. They chose brinkmanship and went on strike. They expected that mass picketing and the consequent disruption of Murdoch's distribution would eventually force him back to talks. They also assumed the co-operation of other unions, in particular of enough NUJ members to impede the papers' production. It was not a reckless assumption. News International was in considerable doubt as to how far to involve its NUJ chapels in contingency plans for a move: this was one group of existing workers that Wapping could not realistically do without. As events moved towards crisis, negotiation became acrimonious, culminating in an NUJ instruction that Wapping should be 'blacked'. Management waited until the last minute, wishing to offer the least amount of time for an anti-Wapping lobby to develop before each individual would have to make his or her own decision. Not until Friday 24 January were the journalists formally told they must move to Wapping, in return for an offer of an extra £2,000 a year plus health benefits. Those refusing to go would be deemed to be on strike – a moot point at law – and would be sacked. Otherwise, they should report to the Tower Hotel in St Katharine's Dock that weekend to be bussed into the fortified works. It was cavalier treatment of men and women traditionally regarded as the heart and soul of a newspaper. Those *Times* writers of a historical disposition grimly recalled the early days of Lord Northcliffe's custodianship.

Journalists on the *Sun* and the *News of the World* voted overwhelmingly to move; those on *The Times* and the *Sunday Times* were evenly split, but enough travelled east to enable continuous production of all titles – with the exception of the loss of the Saturday edition of *The Times* and the *Sun*. On arrival, the staff found desks and terminals waiting for them. American and Australian computer experts were on hand to give instruction. Inside all was eerily calm while outside pickets shouted obscenities. Many journalists had long talked of the day when the chapels that had so often sabotaged their work would be finally challenged and defeated. That day had now arrived and for many it seemed unpleasant and unreal. The writing staff had been treated peremptorily by the management, partly from a concern for secrecy, partly from a longstanding Murdoch inclination to take journalists for granted. A number resigned in protest; others found the Wapping environment unattractive and drifted away. It was an aspect of the move that caused Murdoch increasing trouble subsequently.

As TNT's 34-tonne lorries roared down the Wapping ramp and out through the barbed wire into the night on 25 January and on successive nights thereafter, the reaction of the pickets became more desperate. The full print order was not met for a number of weeks, with the *News of the World* blacked in Manchester and *The Times* supplements blacked for a while in Northampton. Murdoch offered to talk with the unions through ACAS, but only on the partial reopening of his old works. He considered paying up to £15 million into a hardship and re-training fund for his old workers. In April he offered the unions the Grays Inn Road works, lock, stock and barrel, for them to use to print their own paper. In June, these two offers became a formal deal, agreed with the union leaders, for a package of £50 million in compensation plus Grays Inn Road in return for an end to the picketing. Murdoch would not, however, concede recognition for the traditional unions inside Wapping. This package was rejected by the strikers by a clear majority. With most of the original 5,500 now employed elsewhere (SOGAT '82 confirmed it was paying only a third of its sacked members unemployment benefit), the vote appeared to be a combination of no confidence in the union leadership and a continued conviction that Murdoch might yet come up with a better offer. The picketing continued into the autumn, sporadically violent, with the hopelessness of the demonstrators balancing in misery the demoralization of the journalistic staff cooped up behind the wire. In the course of the summer, Murdoch's paper warehouse was burned out, his staff were physically assaulted and his vehicles were constantly vandalized. He might have won a famous victory, but at least the vanquished could prevent him walking free over the battlefield.

The EETPU struck to its guns within the TUC, with Eric Hammond promising only that he would not sign an actual agreement with Murdoch (which would thus formalize any poaching). News International found its production at Wapping lengthening as staff became more proficient. Glasgow was running smoothly. Managers freed from the need to negotiate every move with their chapels could experiment and manoeuvre to increase productivity, and what had seemed an emergency measure was becoming permanent. New capacity was planned at Wapping. Murdoch had no further need for satellite printing in London. He no longer needed British Rail or SOGAT '82 distributors – though both would have been cheaper than TNT. The *UK Press Gazette* estimated News International was saving £65 million on labour costs alone, against an additional £15–20 million on distribution. Interviewed by the *New York Times* in March 1986, Rupert Murdoch could not resist some modest gloating. 'The unions completely messed it up,' he said bluntly. They could have had a deal in 1984 and again in 1985. They had been through the plant and knew what was in store: 'They were victims of their own delusions.' He calculated he would save £60 million annually. He had implemented a technologically complex investment in just ten months and converted a new plant to full working efficiency within a week. By any standards, it was an extraordinary managerial achievement.

Few of Murdoch's Fleet Street rivals saw it that way. However much they may have privately cheered the discomfiture of the unions, and looked forward to exploiting it industrially, their editorial columns were largely mute. Murdoch, bane of their lives for so long, had done what they had so often said was necessary but had never dared to do themselves: stand up to the chapels and ultimately confront them with a green-field option. He had also done it without any of them apparently being aware of it. No newspaper had fully investigated Wapping in the course of 1985, though some had repeated alarmist rumours from the left-wing press (including an accurate one in the September *Socialist Worker*). The *Observer* carried regular gossip about low morale at Times Newspapers and acceded to union pressure to lay off casual staff who worked during the week on Murdoch titles. It refused to print a review by Bernard Levin because he also wrote for *The Times*. The *Guardian* focused attention on the civil rights hardships of the pickets or on shortfalls in News International's circulation. The *Daily Telegraph* refused a Murdoch advertisement. College common rooms and Labour local authorities banned Murdoch titles from their libraries. The Labour party refused to talk to Murdoch journalists. Fleet Street managers generally waited on edge to see how News International would 'spend' its surge in profits: would it slash advertising rates or cover prices or, they fondly hoped, merely pocket the surplus and take it as far away from Fleet Street as possible?

The events at Wapping inevitably stole much of Eddy Shah's thunder. It was perhaps as well. Six weeks after the move to Wapping, *Today* appeared on the streets. With a new staff, new technology and a new production and distribution system, it was plagued with troubles. The colour seemed tawdry alongside the preprinted gravure used by other tabloids as first-day 'spoilers'. Much of the equipment proved too complex and sensitive for the robust needs of a daily paper. *Today* was afflicted with a succession of accidents as stories were lost in the computer, transmission times lengthened and colour pictures appeared out of register. The paper was on sale, settling down in the summer to an as-yet-unaudited circulation of about 400,000. But despite forecasts, this was not enough.

Shah's financial predictions proved as inadequate as his faith in new technology. In June the additional cost of extra staff and shortfalls in sales and advertising revenue led to a cash crisis. Urgent talks were held both with his existing backers and, more ominously, with established Fleet Street groups interested in his new presses. These reportedly included Robert Maxwell, Associated Newspapers and even Rupert Murdoch, as well as such eccentric outsiders as Richard Branson of Virgin Records and the Al Fayed brothers. Eventually Tiny Rowland of Lonrho and the *Observer* came forward to head a £24-million capital restructuring – effectively doubling Shah's original start-up cost. Lonrho took a 35 per cent stake in the paper, generously leaving Shah in formal control. However, the managing director of Lonrho's George Outram publishing company, Terry Cassidy, was moved down from Glasgow to take over the running of the rescued firm. New editorial executives were hired from Fleet Street to bolster the flagging staff and to revamp the paper's appearance. At the same time, Shah conceded the failure of his alternative distribution and joined the orthodox wholesale network, using SOGAT '82 labour. The Sunday *Today*, which had performed worse than the daily, was now clearly vulnerable to a Lonrho decision to move the printing of the *Observer* out of central London on to its presses, a likelihood increased in August when the *Observer* announced that its editorial offices would be going from Queen Victoria Street to Battersea. That month Shah finally sold half of his remaining shares to Lonrho and 'returned' to Cheshire. Fleet Street had struck back, and won.

Eddy Shah suffered the predictable scorn of those he had berated a year earlier. His editor, Brian MacArthur, graciously ate his own words (on rice paper) at an industry conference in Paris in April. Yet *Today* merely confirmed the iron law of new publishing (and broadcasting) ventures: that it is not the first day that matters but the first day of the first relaunch. Shah had a product up and selling. His 400,000 in three months might not have seemed so puny had he not oversold himself in advance. It was a sector of the market, the 'middle ground', that had long been regarded as in terminal decline. The paper itself was editorially ragged and could only improve. A new venture had gained admission to the Fleet Street club, even if an existing member had to grab it exhausted on the steps and drag it through the door.

More significant than Shah's personal fate was that by the summer of 1986 – through his efforts and those of Rupert Murdoch – over a third of the national morning and Sunday newspapers bought in Britain were being produced by non-print union labour. Fleet Street's centuries-old chapel monopoly had been broken. There was understandable acrimony within the unions over who was to blame. The NGA's London Region consultative conference, meeting in March, was a display of angry confusion.* Speakers accepted that direct inputting, even legally binding contracts, had to come. What to chapel members was inexcusable was that the union leadership under Tony Dubbins had lost them control of the new plant and thus conceded a cardinal principle: that Fleet Street titles should never appear except by courtesy of the NGA.

Brenda Dean of SOGAT '82 endured similar recriminations at her June conference. She had felt obliged to opt for a strike because she feared being dragged into one by her militants. Her executive had confidently expected that after months of fierce picketing, Murdoch would sue for peace. As it was, the strike had cost her members not just their jobs but also their redundancy entitlement. The union was deeply divided. Many SOGAT '82 wholesale distributors were gladly handling News International titles. With the union's funds sequestered for much of the summer, SOGAT '82's non-Fleet Street members began to resent bitterly the cost and aggravation which a wealthy and intransigent minority of their number had inflicted on them. Yet still it ran against the grain to admit defeat.

*See the April edition of the NGA journal, *Print*.

Both the chapels and their national leadership – long used to being guided by history – had been confronted by a circumstance for which history offered no precedent: a proprietor able to refuse the asking price for their labour. Some printers accused the national negotiators of straightforward ineptitude, claiming they should have detected the altered balance of power and negotiated the chapels into Wapping at any cost. The electricians had stolen a march on them. Others argued the reverse, that their leaders had already made reckless concessions to get into Wapping, which threatened future agreements across the rest of Fleet Street. The Willis proposals tabled in January were now an embarrassingly public precedent, enticing other hard-pressed proprietors to pick it up. It would have been safer by far to leave Wapping behind its barbed wire and concentrate on preventing its example from spreading. A third of Fleet Street had been lost to the companionships, much as a third of New York's press had been lost in the 1960s, but chapel power, and its capacity to generate individual earnings, survived in the other two-thirds. This should not now be put at risk by foolishly pretending Murdoch could be induced to barter new concessions. While the first viewpoint might have been wise counsel in 1985, by the middle of 1986, the second was the only realistic way of cutting the unions' losses. It acknowledged what appeared to be a *fait accompli* and sought to stabilize a new equilibrium, a point to which we return in chapter eleven.

Why had Murdoch not acted before? The only answer is that not until 1985 had enough pieces of the jigsaw of Fleet Street reform fallen into place. There is no evidence of collusion between Murdoch and Shah – though Murdoch undoubtedly admired Shah's determination and wished him well. Both men staged their challenges to Fleet Street convention independent of the other. Shah even fought shy of using TNT when told of Murdoch's shareholding in it. The EETPU involvement, crucial in both cases, was initiated by the union and its friends separately to each party.

The prospect of Shah – however disappointing the reality – undoubtedly acted as goad not just on Rupert Murdoch but on Robert Maxwell, David Stevens and indeed on the rest of Fleet Street. In 1985 his hyperbolic talk and beguiling prospectus were enough to worry any tabloid proprietor, wrestling as they all were with the tail-end of the bingo war. Behind Shah lay Mrs Thatcher's trade union legislation and her defeat of Arthur Scargill's miners, effected in the spring of 1985. Behind him also was the knowledge that for decades the industry had been open to just such an attack as he and others were now launching.

Yet in the foreground was Rupert Murdoch. Faced with Bruce Matthews's despairing report on the state of his Wapping venture in January of that same year, he could have decided, as he had decided many times before, to back off and play safe. From his desk in New York, he had good reason to treat the London chapels with circumspection, to guard his British assets and concentrate risk on his American adventures. He did not do so. Fleet Street drew him back. The proprietorship of entrepreneurial virility, already detected in Robert Maxwell and David Stevens, found its arch-exponent in Murdoch. Once again he had gambled and won.

# 11

## CONCLUSION: THE MARKET FOR GLORY

For the past century, the idea of the press as the 'fourth estate of the realm' has beguiled proprietor and editor alike. Under Delane, *The Times* in 1852 presented the industry as 'daily and for ever appealing to the enlightened force of public opinion, anticipating if possible the march of events, standing upon the breach between the present and the future, extending its survey to the horizon of the world'. Three years later, Henry Reeve in the *Edinburgh Review* declared that the 'vast and preponderating power' of the press had no less a right than Parliament to democratic credentials: 'If a member of the fourth estate differs with his constituents and incurs their displeasure, then he must abdicate or recant as surely as a member of the Lower House, and far more promptly.' The market place was as democratic a system of accountability as the ballot box. This attractive thesis was happily acknowledged by the two leading proprietorial families of the period, Walter of *The Times* and Levy of the *Daily Telegraph*. It was adopted by the 'press barons' after the turn of the century, who compared circulation with votes (before the universal franchise) and ranked themselves with cabinet ministers. It has remained central to Fleet Street's claim to political significance ever since.

The concept of the press as an independent element in the British constitution is not easy to sustain. Through most of the last century and well into the present one, newspapers were founded or purchased by wealthy syndicates to further a party cause. The press, writes George Boyce, 'was an extension of the political system not a check or balance on Parliament or the executive'.* Those who paid the piper called the tune, and since few serious newspapers before (or even after) the Northcliffe era were financially secure, the tunes were customarily those of party or faction. Where journalists established an independent reputation – and between Delane and C. P. Scott plenty did – it was through the force of their intellect and the generosity of their owners. Editorial independence, long the totem of the professional journalist, has always depended on and been licensed by proprietorial independence, and that in turn requires proprietors with money, whether from internal profits or by access to cross-subsidy.

In the first half of the twentieth century, more papers were able to publish free of the constraints of political subsidy. The new generation of mass-market proprietors could rely on their own profits to give them status as custodians of the fourth estate. They could stand free on Trollope's Mount Olympus, 'whence issue forth fifty thousand nightly edicts for the governance of a subject nation'.† Northcliffe, Rothermere, Beaverbrook, Camrose, Cadbury regarded themselves as political grandees whose large readerships invested in them both a right and a duty to protect the national interest. Some might have been statesmen *manqués*, cravenly seeking honour for themselves and position for their offspring. Most were convinced Conservatives, albeit often disloyal ones. Megalomania might lead them to overact their role: Northcliffe and Rothermere were, as a result, called to account by Lloyd George and Baldwin. Yet the press barons, properly so-called, were collectively distinct from party politics and thus gave the fourth estate a substantive connotation. Their editors might be their paid servants, but they were not the servants of political parties.

---

*For Boyce's reassessment of this period of press history, see bibliography.
†*The Warden.*

However, though profit undoubtedly made proprietors more inclined to political independence, profit was neither a sufficient nor a necessary condition for it. As the century progressed, papers found other sources of cross-subsidy than from political parties. Many of the most 'independent' editors of this century ran financially disastrous publications. All they needed – and by definition found – was a willingness on someone's part to meet their losses. In the 1890s the *Westminster Gazette* enjoyed a stable existence ostensibly free of party subvention. Its subsidy came from the profits on *Titbits*, transferred to the *Gazette* by its owner, George Newnes, who was an enthusiastic Liberal and felt the *Gazette* should be so too. Whether this private-sector support made the paper more or less 'independent' of political interference than, say, the Liberal party's *News Chronicle* or the TUC's *Daily Herald* in the 1930s, is a moot point. When Newnes 'wearied of the *Gazette*' in 1908 and it was sold to a Liberal syndicate later dominated by Lord Cowdray, it did not become more or less Liberal. Nor was the independent *Daily Telegraph* appreciably less Conservative between the wars than its rival, the *Morning Post*, which after 1924 was backed by a group of rich Conservatives.* As both Koss and Boyce point out, the change in the *Morning Post*'s proprietorship from 'independent' to 'party' status saw remarkably little change in the conduct of its editor, H. A. Gwynne. His outlook was that of a man in constant intercourse with the upper echelons of the Conservative party. In 1924 he merely exchanged one source of politically 'die-hard' subsidy for another.

After 1945 cross-subsidy became more rather than less dominant as a feature of Fleet Street. *The Times* required backing from the Astors, from the Thomsons and then from other titles in the News International stable. The *Observer* was supported over six years by ARCO. The *Guardian* received subsidy from the *Manchester Evening News*. Certainly when George Newnes paid for the *Westminster Gazette*

---

*The *Morning Post* was acquired from Lady Bathurst, the only instance I can find in this century of a woman Fleet Street proprietor.

he did so specifically to secure a loyally Liberal publication, whereas ARCO's support of the *Observer* and Thomson's of *The Times* were made to protect their continued editorial independence. Most proprietors seeking to justify cross-subsidy have done so in the cause of editorial independence – usually independence from a rival who might otherwise 'change its existing character' – though Thomson's purchase of *The Times* changed its character drastically. In contrast, the *Daily Telegraph* has been proprietorially independent throughout its history, yet under the Berrys its editorials were far more pleasing to the Conservative leadership than the supposedly 'dependent' *Daily Herald* and *News Chronicle* were to the Labour and Liberal parties respectively. The *Daily Mail* has not taken a penny from the Conservative party, yet it has been subsidized by the Harmsworth family for years as a loyal Conservative newspaper.

The *Guardian* offers even less help towards a definition of press independence in terms of profit or loss. It has long maintained that it is uniquely independent. Its television advertising states that unlike the rest of the press, the *Guardian* has no proprietor, is not a 'puppet on a string' and can therefore 'dance to its own tune'. Its journalists have revelled in their freedom from the need for commercial viability and from the insecurity this might imply. The more left-wing among them have even suggested that this has somehow liberated them from the profit motive, to write whatever they choose. Yet the *Guardian*'s constitution is carefully designed to maintain one of the most clear-cut proprietorial personalities in Fleet Street: the Liberal/radicalism of the Scott family. This has had to be supported by a cross-subsidy from other journalists shackled to the profitability of the *Manchester Evening News*. (A Marxist – not a very good one – might even cite the *Guardian* as an instance of exploitative private capitalism.) To C. P. Scott, its editor from 1872 to 1929, the paper was 'an engine for the moving of opinion'; it would neglect its role as a news-gatherer, not at some risk to its commercial prospects, 'but at the peril of its soul'. This tradition remains vested in the Scott Trustees, formally the proprietors of the newspaper through the Scott Trust, a self-selecting group who are, in the words of one, Charles Scott, 'the sort of people who would read the *Guardian* or appreciate the *Guardian* or in some way be sympathetic to the *Guardian*. I don't think anyone with right-wing views would be appointed to the Trust.'* Each new editor is required on appointment to conduct the paper 'on the same lines and in the same spirit as heretofore', a phrase taken from the will made in 1905 of Scott's cousin and son of the paper's founder, John Edward Taylor. Even the company chairman is required to be in sympathy with what is enigmatically called 'the *Guardian* outlook'.

Both Taylor and Scott were Mancunian liberals who understood perfectly that the high principles of the then *Manchester Guardian* depended on the circulation, revenue and profitability of a commercial concern. As proprietors they chose to devote its profits to a particular cause: the preservation of a newspaper broadly on the left of the political spectrum, cross-subsidized from elsewhere within the business if need be. Since the Second World War, this has meant from the *Manchester Evening News*. Though the company as a whole might not be in business to make money, by definition it could not lose it. The motivation was no different from that proclaimed by Lord Beaverbrook. Like him, the Scott Trust needs secure reserves to make propaganda, though the trustees would never put it so crudely. Unlike Beaverbrook, the business acumen of their managers was enough to protect the paper under its trust deeds. No other paper has gone to such lengths to ensure that its editorial columns remain loyal to the wishes of its original proprietor: not even the Harmsworth family and their *Daily Mail*, whose subsidy from the provincial press exactly paralleled the *Guardian*'s throughout the 1970s. If a *Guardian* editor, once appointed, suffered a brainstorm and decided to back the Conservative party, it is a safe bet that the spirit of Scott would descend and find ways and means to cast him swiftly into oblivion.†

---

*See the *Guardian*, 23 June 1986.
†The *Guardian*, however, is not the only paper to have had a ghost as a proprietor, see page 44.

The bonds that tie a newspaper to its owner depend not on financial viability but on the motives of those who have capital invested in it. The history of these motives since the nineteenth century is often regarded as a progression from egocentricity to banal commercialism. As the press barons departed the scene, they were succeeded by descendants who parodied their public posturing and wasted their assets. They in turn were followed by a new generation of businessmen, often from abroad, whose fortunes had been made outside Fleet Street. These men, so conventional wisdom had it (for instance, among Royal Commissioners), would modernize the industry and prepare it for technological innovation. Many would not be owners as such but, rather, corporate executives, answerable to boards and shareholders. Newspapers would have to be profitable to survive. Many would close.

This synopsis was clearly wrong. The attractions that have drawn men into proprietorship have been largely non-pecuniary up to the present day: from a fascination with politics to a yearning for public recognition, from a desire to prove oneself a tough entrepreneur to a simple bid for admission to that ill-defined but vigorous social organism, the British Establishment. Leonard Woolf summed it up in his autobiography: 'A magnetic field of highly charged importance, influence, and power is created around every newspaper, and everyone connected with it is subjected to its effect and to any vocational delusions to which it gives rise.'* By the Second World War, the bluff of proprietor-as-statesman had been called, if not by Lloyd George and Baldwin at least by the finding of the 1938 study by Political and Economic Planning that a newspaper's political opinions bothered few of its readers. Yet however deluded the claims of the early proprietors, they gave Fleet Street an aura. They turned a commercial product – a popular newspaper – into a national institution and in doing so made a public figure of its manufacturer. This achievement brought in its train half a century of imitators ready to salvage any title, endure any

*Quoted by Boyce, see bibliography.

loss, subsidize any malpractice for the chance to own a national newspaper.

To Roy Thomson, proprietorship of Printing House Square was a similar apotheosis to that enjoyed by Lord Northcliffe and J. J. Astor. To Cecil King, the *Daily Mirror* possessed the same Olympian status on the left as the *Daily Mail* possessed for his uncles on the right. Robert Anderson rescued the *Observer* as an act of philanthropy in terms that might have been scripted by Delane (see page 61). Lord Matthews at the *Daily Express* saw himself as striving for Britain's greatness and revelled in the resulting comparison with Beaverbrook. Like Beaverbrook, he had to make it 'secure in reserves', but it was not reserves that secured him the glory of a coronet. He was ennobled by Mrs Thatcher for keeping the *Daily Express* in being and true to the Tory cause when, in 1980, its losses were still enormous – an old-fashioned political reward for cross-subsidy. Conrad Black's vision of proprietorship at the *Daily Telegraph* might be more sophisticated than that of Lord Camrose, but it would have been recognized, and admired, by his predecessor, Lord Burnham. Robert Maxwell's custodianship of the *Daily Mirror*, apart from keeping it secure for Labour, has at times seemed a carbon copy of that of its founder, Lord Northcliffe. Even Rupert Murdoch, an exception to most Fleet Street rules, was so shocked at his ostracism by the London Establishment that he migrated to America. Yet he returned to try successively for the *Observer*, Beaverbrook Newspapers and *The Times* in what seemed to many a wholly traditional thirst for proprietorial revenge.

Nor did these men behave any less idiosyncratically for being, many of them, subject to public shareholders. Beaverbrook constructed a two-tier share structure to keep hold of voting control when he needed equity capital for expansion. But even when he transferred his voting shares for tax purposes to the trustees of the Beaverbrook Foundation, he rightly remarked, 'I no longer control; I still dominate.'* Lord Matthews and Cecil King, neither of whom technically

*Chester and Fenby, see bibliography.

215

owned their papers, could say the same. Both were ultimately ousted by boards or shareholders, but both behaved within their offices as traditional, omnipotent proprietors. By contrast, Lord Hartwell's sovereignty over the *Daily Telegraph* may have been total, but it evaporated when losses mounted and no source of cross-subsidy was available. The strongly left-wing tradition of the *Daily Mirror* managed to survive the passage of the years and a changing corporate ownership. Indeed the paper with perhaps the most truly 'independent' editorial staff, the *Financial Times*, is one that has been run since the 1950s under the most paternal of family regimes, that of the Pearsons and their relatives, the Hares.

Fleet Street newspapers tend to have a political and editorial personality that is so strong as frequently to dominate those who manage, edit and even own them. It is this that has made them such suitable products for the market for glory. It is also the reason why their proprietors so defy classification. The only reasonably safe conclusion is that proprietorship has changed remarkably little over the period surveyed in this book. The more it has appeared to change, the more it has emerged the same. The clothes of the emperors are magnificent as they march up Fleet Street, waving to the cheering crowds. Only when some turn right into Carey Street* is any nakedness apparent. The tradition of glory established and bequeathed to the industry by the great proprietors was an enduring legacy. It supplied national newspapers with rescue capital through a lean quarter century (1960–85) when commercial logic indicated widespread collapse. It preserved a degree of diversity in the British press which would otherwise have vanished.

Have the events of 1985–6 described in the last chapter shattered this legacy? At first glance, the answer might be yes. After six years of Conservative rule, a handful of brave knights were ready to challenge the dragon of chapel power, armed with the sword of Reuters' gold and the shield of new anti-union laws. They were goaded into action by the rise of

*The traditional home of the bankruptcy court is just off Fleet Street.

Eddy Shah and by the need to modernize their printing capacity. Some of their motives had certainly changed from those of their predecessors. The industrial climate of Britain in the early to mid-1980s was markedly different from that of a quarter-century before. Businessmen could gain public recognition for how they made their money rather than for how they spent it. A Fleet Street proprietor did not have to dabble in politics to achieve access to the Establishment – though it still helped if he gave generously to political funds. The image of the tycoon was no longer that of the Edwardian entrepreneur, moving swiftly from mercantile to landed status, adopting an aristocratic lifestyle and putting his son through Eton to a safe Conservative seat. Mrs Thatcher's Britain gave credit to those prepared to innovate, reorganize, confront traditional practices, be ruthless where necessary (and sometimes where not). By hurling himself at the market place, and specially at the market for unionized labour, the industrialist could demonstrate similar machismo to that with which Northcliffe, Beaverbrook and Rothermere hurled themselves at Asquith or Baldwin.

This implies a change in the nature, if not in the magnetic force, of Fleet Street's appeal in the 1980s. At least the energy and egocentricity were now directed at securing a more efficient and competitive industry. The second wave of new proprietors was not intent, as some had feared, on closing titles and realizing assets. There was no glory in that. They wanted to make their newspapers public monuments to their entrepreneurial talents, as their predecessors wanted monuments to their political power. But it seemed that, for once, the market for glory and the market for newspapers were on converging courses. Not just Rupert Murdoch but David Stevens at the *Daily Express* and Robert Maxwell at the *Daily Mirror* (despite his support for Labour) seemed tailor-made for Mrs Thatcher's new Britain. Their initial declarations were business-like, their chapel confrontations spectacular and their attack on production costs obsessive. Less demonstrative proprietors followed where they had led. The *Financial Times*, the *Guardian*, the *Daily Telegraph*, the *Observer* and the *Daily Mail* produced proposals involving unprecedented concessions by composing-room chapels on new technology (some a revival of the old 1975 plans). This sudden determination in the course of 1985–6 threw the unions into retreat across the entire industry.

Nor were they alone. While born-again proprietors were flexing their muscles, in early 1986 a plethora of new titles promised to pour through the hole that Murdoch and Shah were blasting in the wall of Fleet Street oligopoly. At one point these included a new tabloid (*Good Day*) and a London evening (the *Daily News*) from Robert Maxwell; two other London evenings, the *London News* from the Chequepoint group and possibly a revived *Evening News* from Associated Newspapers; Murdoch's temporarily shelved *London Post*; and a left-wing Sunday paper, the *News on Sunday*, originated by the Mirror group's former chairman, Clive Thornton, and planned for a launch in Manchester in 1987. Much the most ambitious, the *Independent*, was started by Andreas Whittam Smith with a group of defectors from the embattled *Telegraph* and *Times* titles, a sign of the decline of these two ancient giants of Fleet Street in the face of the challenge from the *Guardian* and the *Financial Times*. With £18 million amassed from 100 investors by the bankers, Charterhouse Japhet, and a staff of more than 120 journalists, the *Independent* was the first new 'quality' daily to be launched this century, attacking one of Britain's most entrenched and conservative markets, that for serious journalism. This activity suggested that the perceived cost of entry into Fleet Street was tumbling. There was even heady talk of a new dawn of free communication similar to that which followed the abolition of the Stamp Acts in the middle of the nineteenth century.* Every body of opinion could have its own computer typesetter and run off its own newspaper. Capitalism and free speech were at last in holy alliance.

By the middle of 1986, however, just a year after Murdoch and Shah had embarked on their new projects, there were signs that the revolution might, at best, be partial. Many new proposals began to sink from view. Only the *Independent* and

*Goodhart and Wintour, see bibliography.

the *Daily News* were staffed up for production, planned in October. Shah's baptism by fire was an awful warning to other new entrants, as he conceded SOGAT '82 distribution and eventually surrendered the control of his company to the proprietor of the *Observer*, Tiny Rowland. As his costs rose to cover editorial and technical miscalculations, the gap between his own and more traditional methods of production narrowed. The *Independent* cautiously decided to sub-contract printing and distribution to conventional (print-union) operators. At the *Daily Express* and *Daily Mirror*, chapels that had been forced to concede up to a third of their formal 'jobs' but allowed to keep their negotiating weapons began to recoup on the shop floor what had been conceded in the boardroom. Fleet Street abounded with rumours of redundancy deadlines missed, 'abolished' chapels still in place, savings 'not as great as anticipated'. At the *Financial Times*, the *Guardian* and the *Daily Telegraph*, managements preferred to emphasize their distance from Rupert Murdoch's innovation. 'A revolution, without the conflict' was how the *Financial Times* presented its own deal, which included partial direct inputting in its composing room. All were happy to negotiate a Docklands move with their exist-ing chapels. As Harry Roche, manager of the *Guardian*, told the *UK Press Gazette*, 'We want to go down this path with the traditional unions in the traditional way.' No group pur-sued a single-union deal for their new machine rooms, though at various stages such a cure for many of Fleet Street's past ills might have been achieved, with SOGAT '82 defying the NGA to do its worst. In July 1986 both the *Guardian* and the *Daily Telegraph* confirmed they would not be seeking legally binding agreements with their chapels in Docklands.

As had occurred ten years earlier, proprietorship's cutting edge was blunted by a combination of exhaustion, rising prosperity and, on the part of the newcomers, involvement in the pleasures of editing. The *Guardian* and the *Daily Mail*, long-term loss-makers, anticipated profits in 1986. Execu-tives throughout Fleet Street were struggling against the clock to get agreements in place for when their Docklands plants came on stream, hoping that 'the changed industrial climate' would ensure their enforcement. It was the biggest upheaval in the history of the industry and had already brought them gains beyond the dreams of a decade earlier. Chapel confrontation that might disrupt production was unlikely to be greeted with enthusiasm in the boardroom. Corporate virtue could once more be discovered in managerial weakness. As Lord Goodman, former chairman of the *Observer* and of the NPA, told the 1977 Royal Commission with his characteristic irony, 'some of the greatest moral courage displayed by newspapers has been a readiness to capitulate'. Rupert Murdoch might have shown rival proprietors the fruits of total victory, but for most it meant one battle too many. Besides, David Stevens, Robert Maxwell and Conrad Black were finding, as so many had before, that running newspapers could be fascinating. They worried over their circulations, summoned their editors and 'suggested' improvements. The bug was biting.

To the chapels, battered by the events of the previous year, this was good news. What they needed above all was time: time to cordon off Wapping from the rest of Fleet Street; time to redeploy their 5,500 News International members; time to absorb the 'jobs' shaken out from other titles (by methods examined in chapter four); time to regroup and win back negotiating leverage over new composing technology as they had successfully done at the *Daily Mirror* in the 1970s. While proprietors played short, the chapels could play long, but they needed a breathing space. The drawing-out of the dispute with Murdoch at Wapping thus served a number of purposes. Above all, it made confrontation in Docklands extremely unattractive to other proprietors. Every month that the razor wire and picketing could be sustained at Wapping was a month gained elsewhere. Murdoch's expensive road distribution system stood ready to supplant the SOGAT '82/British Rail network, but only if other titles could be induced to join. Violent picketing forestalled this. The EETPU had shown that traditional printers, apprenticed and trained, were not needed in Docklands. But as long as Murdoch was embattled, other proprietors would have to spend a fortune on security to follow his lead. The chapels still controlled two-thirds of Fleet Street's output and were determined to see no further erosion. With a general election in 1987–8 and the possible succour of a Labour Government, it was a matter of playing for time.

The most serious threat that Murdoch and his fellow innovators posed to the rest of the industry was in the market place. By producing newspapers more cheaply, they could undercut their rivals and worsen their competitive position. *The Times* could steal a march on the *Guardian*'s young readers and push the *Daily Telegraph* even further into loss. The *Sun* could force the *Daily Mirror* and *Daily Express* to a deal, perhaps involving the closure of the *Star*. This threat clearly remains in the background. However, News International soon declared that it would use its increased profit not to cut its advertising rates and thus threaten revenues across the industry, but to improve the newspapers themselves.* As long as Murdoch's rivals were unable to reduce their costs to Wapping levels, he and his managers could enjoy the fruits of their enterprise untroubled and supply useful collateral for his American ventures. The attractions of the 'quiet life' were as potent in post-Wapping Fleet Street as in the rest of British industry.

The British newspaper market appeared largely immune to the upheavals in its industrial structure. Changes were taking place in newspaper production, not in the newspaper as a product. Apart from the promise of later edition times and more colour pages, Eddy Shah's revolution was technological, not editorial. As with the contraptions of Victorian inventors, the ingenuity of an innovation is not a sufficient condition for its market success. The steady decline of the *Daily Mirror* and the *Daily Express* was not halted by spectacular and much-publicized changes in ownership. There was no shortage of bidders for Fleet Street titles throughout the 1970s and 1980s, even when outgoing owners tried to protect the editorial character of their inheritance,

*Address by Bruce Matthews to Press '86 conference in Paris, April 1986.

for instance at *The Times* and the *Daily Mirror*, by attaching strings to their sale. But the success of individual titles in the market place continued to depend, as it had always done, on readers' perception of the product itself, ultimately on its editorial character and quality.

Just as readers reported in 1938 that they were unmoved by the politics of the press barons, so they appeared unmoved by the 'corporate machismo' of 1986. The accustomed paper that appeared each day on the newsstand seemed much the same – albeit 'not quite what it used to be'. The news was still the news. The mirror that Fleet Street held up to the world might appear more tarnished and cracked than before, but it continued to reflect familiar images. By comparison with the events that newspapers normally record, they themselves make a parochial tale. Newspapers have never featured large in the lives of most of their readers, certainly not the biggest-selling ones. The 1977 Royal Commission found most readers of Britain's most popular paper, the *Sun*, regarded it as short on news, sensational in its coverage and inclined to inaccuracy.* They said they would not miss it much if it was not there, but they still bought it because it was 'enjoyable'. When the breakfast table has been cleared and the morning paper turned firmly to the evening's television guide, other distractions soon claim the public's attention.

Fleet Street remains an industry in uneasy equilibrium between militant chapels, conservative readers and proprietorial motivation. Undoubtedly the events of 1985–6 shook that equilibrium. Chapel autonomy was undermined and the conservatism of the market was challenged. The weight attached to proprietorial motivation accordingly rose on the scales. Yet this motivation has not been wholeheartedly directed towards pushing home commercial advantage. The chapels seem certain to recover much of their old vigour. Eddy Shah's experience suggests that British newspaper readers are difficult to entice away from their accustomed

*Report by Social and Community Planning Research for the Royal Commission, see bibliography.

products. Most important, there is no reason to believe that the attractions that have traditionally brought new money to Fleet Street have diminished, despite the 'down-market' drift of tabloid titles and the ever-more-dominant role of broadcast media.

National newspapers remain an important cog in the machine of modern publicity and communication. Owning a newspaper is still a short cut to national prominence. The upheaval will have cut costs and possibly increased the range of competition, but this implies no more than a cheaper subscription to the Fleet Street club. The market for glory may achieve a new equilibrium at a lower price, but this will not diminish its appeal. As long as the magnetism of proprietorship survives, the scales will be tilted in the traditional direction: towards continuity of production and a happy hunting ground for any combination of workers ready to exploit the transient nature of the product.

I have been sceptical of the constitutional claims made for Britain's fourth estate. Far from acting as watchdog on the body politic, Fleet Street has so often served as its lapdog. However proprietorially independent, it has integrated itself into the political Establishment rather than stood over against it. At the same time, its manifest bias towards the right of the political spectrum has had little or no impact on electoral politics. The press has rarely been more pro-Conservative than in 1945 (a Labour landslide) or more pro-Labour than in 1955 (a Conservative landslide). There is no guarantee that a multiplicity of titles yields any particular diversity of opinion, nor that a diffusion of owners yields a constitutional dividend. Five of the six British tabloids (excluding *Today*) are unmistakably Conservative; three are almost carbon copies of each other. By way of contrast, those great American liberal organs, the *New York Times* and the *Washington Post*, enjoy quasi-monopolies in covering American politics, without drowning out the voice of American conservatism. Political access to the press might seem more generous in Britain, but it would be tendentious to argue that America has a less democratic or less open political society as a result.

Indeed, where diversity has led to unstable competition, it can be the enemy of a 'watchdog' press. Many newspapermen feel that Fleet Street's present prosperity has accompanied, if anything, a decline in journalistic performance, certainly in the readiness of the press to act courageously or scrutinize Government. The Fleet Street press is not synonymous with the profession of 'serious journalism': it merely supplies a selection of platforms on to which the journalist must scramble in order to sell his wares. The profession contracts its skills to a newspaper much as a printer contracts his craft.* Political news and comment often survive on sufferance even in the most 'quality' of newspapers. Circulation battles and cost-cutting exercises tend to drive out material not of the widest appeal – hence the pressure on foreign coverage in recent years. To cite America again, newspapers such as the *Washington Post* without close rivals breathing down their necks can afford to devote more space and staff resources to the affairs of Government than their British counterparts. A lack of diversity yields profit and profit can, in the right hands, mean more responsible and thorough journalism.

Demands are made periodically for public subsidy to keep open particular titles or to diversify Fleet Street ownership. In the 1970s it was feared that the *Guardian* might be forced to close and that the *Daily Mirror* might be sold to a proprietor unsympathetic to its Labour tradition, leaving the left with no substantial daily paper to plead its cause. This would certainly have made the subsidy debate more immediate. In the event, the private sector came to the rescue. Schemes suggested by a minority of the 1977 Royal Commission and by Lord McCarthy for the TUC, essentially directed at re-establishing a paper loyal to Labour, have come to nothing. Indeed, it is easier to argue the case for subsidy *ad hoc* than to construct any theory to sustain it. As Colin Seymour-Ure has pointed out in his lucid analysis of the press's relationship to politics,† the more one asks how many

---

*Jeremy Tunstall has drawn useful distinctions between the journalistic profession and newspapers as institutions, see bibliography.
†*The Press, Politics and the Public*, see bibliography.

papers are needed to 'provide an adequate safeguard against the dangerous consequences of bias and distortion . . . the more the exercise becomes ludicrous'. How many titles are enough? How much concentration might yield an improvement in journalistic quality before it yields a restriction in range of opinion? And who decides? If one paper is to be subsidized from the public purse, what about those already subsidized from private sources? Might they claim subsidy? Ultimately, how much weight can be attached to whose opinions to justify a claim to public support?

To the left, and to all who feel the British press pays inadequate attention to their views, the answer lies at present with the will – and whim – of capitalist proprietors, editors and subordinate journalists operating in an oligopolistic market. The only reply to this must be Churchill's sanguine defence of democracy, that the system may be full of imperfections but that all others are worse. It is a valuable activity of the press, whether or not it is defined as a 'constitutional function', to scrutinize, criticize, embarrass and, in the final analysis, even undermine the powers that be. The obstacles to journalism performing this function – including those supplied from within the newspaper industry – are severe enough without the added handicap of cash limits and Treasury monitoring. It may be that one day Fleet Street, like its Swedish counterpart, will be publicly subsidized. As long as politicians are convinced that newspapers are important to their daily work and have public money available to suborn them, subsidy will be on the political agenda. In Britain, that day is still far off. It would be a defeat not just for the private sector's ability to reflect consumer choice, but for the effectiveness of the press as public scrutineer.

Even an oligopoly in the private sector is preferable to a public sector monopoly or to the subtle versions of such a monopoly so far proposed. Editors and journalists may be engaged in a constant struggle – sometimes in league with, sometimes against their proprietors – to obtain the resources to do the job some of them see as central to their calling. Often they may fail. But it is this struggle, rather than the superficial competition between titles, that is central to Fleet

225

Street's constitutional significance. That is subject for another book. In the long term, however, it must be the case that the more proprietors there are, the better. It is a form of security that the industry can attract new capital and new entrepreneurs, whatever their diverse, even devious motivations. In the coverage of public affairs, as in the theatre, both actor and audience need more than one critic. Choice is a necessary condition for John Milton's 'free and open encounter between Truth and Falsehood'. The market for glory may be imperfect, but it supplies a degree of choice and thus a prerequisite for that encounter. It is in rude health.

# APPENDIX

*Selected Fleet Street circulation figures 1930–86 (millions)*

| Newspaper | 1930 | 1937 | 1947 | 1961 | 1966 | 1970 |
|---|---|---|---|---|---|---|
| Daily Herald/Sun | 1.12 | 2.03 | 2.13 | 1.41 | 1.24 | 1.61 |
| Daily Express | 1.69 | 2.20 | 3.06 | 4.32 | 3.98 | 3.56 |
| Daily Mail | 1.85 | 1.58 | 2.08 | 2.65 | 2.32 | 1.90 |
| News Chronicle/Today | 1.45 | 1.32 | 1.62 | | | |
| Daily Mirror | 1.07 | 1.33 | 3.70 | 4.58 | 5.13 | 4.57 |
| Daily Sketch/Daily Star | .93 | .68 | .77 | .99 | .86 | .78 |
| | [2] | [2] | 13.36 | 13.95 | 13.52 | 12.42 |
| The Times | .19 | .19 | .27 | .26 | .28 | .39 |
| Daily Telegraph | .16 | .56[1] | 1.02 | 1.25 | 1.35 | 1.41 |
| Guardian | | | .13 | .24 | .28 | .30 |
| Financial Times | | | .07 | .13 | .15 | .17 |
| | [2] | [2] | 1.49 | 1.88 | 2.07 | 2.27 |
| News of the World | 3.41 | 3.85 | 7.89 | 6.69 | 6.15 | 6.23 |
| Sunday People | 2.50 | 3.41 | 4.67 | 5.45 | 5.56 | 5.14 |
| Sunday Mirror/Pictorial | 1.95 | 1.35 | 4.01 | 5.32 | 5.22 | 4.83 |
| Sunday Express | .93 | 1.35 | 2.58 | 4.11 | 4.18 | 4.26 |
| The Mail on Sunday | | | | | | |
| | [2] | [2] | [2] | 21.57 | 21.11 | 20.46 |
| Observer | .20 | .20 | .38 | .72 | .88 | .83 |
| Sunday Times | .15 | .27 | .57 | .99 | 1.36 | 1.44 |
| Sunday Telegraph | | | | .69 | .65 | .76 |
| | [2] | [2] | .95 | 2.40 | 2.89 | 3.03 |

[1] includes Morning Post
[2] total would include titles now defunct
[3] Times Newspapers closed
[4] *Today*, estimated sales (none available for Sunday edition)

(Source: Audit Bureau of Circulation)

| 1973 | 1976 | 1979 | 1981 | 1982 | 1983 | 1984 | 1985 | 1986 |
|---|---|---|---|---|---|---|---|---|
| 2.97 | 3.71 | 3.79 | 4.14 | 4.08 | 4.17 | 4.19 | 4.07 | 4.06 |
| 3.29 | 2.59 | 2.40 | 2.13 | 2.03 | 1.90 | 1.98 | 1.87 | 1.86 |
| 1.73 | 1.76 | 1.94 | 1.89 | 1.89 | 1.80 | 1.80 | 1.83 | 1.80 |
| | | | | | | | | .40[4] |
| 4.29 | 3.85 | 3.62 | 3.41 | 3.36 | 3.31 | 3.37 | 3.27 | 3.05 |
| | | .94 | 1.50 | 1.39 | 1.34 | 1.37 | 1.43 | 1.42 |
| 12.28 | 11.91 | 12.69 | 13.07 | 12.77 | 12.52 | 12.71 | 12.47 | 12.59 |
| .34 | .31 | [3] — | .30 | .30 | .37 | .38 | .48 | .47 |
| 1.42 | 1.31 | 1.48 | 1.34 | 1.30 | 1.27 | 1.26 | 1.22 | 1.16 |
| .35 | .31 | .38 | .40 | .42 | .44 | .47 | .49 | .52 |
| .19 | .17 | .20 | .20 | .20 | .22 | .22 | .23 | .25 |
| 2.31 | 2.10 | 2.06 | 2.24 | 2.22 | 2.30 | 2.33 | 2.69 | 2.40 |
| 5.94 | 5.14 | 4.67 | 4.23 | 4.31 | 4.07 | 4.28 | 4.79 | 4.85 |
| 4.42 | 4.09 | 3.93 | 3.23 | 3.48 | 3.39 | 3.38 | 3.10 | 3.06 |
| 4.54 | 4.10 | 3.89 | 3.79 | 3.67 | 3.51 | 3.52 | 3.21 | 3.05 |
| 4.10 | 3.45 | 3.26 | 2.99 | 2.93 | 2.61 | 2.60 | 2.40 | 2.38 |
| | | | | | 1.30 | 1.58 | 1.60 | 1.62 |
| 19.00 | 16.78 | 15.65 | 14.25 | 14.39 | 14.88 | 15.36 | 15.10 | 14.96 |
| .79 | .67 | 1.12 | .89 | .84 | .78 | .77 | .75 | .79 |
| 1.52 | 1.38 | [3] — | 1.36 | 1.31 | 1.29 | 1.31 | 1.26 | 1.15 |
| .77 | .76 | 1.28 | .92 | .85 | .74 | .74 | .70 | .68 |
| 3.08 | 2.81 | 2.40 | 3.17 | 2.00 | 2.81 | 2.82 | 2.71 | 2.62 |

# BIBLIOGRAPHY

Baistow, Tom, *Fourth-rate Estate: An Anatomy of Fleet Street*, Comedia, 1985

Beaverbrook, Lord, *Politicians and the Press*, Hutchinson, 1926

Boyce, George and others, *Newspaper History*, Constable, 1978

Braddon, Russell, *Roy Thomson*, Collins, 1965

Brandon, Piers, *The Life and Death of the Press Barons*, Secker and Warburg, 1982

Broackes, Nigel, *A Growing Concern*, Weidenfeld and Nicolson, 1979

Burnham, Lord, *Peterborough Court*, Cassell, 1955

Camrose, Viscount, *British Newspapers and their Controllers*, Cassell, 1947

Chester, Lewis, and Fenby, Jonathan, *The Fall of the House of Beaverbrook*, André Deutsch, 1979

Christiansen, Arthur, *Headlines All My Life*, Heinemann, 1961

Cleverley, Graham, *The Fleet Street Disaster*, Constable, 1976

Cudlipp, Hugh, *Publish and be Damned*, Dakers, 1953
   *At Your Peril*, Weidenfeld and Nicolson, 1962
   *Walking on the Water*, Bodley Head, 1976
   *The Prerogative of the Harlot: Press Barons and Power*, Bodley Head, 1980

Curran, James, and others, *The British Press: A Manifesto*, Macmillan, 1978

Curran James, and Seaton, Jean, *Power without Responsibility*, Fontana, 1981

Economist Intelligence Unit, *The National Newspaper Industry*, EIU, 1966

Evans, Harold, *Good Times, Bad Times*, Weidenfeld and Nicolson, 1983

Ferris, Paul, *The House of Northcliffe*, Weidenfeld and Nicolson, 1971

Glenton, George, and Pattinson, William, *The Last Chronicle of Bouverie Street*, Allen and Unwin, 1976

Goodhart, David, and Wintour, Patrick, *Eddie Shah and the Newspaper Revolution*, Coronet, 1986

Goulden, John, *Newspaper Management*, Heinemann, 1967

Grundy, Bill, *The Press Inside Out*, W. H. Allen, 1976

Henry, Harry, and others, *Behind the Headlines*, Associated Business Press, 1978

  *The Dynamics of the British Press 1961–1984*, Advertising Association, 1986

Heren, Louis, *The Power of the Press*, Orbis, 1985

Hirsch, Fred, and Gordon, David, *Newspaper Money*, Hutchinson, 1975

Jacobs, Eric, *Stop Press, the Inside Story of the Times Dispute*, André Deutsch, 1980

Jenkins, Simon, *Newspapers, the Power and the Money*, Faber, 1979

King, Cecil, *The Cecil King Diaries*, Jonathan Cape, 1972

Koss, Stephen, *The Rise and Fall of the Political Press in Britain*, 2 Vols, Hamish Hamilton, 1981 and 1984

Lawrenson, John, and Barber, Lionel, *The Price of Truth*, Mainstream, 1985

Leapman, Michael, *Barefaced Cheek: Rupert Murdoch*, Hodder & Stoughton, 1983

Lee, Alan, *The Origins of the Popular Press 1855–1914*, Croom Helm, 1976

McDonald, Iverach, *The History of* The Times, *1939–1966*, Times Books, 1984

Margach, James, *The Abuse of Power*, W. H. Allen, 1978

Martin, Roderick, *New Technology and Industrial Relations in Fleet Street*, Oxford University Press, 1981

Munster, George, *Rupert Murdoch, a Paper Prince*, Viking, 1985

Musson, A. E., *The Typographical Association*, Oxford, 1954

Political and Economic Planning, *The British Press*, PEP, 1938

Pound, Reginald, and Harmsworth, Geoffrey, *Northcliffe*, Cassell, 1959

Raskin, A. H., articles on New York press strike, *The New Yorker*, January 1979

Regan, Simon, *Rupert Murdoch, a Business Biography*, Angus and Robertson, 1976

Royal Commissions on the Press, HMSO, 1949, 1962, 1977 (Interim report published in 1976)

Seymour-Ure, Colin, *The Press, Politics and the Public*, Methuen, 1968

Sisson, Keith, *Industrial Relations in Fleet Street*, Blackwell, 1975

Smith, Anthony, *The British Press since the War*, David and Charles, 1974
    *Goodbye Gutenberg*, Oxford, 1980

Social and Community Planning Research, HMSO for Royal Commission, 1977

Swanberg, W. A., *Citizen Hearst*, Scribner's, 1961

Taylor, A. J. P., *Beaverbrook*, Hamish Hamilton, 1972

Thomson, Lord, *After I was Sixty*, Hamish Hamilton, 1975

Tunstall, Jeremy, *The Media in Britain*, Constable, 1983

Walker, Martin, *Power of the Press*, Quartet, 1982

Whale, John, *Journalism and Government*, Macmillan, 1972
    *Politics of the Media*, Fontana, 1977

Williams, Francis, *Dangerous Estate*, Longmans, 1957
    *The Right to Know*, Longmans, 1969

Winsbury, Rex, *New Technology and the Press*, HMSO for Royal Commission, 1975

Wintour, Charles, *Pressures on the Press*, André Deutsch, 1972

Wood, Alan, *The True History of Lord Beaverbrook*, Heinemann, 1965

Woods, Oliver, and Bishop, James, *The Story of* The Times, Michael Joseph, 1983

(Additional material from the *UK Press Gazette*; evidence to the 1947 and 1977 Royal Commissions, especially the studies commissioned by the latter; *Dictionary of National Biography*; newspaper archive files.)

# INDEX